W9-CFV-091

Sanctuary Ranch

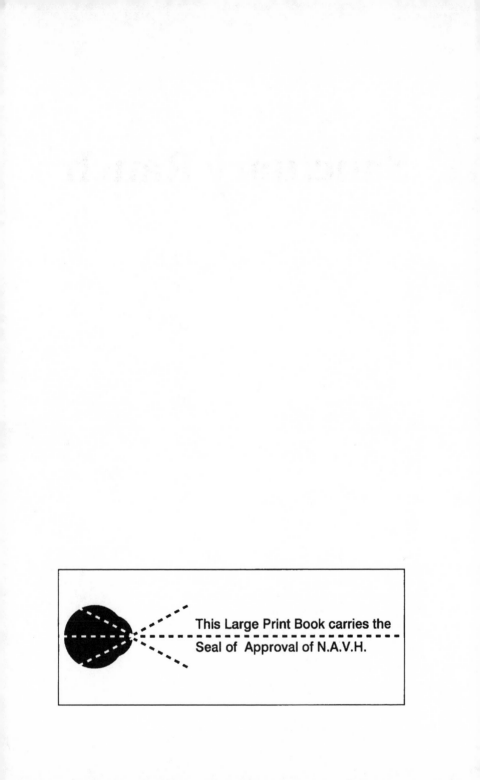

This Large Print Book carries the
Seal of Approval of N.A.V.H.

Sanctuary Ranch

Junior Michael Ray
and Corinne Joy Brown

WHEELER PUBLISHING

Map of Wyoming used by permission of Blackbirch Press, Inc.

Grateful acknowledgment is made for permission to use lyrics
from the following copyrighted works:
"You Just Can't See Him From the Road," Copyright 1992 by
Home At Last Music (BMI) and Just A Secretary Music
(ASCAP). Courtesy of Donnie Blanz, Ed Bruce, and Judith
Bruce. All rights reserved.
"Ride to the Sunset," Copyright 1996 by BMI. Courtesy of
Stan Rood. All rights reserved.
"Carolyn in the Sunset," Copyright 2000 by Barwick's Voice &
Music, BMI. Courtesy of Bill Barwick. All rights reserved.
"Through the Gap," Copyright 1994 by Western Dog
Publishing. Courtesy of Jon Chandler. All rights reserved.

All rights reserved.

This novel is a work of fiction. Names, characters, places and
incidents are either the product of the author's imagination, or,
if real, used fictitiously.

Published in 2006 by arrangement with Tekno Books and
Ed Gorman.

Wheeler Large Print Hardcover.

The text of this Large Print edition is unabridged.
Other aspects of the book may vary from the original edition.

Set in 16 pt. Plantin by Al Chase.

Printed in the United States on permanent paper.

Library of Congress Cataloging-in-Publication Data

Ray, Junior Michael.
    Sanctuary ranch / by Junior Michael Ray and Corinne Joy
Brown.
        p. cm.
    ISBN 1-59722-315-8 (lg. print : hc : alk. paper)
    1. Women country musicians — Fiction.   2. Country
music — Fiction.   I. Brown, Corinne Joy, 1948–   II. Title.
PS3618.A9825S26 2006b
813'.6—dc22   2006014120

This novel, as are all my books, is dedicated to the soldiers I served with — though my time in the service was cut short. Also, to the rodeo hands I went down the road with and rode against. In addition, this story is dedicated to the man who inspired me to follow the rodeo path — my hero, Chris LeDoux. And to the only person who believed in my life as a rodeo man, Lisa.

Junior Michael Ray

This book is dedicated to all the musicians who are keeping the West alive, one great song at a time. Without your voices, many of the greatest stories would be lost. You are the keepers of the old West and the new.

Corinne Joy Brown

Foreword

The West of myth and dreams knows no landscape. For those of us who crave big skies and the promise of open space, the feel of a horse and the solitude of the mountains or prairie, the West is in our hearts. It's within, and also without, somewhere — always waiting. Sanctuary Ranch is that place.

Corinne Joy Brown and Junior Michael Ray met in the summer of 2001 at a writers' conference in a Colorado ranching town called Gunnison. Though they walked distinctly different paths and led entirely separate lives, they had one thing in common: a love of the modern West.

Junior's pursuit of rodeo and Corinne's aspiration to write seemed well-suited to each other. Both knew horses, loved music and read the same authors. Junior, in his late twenties at the time, had a way with a pen as well, and had toyed with a series about his experiences in rodeo. He had an idea for a novel, but sought someone more familiar with a female point of view to help bring it to life. The idea for Sanctuary Ranch was born, and Corinne agreed to co-write a yet undetermined tale with Junior Michael Ray. Little did they know that who they both were and had been in the past would shape the story's characters. Junior had served in the armed forces and ridden bareback, saddle broncs, and bulls in competition; Corinne had worked on a dude ranch and was a longtime musician. Both had loved and lost and, equally, loved and won. In spite of the years between them, the challenge was met, and the resulting book, a story of that West in all its variety and richness, now lies within these pages.

Wyoming

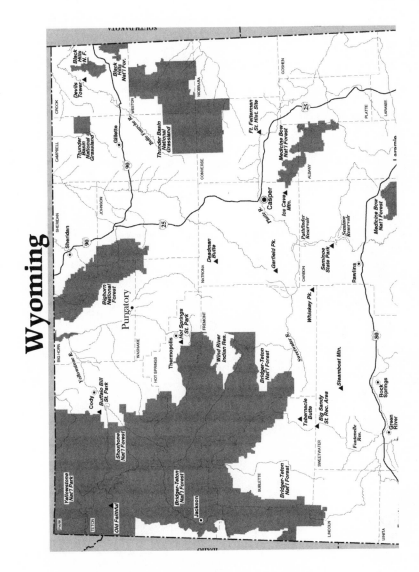

Chapter One

Discovery

The girl with the great big voice and skinny legs shook her long hair, spread her feet in her high-heeled, black patent vinyl boots as far as her denim mini-skirt would allow, and hit the high note she was looking for with a full breath. Throwing her head back, she closed her eyes as the audience cheered. The drummer turned on the heat, the lead guitarist fingered his last lick, and someone hit the lights as the last note died, plunging the audience into total darkness. Applause like thunder rocked the bandstands. Then, the closest thing in Jersey to a Dixie Chick scrambled off the stage into the arms of her adoring fans, laughing hysterically.

"Somebody, get me a beer!"

"Not bad," Mike Foxworthy mused, lighting up a cigarette and blowing out the match.

"She sucks and you know it," answered Marty Heistler, shaking his head. "You brought me all the way out here to hear this? That kid is nothing but a clone. A wannabe if I ever heard one. Except for that big voice, she's recycled pop. Doesn't know crap about singing country. Or western. What's she doing singing our music anyway?"

"That's just her gig," answered Mike. "She really doesn't get it, but loves the sound, the whine and the heartbreak. Come on, she's got that Martina McBride kind of voice, you know it. Listen to that audience. They want more!"

"Don't kid me. This audience is starved for entertainment. Teeny-boppers most of 'em."

"No way. It's a full house, mom and pop, yuppies — the works. That audience, give or take a couple of generations, discovered Madonna and Billy Joel once upon a time. Audiences don't lie. I say she's ready to launch. I want to sign her and reinvent her from top to bottom, Foxy-boy. She's ours. I think the kid is raw material. She just needs some work. We'll revamp the music, do the makeover and send her to the Grand Ole Opry when she's ready. She just might be our way out."

"You're stark-raving nuts," Heistler replied, shaking his head. "You can't send this kid to Nashville. They'd eat her alive."

"I've got money in the bank says they won't," retorted Foxworthy, the one agent on the East Coast who still hung out at county fairs to find new talent. He really liked Fairfield, New Jersey. He really liked twenty-year-old Miss Tawny Talbot, the local rage with the long legs, silky hair and perky breasts. He really liked her voice.

"I think she's a long shot, but a good one," Mike continued. "She needs the right band and the right clothes. Let's face it, she's wearing way too much. Everything that's wrong can be fixed."

Marty Heistler, a youthful thirty-year-old who looked convincingly professional in Lucky jeans and a black T-shirt, eyed his business partner with a look between skepticism and approval. And serious doubt. Would the kid listen to them? Accept an offer?

"How old is she, anyway? Got parents?" he asked. He started to let the prospect simmer, but wanted to know something about the baggage.

"Do I look like a fool?" answered Mike. "She's been on her own since she was sixteen. I got the whole story from the ticket office. What she does have is that witch over there with the big hair who says she's her road manager, supervisor, whatever. She sees money in our little kitten, too, I betcha. No problem getting past her. We just need to get her on our side."

"Let me think about it," Heistler said, watching a pair of sixteen-year-olds in low riders and tube tops walk past, eyeing him as though he were somebody's grandfather. He rolled up the sleeves of his button-down collar, white oxford shirt and rubbed the dust off his Bruno Maglis, squinting at the stage. Marty played off Mike like a straight man in a stand-up act, hiding his lack of experience behind brand names and a manufactured tan. Mike was right. She almost had it all. Youth, a great ass, a great voice, and the possibility of becoming anyone they wanted her to be. Plus, the time was right. As far as they knew, she hadn't been approached or discovered by anybody. She was prime.

"Hey, doll, we'd like to have a chat with you. Got a minute for two big fans of yours?" Mike Foxworthy drawled. They approached Tawny and Terry Ann Hill, the used-up blonde with turquoise eye makeup caked in the creases, faded Levi's, and an expression that could scare vampires.

"We like your little lady's act there, Miss Hill," Heistler chimed in with a breezy smile. He batted his blue eyes and oozed Southern charm. "We'd like to talk about where she can go with it, with our help."

14

"Not now," she snarled, as she watched Tawny disappear into the ladies' room behind the concession stand. "We're about to get out of here. You want to talk? Make an appointment."

"Where's she going in such a hurry?" Marty asked.

"Just out back to do what she does after every show," answered the blonde.

"What's that?" Mike asked, regretting the question.

"Throw up."

Chapter Two

The Deal

The coffee at the Hide-Away Inn near Fairfield tasted like swamp water heated to boiling, but the all-night diner was the closest place they could find without driving to town. Time didn't allow for that.

Marty winced as he swallowed his first sip and ignored the bitter taste, smiling at Terry Ann and staring at Tawny the way an older brother stares down a kid sister.

"Okay, ladies, let me make it real simple. What we do is make music," Mike began. "We make it big. We take little promises like you, Tawny Talbot, and make them into reality. Big time. We're Foxworthy and Associates — the music men." He handed her his card.

"Her real name's Amy, gentlemen," Terry Ann replied.

"Okay, Amy. Whatever. Last concert of the season here, huh? Looks like you've gone about as far as you can go around these parts. What's next?"

Amy squinted at Marty and Mike as if

they were the Men in Black and she was the alien.

"Nothin's next. I'm going to Disneyland. What do you want?"

Her attitude worried Mike. She was playing very cool. They needed a quick fix in a hurry or they'd be out of the business at the rate it was moving. Ever since the mid-nineties, the country music industry had drifted toward Texas and the old Nashville sound they'd been pushing had left them without bookings for over a year. They needed a new act with some sex appeal and a touch of western twang. It didn't matter where it came from. Mike decided to ignore her sarcasm.

"Look, honey, you don't know us and we don't know you. But we like what we saw here tonight and think we might have what you need. We'd like to work together, see how far we can go. And just to prove to you who we are, I'd like to suggest a trial period of engagement. You check us out while we do the same. If we like what's there, we cut a deal."

Mike Heistler cracked his knuckles and tried to look nonchalant.

"Just what are the terms?" Terry Ann inquired, looking doubtfully at both faces and putting her arm around the girl. "We gotta eat."

17

"We want Amy here to team up with a band in Nashville before they head down to Fort Worth. We'd like to hear how her sound fits. If it clicks and we can rearrange some of her material, we'd eventually like to book her on the southern circuit. Nothing major, just some warm-ups and filler acts at first. We go live for six months, and once people catch on, we can talk about a CD when the time's right. The investment's equal. You pay us nothing and we pay you the same until we know we're there. Let's call it a little gamble. You cover your own expenses and we'll handle getting you where you need to go."

Marty inhaled so hard his lungs hurt. He couldn't believe it. How the hell would any-body go for an offer like that? Just because they were so broke they were on their fourth credit card to cover this jaunt, he couldn't imagine coming up with a story like this one. One phone call to anyone in the in-dustry would expose the fact that neither of them had a dime to finance anybody's start, and that they owed everyone in town money for equipment or studio time. Of course, there were plenty of places the kid could play for free, that much was true. If she did, and did well, eventually they could book her into some place that really paid off.

"What do you think, Amy?" Terry Ann asked, drumming her long fingernails against the laminate table. "You wanna give it a try?"

"Play for nothing? I don't know . . . but first of all, nobody 'rearranges' my material," she said with an exasperated tone. "I write what I want and I sing it my way. And I'm not sure I really want to go pure country, anyway. I mean, isn't that what Nashville's all about? But then, I'm not exactly booked. You guys have some nerve, asking me to play for free, even if it is a way through the door. I don't know if I believe a word you've said. But then, I guess I want whatever my boss thinks we ought to do." Amy shrugged her shoulders. "Just let her decide. Meanwhile, excuse me . . ."

As 110 pounds of raw talent went out to the car for her cigarettes, Terry Ann looked at both men and said quietly, "It's very simple, guys. Number one: where she goes, I go. Number two: she needs to be paid. Your plan sounds like a long shot. But I'm glad you can appreciate who she is. The kid's got plenty of talent and I'm here to make sure no one steals it from her. You rethink the offer and when it involves some cash, we might consider it. Meanwhile, we've got things to do and a band to pay.

Let me give you our number. And don't un-derestimate either one of us, Mr. Foxworthy. We're not as dumb as you think."

Chapter Three

Catching Up

The aroma of frying bacon filled the air. As usual, the long wood plank table strained under the weight of the country breakfast set in the main house of the J-Bar-M Ranch, fifty miles southeast of Cody, a long way north and west of Nashville, Tennessee.

A lantern-style chandelier illuminated the dining area like daybreak on the plain, casting a warm glow across the room. Music on the radio from Wyoming's only twenty-four-hour-a-day country-western station drowned out the chorus of sounds filtering from the kitchen. Chris LeDoux's lament about a cowboy on the road started the day with enough angst to make a grown man weep, but David Dallas, head cook at the J-Bar-M, liked his country sad and loud.

Ashley Sharpe had come in early for her turn at housekeeping. As the head horse trainer, she'd fed the stock first, then headed down to the mess hall where she shed her big jacket and boots and took on her morning duties.

The assigned shifts changed every two days. Ashley set down the serving plates loaded with heaping portions of toast and biscuits where she could find a space and shuffled back and forth to the kitchen in her clogs, hoping to beat the crowd. She tossed her bangs repeatedly out of her eyes and her long ponytail bobbed as she hastened to finish bringing out David's steaming morning feast.

David, or Double D, as everyone called him, took everything seriously, from his bronc riding to his housework, but most of all, his cooking. That was the one talent the ranch crew enjoyed most. When it was his turn in the rotation, he made it into a holiday. The oldest son in a family of eleven children from the backwoods of Mississippi, he'd helped his mama cook for her growing family. Giving one last instruction to Ashley regarding the coffee, he smiled, realizing that his timing was perfect. As the percolator began to perk, the sound of the door opening heralded the arrival of the remaining crew.

With their morning ranch duties done, Brenda and Brookes Bowers were the first ones in. Brother and sister, they'd taken refuge on the J-Bar-M when things at home went sour. Brookes, sixteen and a junior in high school, didn't have much time to spare, with a bus leaving in twenty minutes. He had a long ride ahead, almost an hour to his school. His older sister hurried him to the table with motherly care.

Gary Russell, ranch foreman, walked in gingerly. He moved with caution, resulting from a previous day's rodeo practice that didn't quite work out the way he'd hoped. His work clothes covered the bruises he wanted no one to see. He hung his battered Carhartt coveralls on a hook in the mudroom and put his stocking cap and gloves in their spot on the shelf. Heading to the kitchen, he scavenged to find a coffee cup, still shaking off the effects of the bitter Wyoming wind.

"Ashley has coffee on the table, Gary," Double D said in his soft Southern accent.

"Oh, that would explain why my cup ain't here. Sorry, weather froze my brain," Gary replied with a smile, rubbing his hands together. Moving to the table, he sat down and prepared to eat. Double D could hear that almost everyone had gathered round. He picked up the plate containing the layered heaps of bacon and eggs that he'd gone to great lengths to keep warm, then joined them.

"Thank you, Miz Ashley, for settin' the

table, especially since Brookes forgot once again last night to do it before beddin' down." He set the full plate in the last open spot on the table.

Brookes, already at a disadvantage with a full mouth, took the defense. "Hey, too bad. Give me a break, I'm running late."

"Now whose fault might that be? Funny how you talk when Jess or Larry ain't around," Double D said with deadly humor. Brookes tried to snap back but was shot down.

"Don't start, Brookes," Gary cut in. "Especially at the table. The Sarge would have your behind for that alone. And take off that baseball cap. There are ladies here," he added as he leaned into his coffee, his elbows splayed on the table.

"You've been shirking your chores way too much," Gary continued. "Everyone here has a job. Ashley had to cover your butt again, which means when you get home, you get the barn cleaning by yourself. Plus your sister had to help you with feeding this morning because you couldn't get out of bed, which means Double D had to cook by himself. Therefore, you get house cleaning by yourself as well."

Brookes looked for a rebuttal, but Gary threw one more stab. "Before you start to whine and cry as usual, everyone here knows you snuck out last night to see your sweetheart. If you want to live a long life, don't go sneaking away when you live within earshot of the boss, a man who's an ex–combat vet, sleeps light, sleeps armed, and still runs three miles every morning at four a.m. That's just suicide."

Brookes realized he'd lost. Arguing about his punishment seemed futile.

Brenda usually came to the rescue of her immature brother, but his behavior had ruined the whole schedule. She was glad Jess wasn't around to hear about it, or they'd all be sorry. Jess McLain expected mornings on the ranch to run in an efficient, orderly, almost military manner. If they didn't, there'd be hell to pay. The crew could mess up later in the day when he was more relaxed.

Brookes swallowed what he could quickly shovel into his mouth and excused himself. The rest of the group leisurely picked at their meal. Though Jess McLain wouldn't have asked for it, they waited for the last two ranch hands to arrive. Brookes pulled on his boots in the mudroom in an effort to escape, but was caught by the sound of the door opening. He feared the inevitable.

Larry Goodman, ranch foreman and

second in command only to its owner, headed toward Brookes on the bench and began to shed his gear: neck scarf, hat, gloves, jacket and vest. His large frame and 230 pounds took up a better part of the seat. He said nothing, which made Brookes even more nervous and anxious to get to school. He could hear Brenda coming down the hall with his lunch.

"Morning, Bren," said Larry. "Getting your brother out the door, as usual?"

Brookes looked up as the last member of the team finally entered the door. It was Jess McLain. Brookes felt hot, as if he could sweat out a raging winter storm and melt the snow while doing it. The presence of the ranch boss always gave him a queasy feeling. This morning was no different.

Brookes fumbled with his school pack and Brenda stood by, hesitating. Usually she could save her brother, but she sensed there'd be no helping him this time.

"Hey! I hear we have a problem getting our work done around here," Jess said.

Brookes felt as though Jess's blue eyes had bored clear through his soul. Brenda tried to head Jess off, only to be stopped dead. "Jess, he —"

"Brenda, get back to breakfast. Baby-sitting this boy is over. Do I make myself clear?" Sergeant McLain ordered.

"Yes, sir. See you tonight, Brookes," she said and turned away before she could witness her brother's fate.

Jess began to remove his heavy jacket and overalls while he continued the verbal thrashing. McLain didn't believe in cursing excessively but when someone brought out the Army Ranger in him, foul words flowed.

"This conversation stops now! Right fucking now. If you can't do your job, get out. Everyone here works damned hard, and all you do is dick around. I've had it!" Jess cursed loudly enough for the whole house to feel his wrath.

Larry had joined the group and smiled as if he knew something was up. The table conversation continued, lest Jess accuse the crew of being intrusive.

Brenda joined the group and fought back tears. Jess had never yelled at her before. She couldn't help trying extra hard to please everybody, especially Jess McLain, her boss and everybody else's cowboy hero.

"Before you go to school, you have some options," Jess railed. "Two of them. You either get those grades up and do your job around here or it's your ass! Get it? It's my way or the highway!"

Brookes knew he dared not speak and

nodded his head in agreement.

"When Goodman or Russell say jump, you say, 'how high?' and do it with a smile. You understand? I've had it with your immaturity!" Jess stepped back, then turned for one last shot.

"Oh, and if you ever sneak out again, I'll find out, and so help you God, you might as well stay gone or I'll have your ass! You read me, lover boy?"

Done with what he had to do, Jess made his way to the table, eager to sit down and eat.

Earlier that morning, Jess and Larry Goodman had risen early to check fences in the west pasture. With spring approaching, they wanted to get a head start on repairing the damage from a harsh winter. They'd put in a half-day's work before sunrise and Jess was in no mood for slack-offs.

The crew tried to be amiable, but with Brenda's sniffling, it proved difficult. Larry winked at her while filling his plate and smiled reassuringly.

Jess joined the table with a quiet "good morning" to everyone and took his place at the head. Gary and Larry flanked him. He took a sip of coffee and caught a raised eyebrow from both men. He could hear

Brenda trying to hold back her hurt. Seeing that "Don't be an ass" look from both his top hands, he attempted to put an end to the matter.

"Now then, when that boy gets home there'll have to be some punishment," Jess said in a much lighter tone.

"Uh, sir, I already told him that house chores were all his tonight," Gary offered. "And that he had to do Ashley's side of the barn too."

Jess paused a second to consider the punishment. He looked to Goodman for his opinion.

"I see no problem with that," Larry said. "How do the rest of you feel?"

All nodded in agreement. Diplomacy had saved Brookes from McLain's wrath. Jess stopped reloading his plate long enough to begin another tack.

"Well, I won't override your authority, Gary. Thanks for stepping up and dealing with it. And Brenda, I'm not mad at you, but enough is enough. I won't put up with him using you, brother or not. Now, I want your input on his grades. I hear they're not so hot."

Brenda lifted her head and tried not to act stunned. How did Jess know that her brother had been goofing off in school?

"How'd you know he was flunkin', Boss?" Double D asked.

"Same way I found out he slipped out last night. Larry and I ran into Katy's dad this morning. It's easy when the girlfriend lives next door. Her mom works at the school and apparently Brookes and little Ms. Katy are both spending a lot of time out of class together.

"Brenda," Jess advised, "I suggest that there's no girlfriend, no TV and no rodeo until he gets his act together. Look, I know you've been raising him, but if he screws up too much, the state will take over and put him in a home. Plus, I'm tired of him taking advantage of you."

Brenda's eyes lit up when she realized he was concerned for her feelings. "That's fine," she replied. "He told me he would get his grades up, but I think the new rules will be okay. Thanks." Smiling, she sighed in relief.

The shrill ring of the wall-mounted phone cut into their chatter. Normally Jess would just let it go. Meal times were not to be interrupted, but Larry had been expecting a call so he reached back and answered. Figuring it might be the bank, McLain crossed his hand in a slicing motion at his neck, mouthing to Larry that he wasn't there.

Conversation stopped.

"Hello-o," said Larry, with a smile in his voice. He raised his eyebrows once he figured out the identity on the other line. It wasn't a call he expected, and it wasn't the bank either. Goodman asked the other party to hold on and handed the phone to Jess. McLain, not looking pleased, appeared ready to jump whoever was on the phone. Once again the room awaited the burning fuse.

"This is McLain . . ."

"Hey, Jess, what the hell you doin'? It's Heistler," the voice on the other end said cheerily.

"Boy, you're one lucky man! I thought you were the bank interrupting breakfast. What the hell you calling me at seven in the morning for anyway?"

Jess stepped back and looked out the window, letting the table conversation proceed. Once again, the ranch hands conversed among themselves, but all were curious as to who would cause Jess to break one of his strictest rules.

"Been a long time, cowboy. How's things up there?" Marty asked, leaning back at his desk. He stared at a black-and-white picture of himself and Jess that sat on his desk, taken in Heistler's younger days. Jess, fresh out of the Gulf War, stood at attention in dress uniform. Just below, in the same frame, was another shot of both of them taken at Cheyenne Frontier Days Rodeo, a year or so later. These stood out among the many glossy commercial pictures, CD covers, and gold records that filled the over-sized office.

"Well, let's see now. It's seven-thirty a.m., it's still winter out here, and well, gosh — the wind's up. Is that what you wanted? The weather report?"

"Oh, you mean same as every other day, except in the summer when it's hot?" Marty added.

"No kidding. Nah, been a rough year. Hard winter, bank breathing down my neck. When beef dropped, it near killed us. Horses are kinda keepin' us going now. Hoping I get a break soon or I might be in some real deep stuff . . ." Jess continued in a lowered tone.

No one had ever heard McLain speak of ranch troubles on the phone, or to anyone else about them, for that matter. Curiosity filled the room. Larry obviously knew who this person was, and the fact that he still smiled and kept eating calmed the crew.

"I don't know why you insisted on paying me off early, Jess." Marty changed the subject. "Maybe if you got rid of some of those losers out there you could save some money."

"That's why I paid you off early — so I didn't have to take your advice. You might be able to make country stars outta church choirs, but you don't know dick about ranching and rodeo," Jess replied.

"Ouch. We'll see. You should get your ass out here for a visit and let me turn you into somebody and you wouldn't have to worry about money at all anymore."

"No thanks, I take care of stock. I'm not in the mood to be a steer in your business. How goes the star search, anyhow? By the way, thanks for asking, but no to the country-music gig, and no to the reunion. I'm staying right here."

"No surprise. I knew calling this close to the reunion, you wouldn't come. You should let it go, Jess. It all worked out. You got a Silver Star because of them. I know it was a day late and a dollar short, but . . . never mind, let's not go over that again. Anyway, the star search blows. Had two flops. The new crooners just piss me off these days. Our industry shovels them in and out. Some of the crap they pawn off as country music these days belongs in your pasture."

"Sounds like a slaughterhouse."

"About that. Well, since I won't see you at the Rangers' gathering, will I see you at Frontier Days in July? You ridin' this year?" Marty asked, deliberately trying to get underneath McLain's skin.

"Don't start with me. Yeah, I'll be there. No riding, though. Hey, try and call more than once a year and not just when you want something, would ya?" Jess finished. "We're supposed to stay in touch, remember?"

"All right, I'll let you go. Just wanted to see how you were holdin' up. Be good to see ya. Tell that old dog Larry to take care, too. You keep duckin' bullets."

"Okay, Marty, will do. Good hearing from you. Keep your head down. Out, here." Jess hung up the phone.

Marty clicked the receiver and held up another picture lying face down on the desk. An old photo, only this one was of him in uniform standing next to Jerry McLain, Jess's older brother. Two years after that shot was taken, Jerry would be killed in action, this picture his last. A scruffy adolescent Jess stood in front, wearing his brother's black Ranger beret. Marty stared at the photo, opened his top drawer, and carefully replaced it in its usual hidden place.

Chapter Four

Doing the Time

Brookes Bowers tried to work fast and avoid the Wyoming wind. With the sun's departure the temperature had grown brutally cold. The chill cut so deep it was enough to make even young joints ache. Cursing the whole way, he tried to curb his language, for if the boss heard him and a woman was within a mile, all kinds of punishment would ensue. Bowers had had his fill of McLain's overbearing Army Ranger work ethic and discipline, forgetting that it was this very man who allowed him a place to live at the ranch instead of in a foster home. He'd been told that youth and laziness seemed to be a disease that Jess personally set out to cure.

Brookes swore under his breath for fear of being heard, especially since Jess lived in a small loft apartment in the top of the barn and no one ever knew if he was there or not. He assumed Jess bunked there because from that vantage point, it was easier to catch somebody, especially him, slacking off.

"How goes it, young Bowers?" The crackly voice of Larry Goodman broke the night air.

"It sucks. I hate this. I always have to do more than anybody."

"Not so. Everyone here works and works hard, my friend. No exceptions," said Larry. "You're just sore because you can't see that little darlin' of yours until your grades come up. I think if you want to be treated like a man, son, Jess is giving you the chance."

"He treats me like shit. He treats everyone like shit. Sometimes we go for days without seeing him. He's never around. Then when he is, everyone freaks," Brookes said.

Larry knew that Jess had his faults, but he also did favors that no one else would. He believed that the J-Bar-M Ranch, with its motley crew of outlaws and mavericks, proved Jess wasn't a total block of ice.

"As I recall, because of Jess, you and your sister have a place to live. Your sister didn't even have to ask twice for him to help you two out. So you get a roof and food, but no free ride. Gary and Double D — same thing. They showed up here starving, begging for work, when the rodeo went sour for them." Larry hoped he was being understood.

"Ashley got hired on after being dumped by a boyfriend and she needed a hand. Things in life ain't free, son. Jess may be . . . well . . . sometimes abrasive, but you and your sister have it pretty good. You might just want to cool off."

Brookes could barely see through the shivering cold while he chopped horse nuggets that had frozen to the floor of the stall.

"Oh yeah, sure, he's a real saint. Sounds like he uses people down on their luck to run this dump. So, why are you here? What does he hold over your head to get work out of you?" Brookes asked.

Larry and Jess had what was the closest thing to a friendship on the place. For quite some time, most people thought Larry was one of Jess's relatives, but no one knew for sure. He was the only person who always seemed comfortable and relaxed around Jess.

"I'm glad you asked," answered Larry. He decided that the boy needed to know who the man really was. Not just the tyrant that hollered at him and made him work hard. After all, Gary and Double D knew all about their boss — who he'd been in the rodeo world had brought them here in the first place.

Larry grabbed the shoeing bench and set

it inside the stall to have a chat and teach Brookes a lesson about life. "Okay, I'll tell you why I'm here, Mr. Hot Pants. But just a short story, not like my usual fire-diers. Make yourself comfortable."

Brookes leaned on his shovel and settled in to listen.

"Back in 'ninety . . . now, you would have been about six years old, I think, America was in a war in the Middle East with a little sand-filled country called Iraq."

"I know what Iraq is, Larry."

"Good. Anyway, see, wars are fought within wars. My son Jack was in the second Ranger Battalion assigned to all kinds of scary stuff." Larry had the youth's attention.

"Him and another Ranger from his unit were picked to join some Army Green Berets to do a mission. They were pretty young, not too much older than you — nineteen, twenty. They were picked because they knew the area. So anyhow, to make a long story short . . ."

"You can actually make a story short?"

"Don't push it, son. You're workin' for me tomorrow." Larry smiled and spat a long stream of chew spit at the youth's feet, and followed it up with a wide smile.

"So the story goes: some senator's brat

didn't have a combat citation. That's kinda like an award, son. Some damn punk officer that didn't know his ass from a hole in the wall. So the thirteen men were dropped into some nasty business. My son and the other Ranger were the radio operators on the thing." He paused.

"Well, this moron waste-of-sperm officer got them all in a whole heap a shit. Don't ever repeat that word around Jess. They got into one hell of a firefight. Sure, it was never reported, but men died there. To make matters worse, the jackass lieutenant got on my son's radio in a panic and called in an air strike and helicopter evacuation. Somehow, Jack and the other Ranger in the mess got split up. The lieutenant called in the wrong area and the unit took some serious hits by friendly fire. Wiped out all but two Green Berets, Jack, the other Ranger and the limp-dick C.O."

Larry spun out his tale full of energy up to that point. But as he continued, his skin began to pale and his jovial sense of humor disappeared.

"When the helicopter got there, it got ugly. Still under fire, the lieutenant had lost all control. He kept yelling at my son that he'd called in the wrong area to hit. Then, that crybaby was the first one on the chopper. The Berets proceeded to load up their dead with the Rangers' help. No one knows for sure, but my son was hit. Hit bad. They were about to all get into deeper fire and needed to evacuate in a hurry but Rangers don't leave their brothers behind, nor do Greens, son — remember that. The other Ranger jumped out of the helo and went to get my boy. But the officer ordered them to take off. Later on, rumor had it that the Greens worked over that jerk pretty bad. Didn't matter, they left those Rangers behind."

Larry began to swallow hard as he spoke of his son's last hours. "They were out there for twelve hours, fightin' with all they had. The other Ranger could have left my boy, but he stayed. When it was all done, that last Ranger carried my son's dead body through the desert for two days in the heat. He damn near died himself." Larry fought back the bitter feelings of a father whose son had fallen. He looked at Brookes with a hard stare, eyes moist and red-rimmed.

"That hard-ass doesn't owe you or anyone else here a damn thing — he carried my only boy's body because he wouldn't leave a friend behind. You know what they did to him for that?" Larry trembled now as he spoke and beads of sweat formed on his forehead. Pain choked his words.

"They tried to blame it on my dead son who went back to get a man he never knew. But ole Jess, boy, he made me proud. He wouldn't let them do it to my boy." Larry started to weep through his smile. "No, sir! Jess turned that little prick in. But because he was a senator's son they wanted to keep it quiet. No sirree, can't have a senator's son screwing up in a war. So they discharged Jess without reason. An honorable discharge to be sure, but a discharge, nonetheless. After an investigation was done because of the Green Beret's statement, they awarded my boy a citation. Then those hypocrites gave Jess a Purple Heart and a Silver Star. You know what that asshole you call a boss did at my boy's funeral? Do ya, boy?" Goodman's lower lip quivered in pain.

"No, sir." Brookes felt overwhelmed. His brazen attitude had vanished.

"He handed me the flag that covered my boy's body and he cried. He asked for me to forgive him for not getting my son back alive. Said he could have walked faster. That's why I'm here, boy. Jess McLain does things he doesn't have to do. He didn't owe me nothin', he didn't owe me a salute either." Larry wiped his cheek and got up to leave.

41

Brookes stood speechless. This wouldn't be a story they'd all hear around the fireplace tonight, he thought. Maybe ever. Brookes said nothing when Larry turned to give him one more piece to swallow.

"You all owe him. When y'all were hurt, he carried you out. He's carrying you right now, Mr. Hothead. You think about that tonight when you go to sleep. 'Cause I guarantee you, boy, he's living with that every second he's alive."

Larry wiped his eyes with a big bandana as he headed out of the barn. "Hurry up now. Your sister did some fine cookin' tonight."

"Yes, sir. Thank you, sir."

Chapter Five

Nightmare in Nashville

Mike Foxworthy knew it wasn't the Tennessee humidity that had him sweating so badly. Damned if his linen shirt wasn't wet underneath his suit coat. All he had to do was look. Seven highly paid musicians were sitting around the stage of the Dixie Rose Bar, waiting. They'd been there from noon until three p.m., not working. They weren't too happy.

The deal between Talbot, Hill and himself had been put together more quickly than he'd ever imagined and Mike had set about bringing Amy into the scene without wasting any time. But it wasn't easy.

Mike Foxworthy pulled on every favor that was owed to him in order to assemble Nashville's musical cream as backup for his new singer. When Amy turned out to be late, they were peeved. With a test concert in eight hours, Foxworthy had to worry about the musicians' performance. Her no-show had him smoking like a steam engine.

Every musician assembled had either

toured with a big name, was on tour with a big name, or had played on important albums. Their talent was evident by the minimum amount of time it had taken to learn Amy's five originals and the five covers she would do. In just sixty minutes the session players had everything down, just not the timing of their singer.

Robert "Bobby" Dall, possibly the best sound man and producer in Nashville, showed up because of his longtime working relationship with Marty Heistler. Foxworthy, he hardly knew.

The two guitarists, Reggie "Ripper" Williams and his brother Charlie "Chucky", didn't owe the men anything. As the most sought-after lead and bass players in Nashville, possibly in the country, they had superstars putting projects on hold just to wait for them. But it was Bob Dall they owed a favor to, and privately, they had been trying to form their own production company with Marty Heistler in the lead. They'd come on board for some inside business, but were still curious about the new piece of "meat" Mike had found.

"Where the hell did these tunes come from?" Chucky asked Bob Dall who was sitting alone by the set. "Does fat boy think this stuff is going to fly?"

"Screw him and his little novice. We're here for bigger reasons than her," he said and then began to chuckle as he continued. "Did you read these lyrics and see the changes? What a joke."

The music-city vet confessed he hadn't. Chucky looked through his copy like a comic book and the two began to rip apart every piece of Amy's work they read.

"Here. Here, this one's my favorite. Umm — 'I left in December on a north-bound train, makin' tracks through the Dakota rain'! Are you kidding me? Rain in December, in Dakota? Which one? North or South? Oh yeah, she's a country singer all right." He laughed.

Then Dall recited a few pieces himself, reinforcing their disgust with the uneducated rookie. Before long, all seven were gathered in a corner crucifying Amy's work.

Foxworthy paced, smoked and paced some more. Marty appeared to be the only one who was relaxed. He'd seen the possibility of a no-show coming and the issue had become just an "I told you so" waiting to happen. Heistler knew exactly what the musicians were laughing at: cowboy songs, written about places and things that the brat, as he now referred to her, had never been to or seen. He chuckled under his breath, wondering what his old friend Jess in Wyoming would think. His thoughts were interrupted when he caught sight of Amy and Terry Ann.

Amy strolled through the door in sunglasses. Terry Ann hurried her along, holding her arm. Her late arrival gave Marty, the king of deals, the upper hand. With the musicians on his side and Mike Foxworthy's obvious duress, it was time for a loyalty check. He winked at his silent partner Bob Dall and set the trap.

"Okay, fellas, time's up. Pack it up," Dall ordered. The band scattered and began breaking down. Terry Ann made a beeline to the corner, heading for Foxworthy, leaving Amy alone.

Marty could see that through her hangover, Amy was frantic at the sight of the musicians heading out. He knew she and Terry Ann were worried. He gave Bob Dall a wink while Mike paced the room. Marty knew then that he had them, hook, line and sucker.

"Hey, guys, stop!" Mike rushed the stage. "What's going on? She's here!"

Terry Ann and Amy followed, tempers flaring.

"Forget it, Mike," Ripper responded. "I don't do charity. You told us you found a huge prospect. This kid? Some spoiled drunken brat that can't get up before the crack of noon? No way. I ain't playing in front of major record execs with that!" Ripper Williams lived up to his name. The others followed suit.

"We've been sitting here for three hours, Mike. You'll get my bill." Bob Dall dropped the pre-arranged comment.

"Guys, come on. We have a show to-night," Mike begged.

Terry Ann decided her time to speak had come. "Forget it, Mike. We don't need this. Call us when you think you've got some-thing. We don't deal with bullshit. Come on, Amy, we're outta here." Terry Ann turned to reinforce her threat by walking out.

With her comment, Marty mumbled to himself, "Gotcha!" and dropped the bomb. "Ms. Hill, do you have any idea who you're dealing with? Do you?" He made his way to the front of the stage.

Terry Ann started to reply, only to have the truth shoved down her throat.

"That's Bobby Dall up there, plus Chucky and Ripper Williams, the top players in the business. Think about what you're doing here. You made a commit-ment to have the brat play. Now you're committed on paper. But three hours late violates your contract. Read the fine print! You're in breach and the money for these guys is on your tab now." Heistler enjoyed the assault.

"Bobby, what's the total at right now for the three hours the Whiskey Princess ran up?"

"Uh, right now, it's five hundred an hour for the musicians, and you know my fee . . ." Dall didn't have to fake the numbers.

"Bullshit! See if you can get a dime," Amy replied. "So I was a little late."

"You ain't getting a thing from us, paper or not," Terry Ann backed up her girl.

Mike knew Marty had them. This was a scene that they'd played many a time. The only problem he saw now would be keeping the finest musicians in the game staying loyal to his partner. Act two, he mused, and proceeded to his next move.

"Oh really, no problem. I know Marty will see that we get paid one way or another. Let me clue you in on something, little Miss Lush. Walk out that door. If you turn into a no-show in front of Sony, Mercury, and Capitol Records tonight, your career is history."

Bobby hated to admit he found enjoyment in the scam himself, as he waited for her reaction. "Not to mention the contract your so-called manager signed. You let me down, I'll see to it you're buried so deep in legal problems you won't be able to play the Jersey County Fair. You get it?"

It was almost too easy, thought Marty. Even though Mike never really approved of this tactic, desperation warranted its use. They needed Amy all to themselves.

Terry Ann could see that they were in over her head. She found herself playing major league ball with major players. She'd been had, and the link between her and Amy weakened by the second.

"What do we have to do?" Hill asked.

"Hey, Terry Ann never said record companies were going to be here," Amy cut in. "That's not fair!"

Mike Heistler took over. "Sober up and get your ass on that stage. Whatever Bobby asks you to do, do it with a smile. And you, Miss Hill, keep her away from the bottle until the show's over. You're legally responsible."

Back in business, Mike needed to get the show rolling.

"We stay on one condition, Mike," Ripper added. "You dim the lights so the brass doesn't see us playing with this child. And she better not suck. I put off my session with Garth for this. He pays the bills."

Mike shook his head, just happy the musicians would stay.

"Put a trash can on the stage and bring some water and coffee, Terry Ann. We don't stop for people who can't hold their mud." Bobby Dall proved once again why he'd become the big man in Nashville.

Heistler winked to Foxworthy as the club debut got underway and sighed in relief. The band took their places and Amy came out, guitar in hand, to a round of expectant applause. It didn't last.

She started off strong doing her first and best original piece, "Time and Tears," making a great first impression. But from there it imploded. Missed cues, late starts, and wrong chords, she ended up trailing the band and, finally, losing her nerve. She faltered, finally backing offstage after the third number.

The club crowd was stunned. Some booed while others clapped politely, out of embarrassment and pity. Had Amy not started out so strong, sounding like a mixture of Patsy Cline and Terri Clark, all would have been lost.

"Son of a bitch, Mike! Where the hell did you find this kid?" Bobby screeched, fol-

50

lowing the band backstage after Amy's disastrous debut. The show had been a waste, and all the pros knew it. Regardless, Amy and Terry had to endure the brutal meeting scheduled with the only two record labels who stayed and the professional musicians whose opinions could make or break the deal.

"Don't ask me for any more favors, Foxworthy. That was my last one," Chucky Williams said. He started to pack up while the rest of the band found seats. Marty hadn't joined them yet, busy courting the record producers with free drinks. The evaluation meeting started without him.

Perched at the edge of the table, Amy and Terry Ann nervously shared a large rum and Coke.

"Okay. Okay, feedback, folks? Bob? Chucky?" Foxworthy tried to salvage the situation.

Afraid of what they were about to say, Amy drank fast. Terry Ann just listened, looking for an angle that would enable her to regain some power.

"Well, I'll go ahead and speak for everybody," Bob began. "A lot of bad things happened, but that first piece rocked the house. We recovered somewhat with the borrowed material, but to get signed, covers don't cut it. If she'd have spent more time singing and less time puking this afternoon at rehearsal, who knows?" Bob refreshed everyone's memory of the earlier session.

"Okay, that's behind us," Mike interrupted. "What else?" He tried to keep them on track and from attacking his property.

Amy wouldn't look at anyone while she sat and listened, hiding behind her dark glasses. When Terry Ann tried to whisper something, Amy shrugged her off.

"Well, for one thing, that East Coast accent kills her image. Doesn't matter how she sings, image sells," Chucky interjected.

"Kid, I ain't trying to hurt your feelings but if you try to pawn off those lyrics about cowboy and country life, you won't last ten seconds in Texas. They'd boo you off the stage out there." Bob Dall spoke the truth.

"Well, are we dead?" Foxworthy asked.

"No, but close. That first piece was her salvation, though. They dug it," Marty replied, massaging his forehead.

"Bobby, honestly, give it to me," Mike said.

"She has a gift, no bull. That voice soars and is pure country, but I don't know. Right now she's a fake and the audience caught on. She ain't no Terri Clark."

"Too bad she's not more like Jess

McLain," Bob added.

Something sparked Amy to get involved. She saw her dreams fading by the second and realized Terry Ann couldn't do a thing to save them. She removed her glasses and focused. "Who's Jess McLain? What do I need to do to be more like her?" she asked innocently.

"It's not a her, it's a him," Mike answered.

"What about him is so special? Clue me in, if you don't mind," Amy pleaded.

"Jess was once a huge rodeo star," Bobby explained. "He has all the ingredients as far as image goes, plus the voice. He's your all-American cowboy. In addition, he owns a ranch in Wyoming. He sat in with us here about three years ago, wasn't it, Rip? Should have signed him then. He's a friend of Marty's. Ask him. We couldn't beg him to cut an album but he'd go gold if he did. Jess McLain represents everything western music was once: authentic, heartfelt and unpretentious. Jess wrote the music he lived and sang it to people who understood. The problem is, he's just not cut out for the life: won't be owned, won't be played with. Hates middlemen and politics and I can't say that I blame him."

"It's a shame, though. He's good. We

could use his talent now," continued Bobby. "The whole industry's going back to its roots, and at the same time, dividing. Country went commercial and pop, too slick for real rural folks. And western went west, where it oughta be. Just look at the names making it today: LeDoux, Tyson, Edwards — some old timers and plenty of new blood, too. The good news is western music is on the way up and growing hotter by the minute. People want the real thing. Songs about the land, the way of life, those cowboy values people still yearn for. I say we ought to give it to them. That's where we need to be. In McLain's territory. The sound of the West. That's the direction we want to go — if we can."

Bobby looked to Marty and the others in the group. They seemed in agreement with the remark.

"That's what you need, Marty. A great voice, a connection to the cowboy life and a pretty little knockout a cowboy can dream about. Find all that and I'll get on board with you," Bob said.

"I'm trying," answered Marty.

"Hey, guys, she's from Jersey, remember? A cowgirl she's not. Next idea?" Terry Ann interrupted.

Mike looked defeated and returned to

pacing, armed with a cigarette.

"You're right, she's not. Okay, let's just think about it. Bob, thanks for coming out. Chucky, Ripper, thanks, fellas. Ronny, Felix, I'll see to it you all get paid. Appreciate the time." Marty shook Bob's hand.

"Wait, Marty, you know damn well she has the look," Mike gave it one last shot. "And the voice."

"Forget it. This was a mistake from the get-go. A pretty smile just won't cut it. Bob's right, we need a cowgirl. Besides, she drinks."

Marty got up to leave. The battle was over.

Chapter Six

Pleading with Destiny

Please, God, don't let this happen. Damn it, Terry, this is your fault! I couldn't keep up onstage. I know I could have done better. What am I going to do now? You never said record labels would be here. How could I be so stupid? I can't keep playing dumps and fairs. The band just didn't know my stuff.

None of these guys liked me. They all hate me. I didn't try and embarrass them on purpose. God, please don't let this happen. I can't go back to Jersey.

Heistler never liked me either; he was just looking for an excuse. Now Foxworthy doesn't think I can do it either. If they'd let me have a drink before I went onstage everything would have been fine. My lyrics aren't that bad. Maybe if I'd worked the crowd more, like a shorter skirt? Crap! I can't let this chance get away. What do I have to do? I can't go back.

Okay, Amy, take a drink and calm down. There's got to be something. Why are they

so hung up on a guy who won't even sing?
Some redneck from Wyoming. It's 'cause
he's a man, is why. No, no, think, Amy.
Marty's leaving. Okay, okay, they all got ex-
cited about a cowgirl singer. The real deal.
Damn it, there's no reason why I can't be
one. How hard can it be? Just act dumb
and wear a cowboy hat. Sing about horses.
I'm not going to spend my whole life
starving.

"Mr. Heistler? Please wait!" Amy ran after Marty through the empty club. He was halfway down the hall when she stopped him, and he looked extremely annoyed.

"Sir, please. I need this. Don't write me off," Amy pleaded.

"Oh, now it's 'sir.' Look, sweetheart, you had your shot. Those guys that you just embarrassed onstage are some of the most influential people in the entire business. I risked it all on their recommendations and came out smelling like a garbage truck."

"Please, sir, I can do this. I can become whatever you ask. I promise. No more bullshit from me. I'm sorry. I know I screwed up. Please help me. I'll become your female Jess McLain or Chris Le—whoever. Please!"

Marty had been around long enough to

57

know when someone was acting, or if they were really sincere. But even he was beginning to wonder how he could turn someone from Fairfield, New Jersey, into a cowgirl.

"I don't know, kid. You don't even know who Chris LeDoux is. You want to sing country-western, darlin'. He *was* country. And western. You'd have a hard time being him. Or Jess McLain, or anybody authentic, for that matter. It's a long stretch. Plus, that so-called road manager you have, she knows nothing. I don't deal with people like that. And you. You seem to have a little problem." Marty wasn't in the mood for negotiation. "Sorry, kid. Good luck."

"Marty, please." Amy reached out and grabbed his coat. "I know we aren't perfect. Terry picked me up four years ago. I was homeless. She may be a bitch, but she taught me to sing and because of her I have a place to live. I know I drink too much and I blew it, but please, give me another chance. I won't let you down. I'll do whatever you say," Amy pleaded. She'd given all she had. Heistler now held her fate.

"Kid, you have the voice, but if you want to work with me, you're going to have to do exactly what I say, no questions. First, you sign a contract with me and only me. You screw up one time and I'll have your ass in a sling. I'm not bullshitting here. No more second chances. And just so you know I'm serious, I have seven other interviews with acts that would kill to have your spot."

Marty stopped there. A white lie couldn't hurt. Something about her innocent tone pulled on him. This could either be his best risk to date or she could ruin him. He knew he couldn't have another failure.

"What about Terry Ann? I can't leave her behind. Isn't there anything you can do?" Amy asked out of loyalty.

"Not now, to be honest. However, if she'll release all rights to you and your music, I'll see to it she still has a job when you go on tour. That's the best I can do. But rest assured, if she gets in the way of your career, you're gone," Marty warned.

Tears formed in her eyes. Amy smiled and looked as though his words had revived her. She now had control of her destiny and knew she could make it happen or end up on the street. She had to become whatever Heistler asked. Her joy overshadowed the worry she had for Terry Ann's fate. She latched onto Marty and gave him a hug.

"Thank you. I promise I won't let you down. You'll see. I won't blow it," she said, wiping her eyes.

"Okay, kid. I have to do some begging.

Don't screw this up."

"I won't. And thank you."

"Hey, Amy, just out of curiosity. How well do you really know your manager?" Marty asked as he turned to go.

"Really well, why?" Amy said.

"When you two are alone and she's giving you career advice, ask her about a singer from about fifteen years ago named Teresa Ann Hillard. If she doesn't remember, tell her to give me a ring. I do. Stick around the hotel, kid. After I spend tomorrow morning eating crow, I'll be giving you a call." Heistler smiled and left the bar.

Chapter Seven

Ultimatum

Terry Ann didn't know whether she should scream, cry, or just wring Amy Talbot's neck. They'd come that close to losing the one break she could tell was the one they'd been looking for. Ever since she picked the kid up and told her she could stay, and then heard her sing, she knew that, someday, that voice would be heard by somebody who would know it could make money. Big money.

Amy was no Charlotte Church, however. She was a bona-fide wreck, guilty of mood swings, binges, and problem drinking. Maybe she was even a real alcoholic. But she had her reasons. People on the bottle always do. Terry Ann didn't judge. No one could say the life the kid had left behind was worth looking back on and, although she was no angel — and certainly not someone the public could know the truth about — she still had the feeling, power and the ability to make music out of her life, short as it had been. That voice was her salvation.

She could be another Lee Anne Rimes if she got her act together, but Terry knew she had to hurry. A whole world of adult pop stars was up against her if she didn't launch soon.

"What was all that about back in the hall?" Terry Ann asked as they slid into the '92 Dodge she called a car. "You look upset."

"Just about me, making sure I never screw anybody over again if I intend to work for Foxworthy. He was pissed, but he's still talking. Can you believe that?"

"No. You're lucky. You think you want to work for these guys, though?" Terry Ann had her doubts about both men. She'd been around long enough to sense they weren't in it for anybody but themselves.

"Yes, I do. More than anything. I didn't know they'd set me up like this, with big-time musicians. I didn't know I'd piss off the whole world by being late. Why didn't you get me outta there this morning? Why'd you let me screw this one up?"

"Me? Get you outta there? Short of shooting you up, sweetheart, I'd say you owe me thanks for getting you there at all. Do you remember me dragging you half-awake into that cold shower? Let's call it what it is, Amy — you're stuck. I've been pushing you and prodding you and holding you up every single day for the last four years, and even when the world gives you the chance you've been waiting for, you stay up half the night swilling your fear away like there was nothing on the line. I couldn't stop you. You're damned near impossible to figure, and I'm just about at the end of my rope!"

Terry Ann glared at Amy and stuck the key into the ignition. "Crap. Let's go! What happened today was sad. You won't admit it, but you've got a real problem, sweetheart, and I'm sick and tired of helping you hide it and then fixing it for you. You want a career in music, you need to get cleaned up. You can't commit to these guys in the shape you're in. You'll never make it. You need to dry out once and for all. Goddamn it, Amy, I'm tired of the whole thing. I can't be there every time. I'm beginning to wonder if I can be there at all."

Terry pulled out into the traffic and headed back toward the motel they'd rented for the week. All she could think of was sleep.

"What do you mean?" Amy said, panicky. She knew full well she deserved every word she heard, and hated to admit that the one friend she had in the world was telling her the truth.

"I can't keep this up, kid. You're too much. In another year, you'll be legal. Honey, it's time for you to get out on your own. I'll be rooting for you, but I just can't carry you around anymore. Don't have the strength, that's for sure."

"What? But I need you!" Amy secretly breathed a sigh of relief. The deal she agreed to meant that Terry Ann would have to go.

"No, you need real management. And you need a mom. Somebody to handle your life. You need a pro. Somebody who knows how to get you through this stuff. I can get you out on the stage and that's about it. That's all I know. That's all I ever knew."

"But listen, that's just what Heistler offered me, Terry — to take me over. In spite of that disaster in there earlier, he actually wants to manage me and get me where I need to go. Somehow, I have to get it together and prove to him that I'm worth promoting. That I can do it. I just never had a good reason before. I can stop drinking. I know I can. And you've got to be there for me somehow, I can't do it without you."

"I wouldn't be so confident, Amy. This is bigger than you think," Terry responded.

"I know, but it's a chance at a real career."

64

"That's not what I mean. You don't see yourself, Amy. Today was as ugly as it gets. You were outta control. And that stuff about you being a phony — in a way they're right. The material isn't really you, and we know it. We all know you can write. Your music is good, but those guys had a point. It hurt to see them tear your stuff apart and you. Honey, we don't have the time or the money to straighten you out in time for this break. I don't know how you're gonna get where they want you to go but that's what you have to do."

"I can do it. I just have to. Don't back out on me now," Amy pleaded. "I need help. Please, cover for me for a while. I'm waiting for Marty Heistler to draw up a contract. There has to be a way."

Chapter Eight

Fat Chance in Fort Worth

Marty Heistler never liked the game of hide-and-seek as a kid. He hated games. He liked to know exactly what was going to happen. Amy's unexpected performance at the Dallas Dome made him very unhappy.

Passing out just into her fourth song while opening for a big act didn't leave Marty feeling too comfortable. She actually had to be carried offstage after her catastrophic collapse. She was currently with the on-call paramedic and Bobby Dall, backstage at the Dome, trying to recover. Once she came around, Marty could try to focus his business mind and rescue himself.

Heistler wasn't really mad at the kid. He couldn't be. Two hours prior to the show Terry Ann had been unexpectedly rushed to a hospital. An ambulance picked her up when she started to have trouble breathing, leaving Amy fairly frantic. His heart went out to the pretty little thing that had first riveted the Texas crowd with her opening number. She stayed strong through her second, then began to weave and buckle, finally passing out midway through her fourth song, either from fright or too much alcohol.

He couldn't believe it. The long shot of having her play again so soon had proved fatal. Marty had come to terms with the fact that his present project was lost in a downward spiral. Amelia Talbot needed real help. Her rehabilitation had to happen, or else. A re-creation, in fact. His lip bled as he chewed on it while dialing up an old friend. He realized he was being forced to beg for the first time in his entire career.

"J-Bar-M Ranch. This is Ashley speaking."

"Yes, Ms. Ashley, by some chance is Jess McLain around?" Heistler prayed.

"Uh, no, sir, don't expect him back for a week," Ashley Sharpe answered without emotion, following some well-learned instructions.

In the middle of one of his rare appearances at the main house at night in search of a cup of coffee, McLain's attention was caught in mid-pour. Mouthing instructions to Ashley regarding who was on the other end, he waited.

"Well, Ms. Ashley, this is Marty Heistler and I'm calling from Texas. Would you please tell Jess I'm on the phone? That it's not the bank."

Ashley mouthed the name to Jess who immediately got up and took the receiver. He knew this couldn't be a social call. Ash left in a hurry. By the expression on Jess's face, she could tell what was coming wouldn't be a conversation she was welcome to hear.

"This better be some kind of emergency," Jess said to Heistler.

"Hey, buddy, how's the home front?"

"Cut the shit, Marty. What is it this time? Didn't we just have this conversation four days ago? I paid you off and then some. I don't owe you anything, so you better be close to death or something, because I couldn't buy my way out of a shit house, I'm so broke. Don't ask for money." Jess never wasted time getting to the point.

Sweating profusely, Heistler searched for words and knew that if Amy's future was even a prayer, then this call was his Hail Mary.

"Look, I'm sorry to bother you. I don't need money. I need a favor."

"The answer is no, and the next question is?" Experience had taught Jess that Marty didn't do anything unless he had something

68

to gain. "I mean, you can ask, but the answer is still no."

"Jess, damn it. I'm in a real bind. Look, I wouldn't call unless I was about to go under," Heistler said, trying not to sound like a beggar.

"I'm going to regret even asking. You know that one of these days, it's not going to count anymore that you gave me money to buy out my ex-wife on this ranch. But don't play me. It's starting to bore me." Jess was impatient.

"Look," Marty began to explain. "I just signed this young kid. A twenty-year-old with a voice no one can buy. But I'm under the gun to turn her into something, and yesterday." Marty squirmed asking his next question, knowing the answer would most likely prompt a four-letter word or a click.

"Yeah, so what does that have to do with me?" Jess interrupted. "We already had this discussion. I won't sing or play for you."

"No, I know you won't try that again. Look, Jess, she's from Jersey. Her image sucks. I can't make a country star out of a white ghetto baby. I have six months to make the kid into a cowgirl. She drinks too much, sounds East Coast, and needs a makeover. Jess, you're my man. Let me ship her out there for six months. Please, I need you."

The question and answer seemed simultaneous.

"Are you friggin' nuts? Where the hell do you get off even dreaming this shit up? I paid you, with interest. I have a business to save here, and I'm not about to baby-sit some kid. Forget it! End of discussion."

The tension escalated as Marty continued, employing as much guilt as he could muster.

"Look, Jess, I know you don't owe me. I didn't owe you, either, and even though you didn't ask for it, I loaned you the money to make the buyout. Come on, you always have a group of losers there living off you. One more wouldn't hurt. Give me a break, Jess. I need this to work. Give an old friend a hand."

Marty's comment about Jess's staff proved to be the wrong one. He regretted it the minute it slipped out.

"Losers? *Losers?* At least they're ranch hands. Honest and hard-working. They're not backstabbing, lying pieces of shit who use people. This conversation is over. Oh, and by the way, don't think I didn't see the hook with the loan. You thought you could force me into cutting a record for you if I owed you something. Don't fuck with me, Marty. I'm the one who saw combat, not you. You don't have the spine to mess with me. Don't you ever, ever call me again and use the word 'losers' about these kids here or, so help me God, I will find you and make you sorry you ever picked up the phone, get it?"

Marty knew Jess meant business. He was a man who grew calm before the kill. His tone at that moment was placid and controlled, and Marty knew he'd pushed too far.

"Damn, Jess, you're right. I'm sorry. Now you're going to really be pissed. I didn't think you'd say no. I've already booked her on a plane bound for Denver and from there, on up to you. I thought that you . . ." Marty tried his last angle: deceit.

"You didn't think! You're putting a kid on a plane headed west and didn't even have the nerve to call first?"

"Jess, I thought it would be okay. I thought you wouldn't let me down." Marty continued to lie.

"I hope it's a round-trip ticket because she's going right back. You're a real piece of work, you know that? Jerry would roll over in his grave if he could see you now."

Marty stopped. The secluded corner he'd found backstage was beginning to feel like a tomb. His last hope had fallen faster than

Amy Talbot after a bender. He couldn't believe Jess was refusing to play. Mike Foxworthy, meanwhile, had gone behind his back and made further commitments, deals they couldn't fulfill. Maybe now was the time to split from Mike and go it alone. Less to worry about, more control.

"Please, just give her a chance. Jess, I'm begging here."

Click.

"Fuck!" Heistler screamed loud enough for those who he was hiding from to hear.

Chapter Nine

The Rescue

Bob Dall wasn't all business. He actually had a warm heart and was known as one of the most upstanding producers in his field. His finest trait was that he was honest. He'd been sitting with Amy after the show and giving her some much-needed support. Seeing that she didn't need to be upset further, he excused himself and went to investigate Marty Heistler's next move.

Amy sipped Perrier from a bottle. The signs of her breakdown showed in her face: streams of tears ran from her bloodshot eyes, which were darkened by smudges of smeared mascara. She watched furtively as Marty Heistler and Bob Dall talked. Marty grew irate and Dall tried to calm him down. The conversation escalated and with each minute, Marty's face grew redder. Finally, after much argument, Marty finally nodded in agreement, closing the conversation.

Amy wondered if they were discussing how to get rid of her. She'd blown chance number two. Bob appeared to be on her side though. He'd told the whole group that. She should have waited to sign with just him, but Marty insisted. Now she had a contract with Marty Heistler and felt owned by him.

Bob Dall smiled when Marty shook his hand, albeit reluctantly. Then he rummaged through his equipment for his cell phone.

As Amy watched him dial up a call, she was sure her fate had been sealed.

Chapter Ten

Last Call

McLain paced inside the kitchen in fury. The phone conversation had made him fighting mad. The ranch hands could hear him still cursing Marty Heistler's name, followed by a few choice words about Heistler's views on things. The phone rang again and on the fifth ring, Jess picked it up.

"Jess, hey, how goes it? It's Bobby Dall."

"What, Bob? Does Marty have you doing his dirty work now too?"

"Look, Jess, I know Marty can be a puke, but he was under the gun from Foxworthy. This girl is good, but it's beyond that right now," Bob said.

Bob never asked anyone to give him something for nothing. His insight into matters was always clear and accurate. He sensed that Jess might be the only one to have a solution that could help save Amy Talbot. Bob liked Amy, even with her problems and flaws, but he knew all too well that if she didn't change, show business would leave her in and out of rehab for the rest of her life. Or end it. She'd be another Janis Joplin, if she lived long enough. He couldn't see another talent like that get burned.

"Jess, I wouldn't call if I didn't think you were the answer."

"I'm sorry, no! Anyway, I don't care. It's not my problem, nor is Marty's fucked-up life," McLain retorted.

"I know, but this kid is damn near a falling-down drunk. If she were sober, she might be close to what we're looking for. Right now, the recording industry is crying for a real cowgirl. Heistler's convinced her that she could be the one. Jess, they conned her into signing. Now she has to produce. She's got no family, nothing. But she does have talent and lots of it. Oh, yeah, she might make it without help for a while, but she'd be a publicist's nightmare, or worse." Bob spoke honestly. He didn't like it, but the facts were clear.

"My give-a-shit is broke. Don't you get it?"

"Jess, look — me and the Williams brothers are finalizing a deal with the largest player in music to create a subsidiary production company. We're in. And right now, your favorite person Marty is someone I need."

Jess interrupted, "So, take him and

maybe I won't end his life."

"Jess, bear with me. I believe this kid can make it so completely that I've talked it over with Ripper and Chucky. Work with us and we'll make you a twenty percent partner if she goes. Ten grand up front." Dall had his plan mapped out. The angles and approach all seemed to match on this rare occasion.

"Twenty-five percent, not to do shit. I won't lie. I hope you cut an album eventually, but that would be all about you. Right now, I'm mopping up this mess. Plus, under the deal, this kid would become mine and if I say I'll take care of her, you know it's done. But she really needs help, Jess, or she's going to fail."

The silence followed on both ends. Jess thought of how deeply he was in debt and how ten grand would keep the bank off him for a year. Twenty-three grand in the hole, on top of a monthly overhead, was killing him.

"Ten grand, up front. I don't want money out of your pocket to fix that moron's mess," Jess said, calming.

"It's not. The major label actually gave me a hundred grand to set things up and get a few people committed. You know I don't joke. Get her back to me in six months a cowgirl and bone dry. I'll take care of the rest. And because I know you're one of the last men of your word, you've got mine in return. To prove it, the check is on its way and your name is on the contract as partner. If she fails, it's still yours, and the payment will begin soon. I'm already making music money, my friend. I won't pressure you to cut an album. Got my word. I just may inquire once in a while."

Bob wasn't Marty Heistler's biggest fan either, but Marty's contacts were a necessity and with luck, Amy could land a number-one hit in the first year. More money than he and Jess needed. Plus, he was doing a good thing for a good man.

"Okay Bob, if it were Marty, I'd say tuck and roll but, hell, I don't know. You promise you won't let Nashville's grime get to her the way it did to Becky? I don't need to clean up someone's life after they get dumped on again. I've been there. Got your word on that?" Jess asked.

"McLain, I've known you a long time. Becky is the reason I owe you this. And you're a good man. I promise I won't let this kid get ruined. I hope you'll help, being a partner. Ripper is really excited; he even wants to see about having a private studio on your ranch someday. It's up to you, but we could get country music back to where it's supposed to be — in the country. And western music back up front. What do you say? And if you're worried, I'll control Heistler. He won't bug you anymore." Dall awaited a response. He didn't have to, but this was his chance to help two people out who needed it.

"All right. If it's us four, I don't have anything to lose. I need the money and I don't have a choice. I ain't too happy about this, Bob. For the record, I still don't like it."

"Neither do I, but if I can make the best out of this for all of us, then it'll be worth it. Help her, Jess. She's naïve and needs a lot of work. Good luck."

Bobby Dall's company was now in place. "Honesty for a change," he told himself. "Damned if it doesn't work sometimes."

Now it was up to Jess to perform a miracle. "Yeah, well, thanks, Bob. I owe ya. I needed a break."

"No," said Bobby. "We're even — *if* it works."

Jess hung up the phone and set down his coffee cup. Pride threw it across the room.

Chapter Eleven

The Road North

The flight to Colorado took longer than Amy expected. Two connections, the first from Nashville to Denver, then an express plane northbound to Cody, all tempered by Dramamine and Tylenol for the hangover. It had been thirty-six hours since the concert, and Amy still couldn't get over the shame of her crumble at the Country Dome. She should have seen it coming. The band couldn't follow her, the size of the hall made the sound bounce all over, and she broke a guitar string during the warm-up. It took three whiskey sours to get up enough nerve to get back up in front of that band for as long as it lasted.

And then Terry Ann! Did she have to pick that night to go to an emergency room? A phone call told Amy that her blood pressure was so high, Terry couldn't even breathe. They admitted her on the spot and scheduled tests right away. Amy didn't stand a chance getting past that last number with Terry Ann on her mind. And she didn't.

Somebody picked her up off the stage when she passed out, almost falling off the edge in the process. They brought the next act out in a hurry. When she came to, she was in the hands of a paramedic, who made sure she wasn't injured.

At six o'clock the next morning she awoke in her motel room to find a note by her bed instructing her to call Bobby Dall as soon as she came to. Her hands shook as she dialed the number. It was eight o'clock when he picked her up and told her she'd be on a westbound plane by ten that same day, headed for Denver with a connection to Cody, Wyoming.

Amy paced the station. The Greyhound from Cody to Purgatory stood parked at Dock Four, scheduled to leave at five p.m. She resisted boarding, even though the gray-and-blue bus had stood with its doors open since three-thirty. She didn't want to get on.

I can't believe this, she said to herself. *Twenty years old and I'm being shipped off to some rest home for retards like I'm a kid going away to camp. How'd I ever agree to this? What the hell made me say yes, sign over the car, and promise I'd stay clean until Mike rearranged my whole life for an-*

other whack at show business? Wasn't there anything else I could have done?

She stepped over her guitar, put down her rucksack, and lit a cigarette. Pathetic. I'm fucking pathetic. No one's going to reinvent me. Not in six months, not ever. I wonder if they sell Heineken in here? As her eyes scanned the bus station for a bar, she realized she couldn't get a beer there, or anywhere. Marty had confiscated her fake ID and Terry Ann was gone.

A pang of loneliness reminded Amy that Terry Ann had been released from the hospital with instructions to rest for at least a month. Unreal. She couldn't believe she was actually in Wyoming by herself and out on her own. That reality, the separation from the one person who had shaped her life for four years, was starting to sink in. Amy felt anxious and alone. Like an orphan, in fact.

Thinking back, she realized she hadn't seen her father since grade school. He'd walked out one morning after a fight with her mother and never returned. No telling where he was. Then came her mom's gradual breakdown and the unspeakable end. She remembered telling her school friends that her mother had just died. She was too ashamed to use the word "suicide."

With no immediate family to turn to, social workers had arranged for a foster home and relocation with strangers. Amy refused to accept the decision, and before anyone could stop her, she'd packed up and hit the road. She found herself one town over and hunkered down at the local country-western watering hole her mom had taken her to occasionally to hear the music they both loved. Amy tried to look as if she was just waiting for someone and sat in a booth by herself until midnight, afraid to move.

Terry Ann had noticed the girl when she came in and served her a large Coke. She refilled it often.

"Can I get you anything from the kitchen, sweetie?" she asked. "The bar's off limits, I'm afraid."

"I know, and no thanks," said Amy. She fidgeted and looked at the menu in earnest. "Maybe later."

By closing time, while picking up tabs and the last round of drinks for the regulars, Terry decided to approach the teen again, still parked in the booth by herself.

"I've seen you in here before," she said, eyeing her suspiciously. "What's up?"

Amy didn't dare speak, she was so afraid of being turned in. The older woman slid onto the seat across from her and said,

"Hey, you shouldn't be in here. You know that and so do I. We're closing, honey. You need a place to crash?"

And that was it. Sister, girlfriend, mother — Terry Ann Hill had taken Amy in and given her a home, even handled the legal rights that let her stay. She gave her a chance to sing and play the guitar and jam as often as she wanted to, right at the bar, before it opened, of course. The bands passing through tolerated the spunky teenager who tried to learn every riff and tune and sang along whenever they'd let her. And Amy dreamed of being a girl singer in a band. And at eighteen, thanks to Terry, she finally got the chance.

Terry saw to it that Amy's education focused solely on her talent, which seemed inexhaustible. During the day, Amy helped out by cleaning the bar or doing short-order cooking in the kitchen. No one had money for college, and Amy had dropped out of high school one semester short of her senior year.

Evenings, she practiced guitar and sang with a local band. Besides, Terry was sure the kid was on the fast track to the music world. She had tons more talent than she herself ever had. She never told her, though. Never told her a word about her own career before it ended. That hurt way too much to even think about. Instead, she pushed Amy to go after her dream before she lost it.

Hell, she can always get a GED later on, Terry said to herself. *Let the kid sing. Just let her sing.*

Chapter Twelve

Road Trip

The bus engines rumbled and the smell of diesel filled the station from one end to the other as Amy started up the bus steps. She found herself jostled by a stringy-haired teen in a blue parka, carrying a backpack and a CD player.

" 'Scuse me. Sorry." Brenda Bowers clambered in and shoved her belongings above the front seat, arranging her earphones on her head and plugging in to whatever it was that drowned out the outside world.

Amy took the next seat over in the front by the door, and piled her belongings next to her so as to discourage anyone from sitting beside her. She wasn't in the mood for strangers or small talk. She wasn't in the mood for much of anything.

Luckily, the bus was barely filled that afternoon, and the doors closed with not more than a dozen aboard. Amy heaved a sigh of relief and settled in, looking blankly out the window.

"Where you headed?" The driver turned toward Amy with a smile. "End of the line?"

"I'm not sure. Some place called the J-Bar-M Ranch. How far is that?"

"I'm glad you asked, little lady. Purgatory. That's actually one stop past the last stop. I do that one as a favor now and then. Just for special folks." He winked, and rubbed his right thigh slowly with his hand as he pulled the steering wheel with his left. "Yep, that one's by special request only. No tips unless you insist." He leered.

"That's bullshit," came a muffled voice from the other seat. Brenda Bowers had scrunched down on the vinyl bench with her feet up on the metal seat arm and her coat over her head, intending on catching a nap on the way home. She sat up and said, "He's pulling your leg. The J-Bar-M is the last stop. I'm getting off there, too, and then my friend Larry picks me up. But . . . um . . . do you know someone up there? There's no rental car or nothin'. It's just a truck stop. You've got to have wheels. The J-Bar-M is where I live."

Amy never imagined that a kid like this could be living at the godforsaken rehab center too, if that's what it really was. She still wasn't sure where Marty had come up with this idea of sending her all the way to some cowboy hideout in Nowheresville for "treatment," as he called it, when he gave her the ultimatum. A place that would clean out her system and clear out her head while it taught her some western geography. If she wanted to sing country-western, he explained, she might as well get a crash course on the western part. That way, when the time came to present her, she would come right out of the West. That's where the action was, he'd said. The music with romance, roots and lots of fans. The ranch was on the Wyoming-Montana border, somewhere, far away from everywhere. But he never mentioned that it came with kids.

"Oh, thanks. What were you doing in town?" Amy asked, hoping to learn something about her options if she needed a quick getaway.

"I work there. Part-time. At the feed store — just a half-day, five days a week. I'm saving up to go to a junior college in Powell next semester and trying to earn some cash to pay my tuition. My younger brother lives with me on the ranch too. I mean, we both do. With Jess. It's temporary."

Amy could barely keep up. "Jess?" Of course, the superstar Marty had told her about. Her new boss.

"Mr. Jess McLain, the rancher who let us

move in while my parents were trying to decide who gets custody. We just said chuck it while they fought it out. Dad travels a lot anyway and my mom works nights so when they decided to sell the house and it turned out there wasn't room in Mom's apartment, we just said to hell with it and — Oh! I'm sorry. You don't care about all this stuff. Hey, my name's Brenda Bowers. You must think I'm nuts."

"Hi, Brenda," Amy answered. "I'm Amy. Amelia Talbot, actually, and no, I don't think you're nuts. Take it easy. You're fine." The name Jess reverberated again. Everybody's superman.

"What are you doing heading up to the ranch?" Brenda asked.

"Oh, me? Let's just say I'm on my way up for a geography lesson."

"What?" the girl asked, screwing up her face. "You're kidding me. There's no geography up there!"

Amy laughed. "Okay, never believe everything you hear. And listen, didn't anybody ever tell you? Don't talk to strangers. It's not safe. But it just so happens I'll be joining you and your brother and whoever else is up there for a little while. Got some work to do."

"That your guitar?"

"Yes."

"Wow. Jess plays guitar. He's really good. Do you sing too?"

"Anybody ever tell you that you ask a lot of questions? Yes, I sing," Amy answered. She felt for her notebook in her jacket pocket. She'd been writing lyrics on the plane, trying to work out her feelings about heading west, into a world she'd mostly imagined and barely remembered, but the stuff many of her songs were made of.

She'd been west once before, a long time before. Her parents took her to Yellowstone when she was eight years old, probably the year her father walked out. But they were together then. Her mother, her father, and herself: a magical memory of a family and a happy, scar-free time. They'd taken Amy on one of those long summer car trips kids hate and usually forget, but she never did. The Grand Tetons and the buffalo and the grassy plains stayed etched inside her memory. She remembered the horses and the campfires and the ranger who told stories under the sparkling stars at night, and her parents, unimaginably, actually together, loving each other, way back then. She grew up writing and singing about a place she barely had a name for, but felt deeply connected to. Year after year, she wrote and explored a mythic world where landscape and the concept of security had fused. In that place she'd acquired the clear knowledge that love can be safe — in fact, that love was even possible. As she grew up, the far West and that knowledge had become one and the same. She pulled out her notebook and looked at her last entry:

Headin' west
In a cold wind:
Heading back to the place that I
  belong:
Riding down the winding road
On the back of my old roan,
Don't ask me where I'm bound,
I know it's home.

Headin' west,
In a cold wind
Never mind that the trail is swept by
  snow,
The fire that's burning in my heart
Is as hot as a roaring hearth,
Don't ask when I'll be home,
I'm sure you'll know. . . .

She wasn't sure she believed any of it. What did she know about home? She knew where Purgatory was now. That was all that mattered.

"I'm glad you're coming to live with us," Brenda started. "There's so much to do. Maybe you can help. Then again, maybe you won't have to do any work."

"Work? What do you mean?"

"Well, Jess makes sure everybody pulls their own weight. Everybody has a job, so I kind of have two jobs, the one in town, and then I do ranch work for Jess too, but I don't mind, too much."

Amy looked at the dark circles under the girl's eyes. She couldn't have been more than seventeen or eighteen, but she looked old and tired.

"Yeah, right. Well, sounds like you're pretty responsible. You're a good kid. Or this Jess is one hell of a jerk to make you work so hard."

Brenda smiled and didn't answer.

Amy thought about herself and how she'd never felt motivated to go back to school, never figured out how to support herself, really. She relied on Terry to do everything. She was supposed to sing. That's what Terry said.

"It's about thirty minutes before we get there. I'm gonna catch some sleep, okay?"

"Sure," answered Amy. She reached for a cigarette and noticed the bus had a "No Smoking" sign lit up right over the driver.

He caught her eye in the rearview mirror as she was studied the sign, and winked at her again.

"Yep, for you, little darlin'," he said into the mirror, "I might even drive all the way to the ranch."

Chapter Thirteen

Drop Zone

The Ford rolled down the long dirt road bound for the J-Bar-M. The sun had set and only a hint of daylight remained. Spring in Wyoming was on the calendar but winter still held a grip on the land. Beneath a gray, chilly sky, the dead yellow grass covering the rolling plains still had blemishes of snow scattered here and there.

The ranch could be seen off in the distance, lights indicating its remote location. Amy was struck by how isolated it appeared — no other vehicles, buildings or landmarks. Soon the early evening moon would rise, giving more illumination to the surrounding barns, feed stores and stables.

Brenda was impatient, but excited and wired. She chatted and supplied Amy with all kinds of details about life on the J-Bar-M, feeling extremely important.

Larry chose to remain silent. Besides, Brenda continued to gab the whole time. When they rolled up in front of the house, however, both Larry's and Brenda's attitude seemed to change. Amy felt the tension and tried to ignore it.

From inside the indoor arena, the ranch crew watched with mild interest.

"Guess the new meat is here. Gary, take a look," Double D pointed out the window to his friend. They'd finished their day's work and were making their way from the large building to the main house. "Must be. Boss waited around the whole day for this one. Can't remember when we saw him in the ranch house for that long a time. I reckon he ain't too happy 'bout her," he added. "Normally he relaxes after noon, but today he was ugly all day."

"All I know is," said Gary, "I think I'm going to make my ass scarce tonight. Haven't seen him like this in a spell."

"Gary, Dallas . . ." a voice called from inside the open barn door. The two hands stopped and waited. Jess McLain walked through the doorway to meet them.

"Look, boys, I want you guys to be around tonight. You both know we got a new hand in." Jess's faded buckskin leather chaps brushed softly when he walked, their scarred surface proof of long hours on the trail in the saddle. His cowboy boots and hat, both black and worn, gave evidence they had seen as many days on the trail as the man that wore them. He wore a sheepskin-lined, denim jean-jacket, his familiar trademark. Leather riding gloves still covered his hands and the spurs on the heels of his buckaroo-heeled boots jingled, adding a magical sound when he walked. Blue eyes gleamed cold as a prairie night.

"Damn, Mr. Jess, you scared the plum hell outta me!" Dallas said, grabbing his chest.

Tickled by the remark, Jess smiled for the first time that day. "Sorry. Look, boys, this kid is a hard case. Some spoiled brat from New Jersey."

"Jersey? She's coming to work here? Doggone, boss, we got roundup coming, rodeo season, calving and stock to sell. What we gonna do with a city kid?" Dallas asked in his heavy Mississippi accent.

"Well, I don't know. I got blind-sided with it. If she leaves, it's not our problem. But Larry knows and now you do too. The kid's got baggage. She's gonna be dryin' out and dryin' up. Gary, I want you to help me break this one."

Gary, being third in command, rarely questioned his orders. "Yes, sir, but why?"

"Well, I don't necessarily think you'll understand, but when a person is one way their

96

whole life, and you want to change that, then you have to break them. Kill that side of them, make them reborn, so to speak. I don't owe this kid nothin', but if she's gonna be here, we're all gonna make her a cowgirl, or she can get the hell out. Savvy?"

Jess trusted his hands with the secret agenda. Gary and Dallas had helped him shape a few people up before and this would be no different, only they both got the feeling that the dark side of McLain was about to be seen.

"So, what I need from you two is a little extra discipline. You become that which you are around. The kid either gets on board here or leaves. Either way, just as good." Jess proceeded to complete his lockdown of the ranch.

"Yes, sir. You's can count on us, Massah." Dallas hoped to poke fun one last time while they could. Gary smiled and tried not to laugh.

Jess shook his head and smirked himself. "Okay, smart ass, get to the house, would you? I'll be there shortly, after I give the new rookie the McLain tour."

Jess disappeared inside the barn. Both men stopped smiling. They had seen the tour before. It wasn't pretty and they thanked God every time that it had never happened to them. To date, no one who had received the tour had lasted more than five days before they left. Gary turned to Dallas as they made their way to the house.

"You know, my whole life I wanted to be a cowboy. It may suck sometimes, but God, I love it here. If there's a definition of a real cowboy, Boss is it. Don't know if there's any harder man, but he's as good as they get. Sure hope someone says that about me someday," Gary sighed.

"Amen, brother. No one in Mississippi said a black man could ride broncs. He's the only one that would teach me. Believed in me. Well, guess we get to teach Miss Jersey here how to be a cowgirl. This gonna be fun," Dallas replied. They both scowled so as to give that hardened look when they walked by the new rookie.

"God damn, it's cold. Why can't we go inside? Shit!" Amy said as they stood outside the truck.

Larry watched Dallas and Gary walking toward the house. Brenda quickly taught Amy her first lesson on the ranch. "Amy, don't talk like that here. The boss will explode. He expects ladies to be ladies and men to treat them that way. If a hand talks around here like that, Jess is liable to dock him."

"Don't worry, hon, I can handle myself. Damn, it's cold," Amy complained.

Larry rolled his eyes and knew that this little girl was in for a shock. As Dallas and Gary approached, they acted reserved and sullen. They tipped their hats to the ladies without a word and gave Larry the report of the day.

Amy felt tired. She paced and fidgeted in the cold wind, her hands punched down into the pockets of her jeans. She hadn't had a drink since just before the flight, and the itch crawled up her back like a spider. Feeling as though she were in some kind of a TV western, she just shook her head, keeping her amusement and frustration to herself. She reached in her pocket, pulled her cigarettes out and went through the process of lighting one. The four ranch hands watched her light it, feigning discomfort. Brenda was the only one that made a comment.

"Oh, no!"

"What? It's just a smoke. You never seen one?" Amy asked.

Spurs jingled somewhere in the distance and out of the gloom, the image of a cowboy appeared. Jess, approaching six feet in height, his skin brown from hours in the sun, had a strong profile and square jaw easily discernable in the twilight shadows. This evening, his black hat nearly covered his eyes. Gary and Dallas forced themselves not to laugh, but it appeared that a show-down was inevitable. The boss walked into the yard.

Brenda almost swooned. Jess always made her knees tremble. She decided to join the rest of her group, leaving Amy deserted.

Amy tried to look confident, but fear engulfed her. She puffed long and hard on her smoke and stared at the man heading her way. Before she could finish, the wraith stood in front of her and pinned her with a hard stare. As she attempted to remove the cigarette, he snatched it violently from her lips.

"Hey, what the —"

"Rule number one: you don't smoke on my ranch. Do you know what a burning butt does to a barn full of hay? Didn't think so. Pack, now." Jess motioned to the car with his thumb.

"Who the hell are you?" Amy had now crossed into McLain's world. The group knew it would be a long night for her.

"Give me that fuckin' pack of cigarettes — now!" Jess held his palm out in front of her. "Or it's my foot in your ass. Do you understand me?"

The ranch hands knew that if Jess was cursing at a woman in the presence of a woman, he was dead serious. Amy looked at him in complete disdain and disbelief. Nonetheless, she pulled out the pack from her coat pocket and handed it over with a smirk. The ranch veterans wished they could tell her to just give up now and life would be much easier, but her fate was sealed. Jess took the pack and crushed the box.

"Hey! Those are expensive!"

"First off, shut your trap. When I want you to speak, I'll tell you. Rules are simple here. You work and you work hard, or you don't eat. You've met Larry and Brenda. You're lucky Larry had an errand to run or I would have let your ass walk. Those other two are David Dallas on the right. He's in charge of the kitchen. And Gary Russell there, on the left, is in charge of all my staff. Whatever they ask, you do it with a smile."

Jess and the outlaws glared at her.

"Great, typical. I get to answer to men. How new," Amy sassed in defense.

"I said don't talk! What about that don't you understand?" Jess barked, intimidating her as best he could.

"Brenda, would you get Brookes's little ass out here to get Jersey's things. She's got work to do," Jess said.

Amy tried to figure out what she was doing here. The whole scene was someone else's nightmare. Maybe being a singer wasn't worth it.

"Work? I haven't eaten in hours. I'm starved. Fuck, I just got here. I don't need this."

The group shook their heads, knowing Amy was in deep water. Almost amused, they watched Jess go to the next level.

"Excuse me. You have a hard time understanding orders. Well, no problem." Jess pushed her out of the way and reached into the extended cab of the truck and ripped her things out. Taking her rucksack and guitar, he placed them behind her, a good distance towards the road.

"Then take your load and haul ass! I don't want you here. Nor did I ask you to come. You're so worthless they sent you here to get rid of you. So, pick up and go. Town is twenty miles that way. Head left at the end of the drive." Jess turned away to walk to the house. Those who knew him well understood that the meaner he behaved, the more the person needed help. This was the worst they'd ever seen.

Amy struggled with her emotions. What she didn't know was that it was all planned.

Keeping her in the cold and wind was done on purpose, letting her know how rough was the land. She would never make it to town. Already shivering, she went to get her things. She picked them up and, in a second, made her first important life-changing decision. Walking to the front of the group, she put her things down. She waited to be noticed.

Finally, Jess turned to speak. "The road is that way."

"I want to stay."

"Excuse me, I don't think I heard you right." Jess squinted at her.

"Please, this may be my last chance. I need it. Please let me stay," Amy said softly.

"Gary, tell Mr. Brookes to take Ms. Jersey's things to Ms. Ashley's room. Mr. Russell, the rules, please." Jess stood with his arms folded across his chest, staring Amy in the eye. Gary began to recite the rules and the others joined him.

"One: No booze, no drugs, no smoking, or you're gone. Two: Once your job has begun, never leave it till it's done. Do your labor, big or small, do it right, or don't do it at all, or you're gone. Three: You break it, you lose it, you pay for it, or you're gone. Four: Livestock is off-limits until you're a ranch hand. You don't ride until shown or you're gone. Five: Get in trouble with the law or in town, you are gone. Six: All hands are high-school grads or are in school, no exceptions. Seven: Only days off are to rodeo or you're gone. Eight: No guests at the ranch unless all agree. Nine: Chores are not an option. Ten: Ladies will be ladies and gentlemen will act accordingly."

Gary paused and then looked to Jess. "Did I leave anything out, sir?"

"One."

"Oh, sorry. It's McLain's way or the highway, no exceptions." Gary finished and turned to the hands. Together they all went into the main house.

"Memorize them," Jess said to Amy. "You're to know them all in two days. Any questions?"

"No, I'm just real cold."

"I'll take care of that. Follow me and listen, 'cause I only say things once and don't give second chances." Jess made his way to the barn. Amy followed, shivering. Her clothes were not Wyoming-proof and the wind chafed at her bones.

"We take care of each other here. We all work together. You don't lie, you don't cheat. You don't cut corners, or I'll get your ass up at midnight and make you do it again. You want to play guitar and sing, do it on your own time, not mine. You leave, you don't come back, period." Jess held the door to the barn open.

They entered and not one word was said. The pungent aroma of livestock and animal droppings was so foreign to Amy she almost felt sick. Jess went into a small tack room and returned with a few items. He handed her some lined overalls and gloves. With no further instructions, he then proceeded to walk behind her and open a stall door. She struggled to put on the overalls as he spoke.

"I have a mare who's foaling early. She's due any day. I want this stall cleaned and mopped. Fresh straw inside when you're done. Leave the horse shit in the wheelbarrow there. Shovels are in that room. Mop it, wall to wall. Then take those bales of straw there and spread them out. I want her comfortable. When you're done, shut the door and come in. That'll be enough work for a meal."

Jess turned to leave. His eyes met hers for an instant and Amy could see nothing but a hard stare.

Suddenly she was alone in the barn. Amy feared her new surroundings and wanted to break down and cry. Jess had given her some advice on his way out. He wasn't completely blind to the fact she was scared. Life is tough and the world is hard.

"If you want it, you'll make it."

"I hope so. Jess, I don't want to fail at this, but just being here, I already broke one of your rules."

He stopped. "Which one?"

"I never graduated from high school," she said apologetically.

"Well, that's your problem right now. Looks like you have some work to do. It's up to you to fix it. Get this job done and get in and eat. Dinner's at seven p.m. Your day starts at four in the morning."

He turned and left.

Gary and Ashley looked out the window and saw the light on in the barn. Wishing they were flies on the wall of the stall, they spoke between themselves as the others prepared for dinner.

"So, the boss really let her have it, huh?" Ashley asked.

"I ain't ever seen him lay into a rookie like that before. But when you see her, you can tell she's a real screwup. Boy, you should have seen him snatch that cig out of her mouth. Almost pissed myself," Russell said.

"Must be why he was ticked off all day. Not to me, but just in general. Still don't understand why he had me dump all the horse manure from the evening cleaning into the birthing stall. But I don't ask questions. I don't get paid to think," Ashley replied. She put her hand on Gary's shoulder. "Whatever. It's dinnertime. Let's go eat."

Chapter Fourteen

Mess Hall

Amy walked into the ranch house hesitantly, rubbing her aching hands together in the cold. It was only seven-thirty, and already the night temperatures had dropped to near freezing. She was hungry. The warm light through the log house windows glowed brightly, and she hastened to get indoors after her brisk walk from the bunkhouse. She'd managed to clean out the foaling stall quickly as instructed, sweep the barn, and get moved into a top bunk in a small cabin where someone else was apparently already installed. Then, she showered and tried to make herself presentable.

She pushed open the door and walked into the ranch house, stopping at the threshold. No one said a word. She looked at the knothole clock on the far wall and remembered that someone had said dinner was at seven.

Damn, she was late. As she took off her jacket, seven pairs of eyes followed, most with a suffering look of impatience.

"Dinner bell rings at seven p.m. sharp around here, Miss Talbot," said Larry curtly. "We don't tolerate tardiness. You've kept some hard-working folk from eating, and I don't think any one of 'em is too happy about it."

"Oh my God, I'm sorry."

"Sorry ain't good enough, Jersey," retorted Jess. "To survive here you need a good memory. There's a lot of people depending on your memory for their survival, get it? This is the last time we wait on you. Next time you can't make it to the table on time, don't bother to come at all. Is that clear?"

Amy took her place at the one empty chair at the far end of the plank table. Paper placemats under china plates dressed things up slightly, but not enough to hide the fact that the fare was simple. Stacks of sandwich bread, bowls of beans and platters of roast meat were passed around, followed by corn on the cob. Amy was too humiliated to eat much. She sat in her chair with tears in her eyes, just wet enough to make her eye makeup run. She didn't want anyone to see her cry.

"Hey," whispered Ashley Sharpe. "It's all right. Take it easy." A lanky strawberry blonde in a denim work shirt and a turtleneck, Ash was chief trainer for the working stock on Jess's ranch. The rest of the horses were all rough stock, bred and sold for rodeo contractors. She'd come on board as a ranch hand to work off her payments for her own barrel horse and trailer. When she wasn't working horses, she competed in professional rodeo for the money. Jess encouraged all of them to ride and compete. He liked it when they won.

"Hey, forget it. Just eat," she continued. "I'm Ashley. Glad to meet you. We're sharing a cabin together."

Their eyes met and Amy smiled gratefully. She might make it after all. Slowly she scanned the faces at the table and tried to analyze what she saw. Next to Ashley sat Brookes Bowers, the sixteen-year-old brother of Brenda. A sandy blond teen with a bowl haircut, he appeared sullen, self-absorbed and definitely not interested in Amy.

On the other side of the table sat Gary Russell, the young rising rodeo star who came to the J-Bar-M to be mentored by Jess. He was the top hand at the ranch and third in command when it came to giving orders. Tanned and wiry, he looked like a man on mission, ready to spring. He ate with his mouth open and winked at Amy when she stared at him.

Next to Gary sat David Dallas, his skin a dark mocha brown, decked out in a plaid western shirt with pearl snap buttons and a red bandana. He had denim overalls on over the shirt and a flashy smile. He grinned at Amy broadly, as if to say, "Don't worry."

David had left Tupelo to learn to be a saddle bronc rider. He'd heard that the black rodeo circuit had money for the brave and willing and he aimed to follow it. Jess and the horses at the J-Bar could teach him how.

On either end sat the head honchos, Jess McLain and the "godfather," Larry Goodman, each representing the voice of authority. One carried the whip, the other decreed how many lashes it could give. Amy feared them both, although Larry appeared to be the more approachable.

How in the world did I ever get into this picture? she wondered. *How much of this can I stand?* Her head throbbed for the want of nicotine and her throat ached for a drop of something with a buzz. She drank a lukewarm Coke and imagined the kick she hoped she would feel.

"Ladies and gentlemen, if you haven't met the latest ranch hand, do it now," interrupted Jess, standing up at the table and gesturing Amy's way. "Miss Amelia Talbot,

111

otherwise known as Jersey. She's on the job here as of this minute. Any questions on her part, kindly direct them to me. If I'm not around, Larry here is the man with the answers. Nobody, and I mean nobody, tells her what to do or how to do it. We got stock to care for," he continued, "round-the-clock maintenance on the place, calving season coming up, several horses looking to drop early spring, and animals to haul. In other words, we got a ranch to run. Little Miss Jersey, you're gonna set that alarm for four tonight. I suggest you hit the sack in a hurry. I expect to see you in here by four-ten, ready to run. Welcome to the J-Bar-M."

Chapter Fifteen

Boot Camp

Amy's first ten days flew by in a blur. She wasn't allowed much contact with the other hands, most likely for the better. Borderline delirium tremors and occasional purging haunted her, as she suffered without the infusion of liquor. Her head ached. Her body dragged. Her nose dripped. If there were a hell, she'd found it. Fatigue dogged her every move. Unused muscles screamed from overuse. Her work seemed to take longer than it took the others and her meals tended to be eaten alone, late and cold. Showing up tardy to dinner was unavoidable. They eventually overlooked it. Jess was usually not too far from her and on her back the second she faltered or stopped.

Amy had never worked so hard. On day four she was awakened by Jess at three-forty-five a.m. with the instructions only to throw on some sweats he'd given her and be out front of the bunkhouse in five minutes. This command was followed by a warning that if lights came on or people were awakened there would be hell to pay.

The frozen morning of Wyoming can be brutal. This one was no exception. Amy hadn't adjusted to the altitude yet and still got winded easily. Outside, Jess stood waiting, looking like a drill sergeant and, once she emerged, he informed her that this would be her daily start: the morning run. But she never made the three miles.

After the first mile, she fell so far behind she could no longer see Jess. Not that she could look up from vomiting anyway. The running made her heave, no matter how hard she tried not to. On the way back, Jess had to help her the whole way.

Amy had been advised to carry around a canteen full of water at all times. She was ordered to have it full and within reach. Usually she threw up the water, but McLain's theory was that it was better to throw up water than to dry heave. She made sure she filled it before every run.

The rest of the ranch hands had grown curious about their new addition. Jess appeared to be on a mission to break this rookie and do it early. Ironically, the usually happy-go-lucky Larry aided him every step of the way and was just as hard on her on occasion.

The nights were the most difficult for

Amy. Her bunkmate, Ashley, was a loner herself, and not much for conversation. As busy and stressed as Amy was, she barely had time to think, let alone write music or play. She ran from job to job so exhausted and sore that by day's end, she often prayed to die. Sleepless nights because of discomfort, pain, and the effects of drying out gave her plenty of hours to contemplate her life.

"I wonder how long she can hold on, boss? She doesn't even cry anymore," Gary Russell asked, leaning over a corral fence. "Just wanders around like a zombie. How long you going to keep this up?"

He and Jess watched from afar while Amy moved bales of hay. Barely able to lift them on end, she struggled to get them up on a flatbed trailer.

"Till she breaks down. Till her body quits on her. Right now she's thinking about dying. Stubborn though. Didn't think it would take almost ten days. But she's almost there. Now the key to this is — when she does, you all have to pick her up. Let her know these are the people she can count on. I'm pretty sure the booze is out of her system by now," Jess explained.

"Whatever you say, boss. Kinda hard to watch her go through it, though."

"Yeah, I hear ya. Not right for a lady to suffer. But if something doesn't happen to that kid now, they'll eat her alive in the world she's headed for. Sometimes you have to hit the bottom to realize you don't want to be there again. So you stay off the bottle or whatever and you stay straight. Just like I told you and Dallas. You can rodeo, but if you want to be great, stay away from the booze."

"What's next on the plan, sarge?"

"Think of a job that will break her. I don't want this to take much longer. Turns my stomach."

They both thought long and hard before looking at each other and saying simultaneously, "Hauling wood."

Gary had given the order and several hours had passed. Two cords of wood down and three to go, twilight was on the way. Amy barely shuffled from the woodpile, fifty yards to the house. Of course, a wheelbarrow would have helped, but she never asked and so they let her be. Gary went to find Jess at the arena as the sun went down. He told him that their subject was crying profusely and barely able to walk. This was it. McLain gave his instructions to give everybody the heads up. The time had come.

Amy felt as though she was fainting. She couldn't feel her feet and her hands ached. *If he wanted me to fail then he got his way,* she said to herself. She made it back to the woodpile and dropped to her knees, knowing full well the unscheduled break would bring a verbal thrashing to get up and get back to work. She cried silently and waited for her punishment. The sound of footsteps grew closer. She didn't even feel strong enough to turn and meet her fate.

"Wood doesn't get moved by just sitting there." Jess's voice further tortured her. Her sobs grew audible and cold lips muffled her answer. "I can't do any more. I can't take this. Why are you doing this to me?"

"I'm sorry. Did you say you wanted to quit?" Jess asked. She still had not turned to face him.

"I can't move. I don't know what I'm doing. Nobody talks to me. I hate this. Please, I can't take it. I want to go home," she confessed.

"Do you really?" McLain's change in voice and next statement caused Amy to muster up what strength she had to turn and face him, still kneeling on the ground. His tone could have been mistaken for compassion.

"So ask. Sometimes asking is the

117

hardest thing to do."

Amy turned around and saw everyone standing behind Jess. The most evil man she had ever known now had empathy in his voice. The crew didn't seem to be angry either. Brenda moved closer to Jess and then held out her hand. Confused and cold, Amy didn't understand. Jess stretched out his arm as if to keep Brenda back, preventing her from helping.

"No, she has to ask for it," he said.

"Ask for what? What do you want from me?" Amy cried.

"What is it you want right now? You want a drink? I can get you one. A smoke? I can find one of those too. What is it you want right now?" McLain demanded.

Amy broke down and sobbed out of control. "I just want to stop!"

"Wrong answer. Everyone inside," Jess instructed. The ranch hands started to straggle away, disappointed at the outcome. Brenda turned last and Jess put his arm over her shoulder as if to say it would be okay.

Amy screamed at the desertion. "Why won't any of you help me? Please, why?"

They stopped and waited. Jess turned and walked over to where Amy knelt on the ground, just out of reach. She stared at him with tears in her eyes. Her whining stopped.

"All you had to do is ask for help. But once you ask for it, it's up to you to make the effort." McLain held out his hand. He stood far enough back so she had to reach.

"Please help me. I can't finish this," Amy said.

"We'll help you out, Amy," Gary offered.

"I got done early, so I could move some wood too," Dallas added.

"Look, around here, nobody can do it alone. Right here are the only people you can count on. But they need to be able to count on you. Bet that hurt. I'll bet you never asked for help a day in your life. Here, take my hand," Jess said in a tone that most had never heard from him.

Amy said nothing as the rest made their way to the woodpile. With fast-paced teamwork, they began to move the rest of the wood to the new stack. Amy saw through it all. They owed her nothing, but did it anyway. A day would come when they might need her. The pain in her legs gushed through her body but she reached for Jess. Struggling to stand, she still sobbed, thanking everyone for the help. The woodpile grew rapidly and Amy held McLain's hand briefly before things finally went black.

Collapsing, Amy fell into Jess's arms.

She'd broken. He scooped her up as she faded in and out. But she was conscious enough to know that he'd caught her and was carrying her in the house. Holding her, he gave his last orders for the evening.

"Tomorrow let her sleep. When she gets up tell her she's going into town. You all take what you have in your hands to the pile and call it a night. I'll finish it."

Confused, Double D and Gary pondered the huge pile of wood, still waiting to be stacked.

Larry questioned the boss. "But, Jess, there's three cords here."

"Call it a night, Larry. I know," answered Jess.

Chapter Sixteen

Headed to Town

Amy slept until noon and might have continued until noon the next day, if not for her roommate. Ashley woke Amy as gently as she could. As she rubbed her shoulder, it took some time and persistence to bring her back to life. All appeared to be working well until Jax, the wily dog that seemed to roam the ranch on his own, jumped on the bed, barking, forcing Amy to wake up.

Jax looked like a reddish-blond wolf but was only knee-high like a fox. Mean and shadow-like, he had a habit of disappearing suddenly. The ranch hands called him "little Jess" because of how he followed people around the ranch and then vanished, as if invisible. Crouched on top of Ashley's bunk, he continued to bark at Amy.

"Jax, shut up," Ashley ordered. The dog gave a quizzical look and stayed where he was as if to say, "Make me."

"What the — ? Oh shit, the sun is up. I'm late," Amy shrieked in fear.

"Jersey! Relax. The boss let you sleep, but

you need to get up because you're supposed to go into town in an hour."

Still not realizing she could relax, adrenaline flowed through Amy's body. Spooked like a wild horse, she forced her way out of bed. As she pushed the covers away, she noticed her clothes had been changed. She looked at Ashley in confusion.

"Jess brought you up here," Ashley explained. "You passed out last night from exhaustion. I got your ranch clothes off. Men here are gentlemen, little sister, don't worry."

"God, I'm so sore. He said I could sleep in?" Amy asked in disbelief. She walked over to the window and picked up her clean, folded clothes. She didn't recognize the sweatshirt and shorts she had on. They must have been Ashley's. Peering out the window she noticed all the wood was stacked properly and her shabby job had been brushed up.

"You all helped me. Thanks. I know you didn't have to do it. I know that now."

"Well, with the clothes, I did. The wood, no — we didn't. We offered, but we didn't do it. Jess brought you in here and then finished it all by himself. He wouldn't let us spend most of the night getting it done," Ashley explained.

Amy felt more in the dark than ever. "Why? I thought all he wanted to do was to get me to leave."

"Wrong. Jess McLain may be the hardest, roughest man you'll ever know, but he does things for a reason. We all treated you that way because you needed it," Ashley said as she sat on her bed. Jax lay by her as if on guard.

"Yeah, I needed to be worked to death."

"No, you needed to learn to ask for help and know your limitations," Ashley explained. "Jess didn't want you here and I'm not sure why, but it seems like he does want to help you out. We don't really know your story, but his comment, when he pitched a cup across the room, was that if you were coming, you were getting fixed. There's lots of ways to do that."

"Really? Like what?" Amy asked as she dressed hastily.

"You learn to be part of a team. You learn that other people can depend on you. It's easy to blow your own life, but much harder to screw up someone else's. That's because you have to watch them suffer. Now hurry. Jess is taking a rare field trip into town and we're all going too, so do us a favor and hurry. See you outside."

Amy didn't feel comfortable around the

dog, who decided to stay. It had lain down to watch her with a baleful expression, its eyes narrowed and its head cocked to one side. She had overheard the other hands talk about how Jax was, in fact, McLain's eyes and ears as well as the ranch sheriff. She dressed and tried to hide from him.

"All right, everybody pile into the Dually, I'll follow in Old Paint," Jess instructed his group.

Trips to town were rare and even Larry got a little excited that they were all going. All five hands mashed into the four-door Ford, except for Amy. The outcast stood outside and waited to see how she would make it.

"Jersey, you'll ride with me. Ya'll follow. Larry, do me a favor, and let Brenda drive. Tired of her taking the damn bus," Jess said.

Amy shuffled quietly to the late model Ford extended cab.

"Jax, you going to town or you staying?" Jess asked the dog.

Amy thought it odd that someone would ask a dog a question like that. Jax stood and barked hard at Jess, then took off across the yard and out into the field. Jess continued the conversation.

"That's fine. Don't stay out too late. Her

father catches you, you're toast."

The truck had pulled out on to the highway and led the caravan of ranch hands west for the hour drive to Cody. The silence of the cab was broken only by the radio. Amy couldn't handle it for long and had to start a conversation. The tension was thick and her discomfort made her sweat.

"Uh, thanks for letting me sleep in today. Thanks for finishing my work."

Jess glanced at her out of the corner of his eye and returned his gaze back to the road. He nodded as if saying, "You're welcome," but didn't talk.

Amy wouldn't let up. She couldn't handle the silence, or a man with a presence as overwhelming as Jess's.

"You don't talk much, do you? Or, you don't like me, is that right? I mean, it's all right if you don't like me." Amy was blunt and shot straight.

Jess pondered before answering.

"I don't know you, only of you. I know you have a drinking problem. I know you're under-educated. I also know those bastards will chew you up and leave you for dead if you don't get tough," Jess replied.

"Well, all I know about you is that everyone is afraid of you. You own the ranch and I have to live with you for six months."

"That's right, then you can go back and be a piece of shit like you were when you got here."

Amy didn't recognize the hostile tone in his voice.

"Ashley said that you only swear when you are serious and are fighting mad about something. It's hard for me to —"

"To act like a lady? Not to have a mouth like a sailor? Yes, I'm a hard ass. I'm mean, tired and nasty. But you're either gonna walk away from here someone different or you're gonna leave. I don't have time for losers," Jess said in a more familiar tone.

"I really want this to work. I may never have another chance like this one." Amy opened up a little.

"Bull. So what? You're going to become something you're not and if they don't sign you, what then? They wasted a year of your life and hung you out to dry. If you change, you do it for yourself and no one else. In the end, only God and yourself are who you need to please," Jess said sternly.

"I don't really talk to God much," Amy confessed.

"Better fix that. When stuff gets bad, sometimes He's the only one you can count on. And you can always count on God."

The conversation died.

"So I hear they wanted you to cut a record. Is that true?" Amy began again.

"You ask a lot of questions, don't you? Yes. But I won't have anything to do with that scene. Plus, Marty Heistler would use his own mother to make a buck. No thanks," Jess said, revealing some of his past.

"Really? Marty acted as though you were brothers," Amy replied.

"Marty is a man whose only god is money. We go back, yes, and he got me out of a jam one time, but he helped me with ulterior motives in mind, so it wasn't the act of a friend. That's all I have to say about that." McLain was obviously not in the mood to elaborate on the issue. Amy didn't want to provoke him, so she dropped the subject.

"You said you were in the Army?"

"Yep, and I don't talk about that, either, so let that die right now and you won't be disappointed," Jess retorted.

"Sorry."

"Don't be. Just don't ask. Yes, I did a lot of things. Past is past. You leave it there," Jess added, knowing that she was only trying to make small talk.

"So why are we going to town?"

"To get you some clothes so you don't die in the cold. Something that doesn't say

127

gunsel, or rookie, and that will last." Jess hinted at a smile, the first one he'd offered to her.

"Why didn't we do it earlier? I wouldn't have had to freeze," Amy inquired.

"Because you didn't ask. That's why."

"I still haven't asked." Amy thought she would enlighten him, only to be shot down again.

"I know. The other hands asked for you," Jess told her.

"Oh."

Jess went into the western store only to give the final approval. Brenda and Ashley towed Amy toward the clothing section and, like little girls playing dress-up, Brenda brought clothes for Amy to try on. She never even got to look at the racks herself. Jess would simply shake his head "no" or nod "yes" as to what he saw. After several pairs of Wrangler jeans (one for going out and some for working, as the girls said) and several understated western work shirts, the girls felt their job was done.

Next, Amy was whisked away to the boot section with Gary and David. Ashley and Brenda argued with the two men as to what looked better. Amy's opinion didn't seem to count. Finally, after an hour of discussion, they bought two pair, one for work and riding, and once again, one for going out. From there, Jess and Larry took their turn at the hats. They picked one out and once again, Amy didn't have a say. Larry and Jess seemed to study her. With every hat they found a fit.

She wouldn't admit it, but Amy loved every minute of the experience. No one had ever done anything like this for her. Growing up, she'd never had much. No man had ever bought her anything unless he wanted to get into her pants. Her prize possession was her guitar, one that Terry found in a pawnshop. All her clothes were secondhand.

Amy had noticed the J-Bar-M jackets. They were all the same and had the ranch name on them. Everywhere they'd gone in the town, people knew who they were. In addition, each hand had his or her name embroidered on the front. The deep olive-green barn coats stopped at mid-thigh and were vented in the back for riding. They tapered at the waist and had a brown leather collar. Amy looked at them enviously, only to have her wish crushed.

"Sorry, you have to earn that one," Jess told her as they picked out a coat, work gloves, and insulated overalls.

Wearing one of the new outfits, Amy stood with the girls, hoping she wouldn't stick out. She watched the girl behind the counter who was older and pretty and who kept giving Jess the eye as she rang up the sale. The girls just laughed and whispered to her that it happened all the time. Amy noticed how McLain didn't even bat an eye, avoiding the flirtation. But her thoughts were interrupted when she heard the cashier announce the sale total out loud. A total of eight hundred dollars and some change.

Amy looked at Brenda and Ashley as if she feared something would explode. Jess started paying for the bill when she finally spoke up.

"Jess?" Amy said, but both girls coughed under their breath and Ashley tapped her on the back. Amy hesitated. "Sorry, Mr. McLain. But you don't have to buy me all this."

"I'm not. You're working it off. Except the hat. I buy all my employees a hat. The rest you work off. You owe me," he said as he motioned for the group to gather up whatever they bought as well as Amy's things. They all piled out the door and the pretty cashier said goodbye to Jess with a smile. Brenda almost acted offended.

Amy didn't understand, but thought it

strange. Where she came from, men would take everything they could get coming their way. Jess barely smiled back, tipped his hat, and left.

Chapter Seventeen

Test Drive

Dinner in town was the most fun Amy'd had since she arrived. The group seemed to cut loose for the first time, except for McLain, who remained quiet. The Trough Bar and Restaurant was a modest hole, but served sumptuous food to a mix of people the likes of which she'd never seen. Cowboys, ranchers, bikers, truckers — the works. Amy couldn't stop staring.

Once the meal ended, Ashley, Gary and David all ordered a beer and Larry ordered a rum and Coke. Jess drank nothing. Amy felt uncomfortable. She'd discovered that drying out had been fairly easy to this point, but mostly because temptation hadn't been there. Now it was everywhere.

The band started up and Gary and Ashley spent most of their time on the dance floor. Dallas did the same with Brenda. Even Larry took time to get up and have a whirl now and then. Brookes was scarce, hanging out with the younger crowd, leaving Jess alone with Amy. Jess watched her closely.

"It's hard when temptation is so close, isn't it, Jersey?"

"What?" Amy answered.

"Don't play dumb with me. You've been staring at the booze since it was ordered. Easy when it's not around, but not when it's in front of you. Well, you'll be tempted more and more. Saying no will be a challenge every time. Give in now and you're right back to where you were."

Amy knew he had her pinned. She figured this was another lesson.

"It's just hard. I guess you're right," she admitted.

A stranger, a man in jeans, biker boots, and a leather vest interrupted their conversation. He looked old enough to be Amy's father. He stepped up to the table, eyeing Amy, and stood before them smiling. When the man asked her to dance, Amy politely declined.

McLain watched as the man tried to barter with her but she wouldn't give in. He finally left and went to the bar to get a drink. Jess dropped the conversation but kept the stranger in his sights.

Amy, relieved, sat back and studied Jess. She thought of how Jax had looked at her and how dog and owner looked the same.

After a short while, the stranger approached Brenda who was dancing with Double D. Jess couldn't hear the conversation but could tell he was trying to cut in, but David Dallas wouldn't have it. Then the conversation turned tense, yet Jess sat steadfast in his chair.

David escorted Brenda back to the table and when the stranger followed, Jess watched, perfectly still, unruffled as a calm lake in the morning.

"Come on, one of you ladies has to dance with me," the stranger said, the effect of liquor slurring his speech.

Dallas stepped in. "The lady politely said no, sir. I think you need to leave. Thank you."

The stranger bristled.

"Hey, black boy, I didn't ask you. I suggest you fuck off." Then he put his hand on Dallas's shoulder.

Jess finally interrupted.

"Around here, my friend, we don't talk like that in front of ladies. I suggest you apologize for your language."

The regulars in the bar knew Jess and his crew, so this turn of events got everyone's attention. Conversation ceased throughout the place. McLain still didn't stand.

"I don't apologize to anyone and I wasn't talking to you. Nigger boy here and I are having a word," the stranger said, heading toward Jess.

Jess now stood and glared, giving Dallas instructions.

"Go ahead and have a seat, Dave," Jess said and walked around to their side of the table. Dallas did as he was asked.

"Oh, you do what he says, boy." The slurred words continued.

Jess stood up and confronted the intruder. He never lost his tone or calm.

"You have two choices. Apologize for your language to the ladies and to my ranch hand here, or deal with me. Your choice."

Tension flowed through the bar. The man appeared to be unfazed by the request.

"Deal with you? You must want an ass kickin', hick."

"You might want to watch that, bud. That man asked you something and most Rangers don't ask twice," Larry offered, moving next to Jess.

"Wha'? Is that supposed to scare me?"

"Then do something, fat ass," replied Jess. "I don't have time to sit here and watch you talk yourself into a fight. You're testing my patience. Either apologize or I'll see to it you spend the next six months learning to walk again, eating three square meals a day through a straw. I've killed more men than you can dream of. So throw down or get out." Jess stood square before him, both fists loosely clenched.

The stranger had whiskey courage but McLain's presence was intimidating. Anyone could see his confidence came from experience and not just talk. The stranger figured he might have gotten in too deep, so he started to back up, ruffled by the Ranger's advance.

"Uh, you forgot to apologize. Do it now, or on all that is holy, you won't walk out that door tonight. Tonight, or tomorrow for that matter."

Jess got closer. The stranger appeared to ponder the situation for a few minutes, but finally gave in. Once he did and headed for the door, Jess didn't move until he was gone.

The music started up again. Amy was unnerved by the incident and questions filled her head. Jess's comment about killing men troubled her, but she didn't dare ask.

McLain returned to his seat and placed his feet up on an empty chair. He leaned back, expressionless.

Amy noticed Brenda smiling in approval from an adjoining table and batting her eyes in adoration. Amy didn't say a word and waited until Jess excused himself to go to the john before asking anything.

Turning to Brenda, she asked, "Do all cowboys act like that?"

"No, but real ones do," Brenda answered.

"Why did he do that?"

"Jess takes care of all of us. He may act like an ass, but he'd stand up for any of us."

"Really," Amy said. She began to hum along with the music and refilled her glass with Diet Coke.

Chapter Eighteen

The Truth

Sunrise wouldn't lighten the sky for another hour and Amy found quiet sanctuary in the early morning, cleaning the barn. She had grown to love the scent of the horses, the sounds they made, and the secure feeling she felt amidst the leather tack, hay bales and wooden stalls. She'd finally been moved to a position of ranch hand and enjoyed being a part of the group. Even though they'd had a late night the night before going into town, she felt recharged. She pondered the previous night's events, disappointed that she'd ridden back with the crew and not alone with Jess.

Amy followed all of Larry's morning instructions, except that she didn't put on the new pair of work boots that hurt her feet. She did sport the new Carhartt insulated overalls, jacket, and work gloves. The protective garments were a welcome and needed change.

She was almost done when Larry joined her to check on her progress. Amy worked fast, fully intent on proving herself a hand, an important word and title that now seemed to have such deep meaning. Breathing hard from the sprint cleaning, she just smiled at Larry as he checked on the stalls she'd finished up to that point. As she opened the door to the last one, Larry stopped her.

"No, no, hon, not that one. Don't ever do that one," Larry said.

"Oh, sorry. Why not? Doesn't this stall need to be cleaned too?" Amy asked, proud of her speed in completing her task.

"Well, Ms. Fireball, yes, but Jess is the only one allowed in there. That's his horse. Damn near a man-killer too. You're doing a good job, Amy. But you'd best slow down before you burn yourself out."

"I know, I just wanted —"

"To prove yourself? We can all see that, Jersey, and Jess is starting to see it too. Relax. You're doing fine," Larry said and patted her on the back.

Amy knew she had time before breakfast, so she hoped Goodman would answer a few more questions. Ones that haunted her. "I never see him ride that horse. And why nobody but him?"

"That's the horse that ended his rodeo career. He bought her, because . . . well . . .

that's another story." Larry stalled.

"Please, Larry, no one here tells me anything about McLain."

"Well, before the boss bought the J-Bar-M . . . now this goes all the way back to the big rodeo in Fort Worth, this horse, Dancing Wind, was bucking horse of the year, and Jess was on his way to being the best damned all-around hand in pro rodeo. Hell, he can't go anywhere and not have people still want an autograph. That ride was a saddle bronc ride like I never seen, but this old girl here took a wrong turn and he and she crashed into the arena wall. Make a long story short, which I never do, he and this horse here were messed up all kinds of ways. It ended her career and his too, sort of. He could go back, but he doesn't. Hope he does someday. So you see, these two is married to each other in a strange kinda way."

As if on cue, the blue roan wandered into the stall from her corral. She was big, powerful, and beautiful. Her very aura had a presence that suggested greatness.

"Why won't he go back?" Amy asked. Larry shrugged off the question, telling her it wasn't his place to say. Amy stared at the horse, saying nothing. She had to ask and this could be her only time.

"Larry, I heard you say last night Jess had killed someone." Amy prayed he wouldn't get mad. Larry had watched her the night before and figured as much. Just like with Brookes, the time had come to tell her.

"Simple, Jess was a soldier. He was at war. It was his job. He'd done enough fightin', that's why he didn't send that city boy to the Promised Land last night. But he won't stand for injustice," Larry said.

Amy turned and sat next to Larry, inviting his trust. Slowly, he told her the tale of how the Army betrayed Jess and the horrifying battle that cost his son's life. And the incredible tale of the journey McLain endured, carrying his son's lifeless body. He told her of the apology for not saving him.

Amy listened spellbound. Larry told of how Jess and his son fought for their lives and how much death surrounded them. How McLain wouldn't let his son be the scapegoat and took the fall with honor, later awarded a Silver Star and Purple Heart. He also told her never to speak of it.

"He wakes up with that memory every day, little Ms. Curious," Larry ended.

"Is that why he lives above the barn and not in the house?" She figured she would get as much as she could.

"No, ever since Becky ran off, he hasn't

lived in the main house. Jess — well, Jess is Jess, that's about it. Too much bad stuff in life and I guess he would just as soon be alone. Well, that's enough for now. Breakfast should be ready and since Jess ain't here, we can eat right away," Larry said and got up to leave.

Amy had learned more than she really wanted. She always felt sorry for herself about her own life, but hearing of Larry's son and Jess, she thought hers may not have been half-bad.

"Larry, would he have hurt that guy last night?"

"For cursing in front of ladies and saying what he did to Dallas? Maybe. You don't mess with a friend of Jess. That's a part of him I hope you never see. You're doing good, Jersey. Keep up the hard work. Enough bull shootin'. We got a ranch to run. By the way, Jess wants Ashley to start teaching you to ride today," Larry said as he made his way out.

"What? A horse?" Amy felt a wave of fear.

"No. Jax. Of course a horse! Roundup is coming and all hands ride for the brand. You too. No questions."

Chapter Nineteen

Checkpoint

Larry handed the phone to Amy as she came in for breakfast.

"Good timing," he said. "It's for you."

"Hey, kid, I finally got you! How's it going?" The voice on the other end of the phone sounded hoarse and foreign.

"Who is this?" Amy asked. "Who were you calling?"

"Hey, sugar, it's me! Terry Ann. Forget about me so fast?"

Amy couldn't believe what or whom she was hearing: a raspy voice that sounded nothing like the low, full-throated one she remembered. Terry always had a wonderful, full, warm sound. This person sounded shallow and rough.

"Yeah, it's me, honey. Your old friend. At least, I used to be. You still there?"

Amy released a sigh. "Yes, I'm still here. You surprised me, that's all. It's been so long. What's wrong, Terry? You don't sound like you. Where've you been? I haven't heard from you for weeks."

"I told you I'd call," Terry replied. "And I have. I told you not to worry."

"Where are you?"

"At Saint Catherine's, in Memphis."

"What's that?"

"A nursing hospital. It's all I could afford."

"What? Oh, gee, Terry, don't tell me you're not better. You were supposed to go back to Fairfield. You said all you had was high blood pressure. People don't stay in hospitals for that . . ."

"No, honey, I won't tell you that I'm not better. I don't have to. While I was being monitored for high blood pressure, some nosey little bitch had to go do some extra blood work and found out I was kind of running on empty. Blood count was down. Not enough of anything that was supposed to be there. They call it leukemia. But I'll be okay. You'll see."

Amy stood against the kitchen wall, holding on to the old phone box like it was a life preserver. She blinked back tears.

"Okay, so what does that mean?"

"Nothing, really, honey. Nothing much."

"What, goddamn it!"

"I'll be getting transfusions down here every day for a while. They'll know in a few weeks if it's helping. They say chemo is next if not. Hey, don't be giving me grief, Amy. I don't want to talk about it. I called to find out how you are. How's it going?"

Amy fought back the urge to scream. The thought of the most energetic woman she'd ever known hooked up to a plasma bag turned her stomach. She couldn't imagine her headed for chemo. This had to be some kind of a joke.

"Okay, you've made my day. And now I'm not supposed to think about you. Well, okay. How about me? Well, let's see. It's going like hell. I work like a common laborer at every imaginable menial job Jess McLain can think of. My hands are blistered and calloused. My back hurts. I wore out my Nikes two weeks ago and wear shit kickers now. What did you think? This McLain guy cut some kind of deal that says I have to suffer before they can re-invent me. The worst part is I suppose they're right. And it wouldn't be so unbearable if it weren't for the thirst, Terry. I still can't control it. That is, when it's not around, I can. But when it's in front of me, I just can't. It's been real uneven, up and down. They watch me all the time now."

"What happened?"

"Two nights ago, after six weeks of being on the wagon since I left Texas, I broke down and had a drink at this bar in town.

Jess took a bunch of us to hear a band there. We've been there before. He thought I might be able to sing. I did and people really loved it. Anyway, it was the second time I'd been in a bar since I left. We were all drinking sodas and beer and, like, somebody pushed me, I had to go steal a half-finished bottle of Coors off a table behind everybody's back. I just couldn't help it."

"Oh, Christ, honey."

"I just couldn't control myself. I got this empty feeling after I got through playing. Like maybe I wasn't good enough, you know? Jess saw me do it and practically dragged me outside. He came just short of slapping me, I swear, Terry. I thought I was going to wet my pants. He scares me to death, he's got the worst temper you ever saw."

"What'd you do?"

"I just dropped to my knees and started to cry. I didn't know what else to do. He told everybody to get in the truck and we headed for the ranch. About ten miles out, he made me get out. He threw me my jacket. It was just unreal. Hell, I stood there like an idiot on the road in the dark while everybody watched. Then I had to walk the last ten miles back to the ranch in the cold. I got home at two in the morning with a sore shoulder, fingers frozen stiff, and my feet looking like raw meat when I took off my boots. Son of a bitch."

"Bet you won't do that again."

"No. I won't. Hey, Terry . . ."

Amy stopped. The words didn't want to come. A lump rose in her throat. "God, I really miss you. I miss you a lot."

"I miss you too, honey. But look, we did the right thing. You're going to get through this. I know you are. Marty says you'll be fine. You know, he's paying my hospital bills right now, and has become a real friend. Say, did he tell you that he used to know me?"

"Yeah, he did."

"Okay, then he wasn't lying. I couldn't believe he'd intrude on me like that. Damn him. Oh well, I guess now you know all about me, too."

"Well, not all."

"One of these days, honey, when we're together again, I'll tell you the whole story."

"How come you kept it from me?"

"Didn't keep it from you. I was just waiting for the right time."

"Okay. Whatever you say. Hey, how can I reach you?"

"Here, take this number down. Looks like I'll be here a while longer."

Amy fumbled for the blunt-tipped pencil tied to a string that Jess always left hanging on the phone. No pad. He just wrote whatever he needed to remember on the wall. The graffiti ran up and down from floor to ceiling. Once every few months someone sprayed the whole thing with degreaser and wiped it off, only to start all over again. Amy found an empty spot and poised the pencil on the wall. She wiped tears from her eyes with the back of her hand and said, "Go ahead."

Terry Ann gave her the number slowly, and then said, muffled, "God, I love you, sweetheart."

"I love you too, Terry," Amy replied. "Take care of yourself. And be patient with me. I can't wait to get out of this place, but I'll get it right. I will. And . . . oh Terry, guess what? I almost forgot. Not everything is all that bad. Jess bought me some real cowgirl clothes last month. And this week I'm learning how to ride!"

Chapter Twenty

Hold On

Ashley snored ever so slightly, keeping Amy awake in spite of her exhaustion. The day had been interminably long, starting sometime before dawn and not ending until half-past nine. The mare in foal finally decided to drop her colt and had more than enough problems to keep three people pushing, twisting and re-adjusting her for several hours. Gary had cussed and wheedled and helped her through it with Ashley and Amy on call.

Amy had never seen a horse give birth before. Not breech or otherwise. She left the barn smiling, worn out but exhilarated, and as soaked with sweat as the mare herself. Ashley stayed on to clean up.

Perhaps it was the sight of the gangly black colt, finally up on his feet, or the red-stained, blood-soaked straw, or just the whole miraculous ordeal that took Amy so far out of herself. When she finally got up, she realized that she'd forgotten how long they'd been sitting in that stall, how cold it was outside, and the fact that she hadn't eaten since breakfast. But she just couldn't imagine leaving. The mare needed her. At least, that's what she thought. She sat near the stall door, keeping the warming light steady and rewarding her with every push and groan. Amy felt as though she'd birthed that foal herself.

Hours later, in the middle of the night, the sight of that newborn foal came to Amy over and over again, keeping her from sleep.

"Ashley, are you awake?" she asked. She dared to disturb the woman who lay as good as dead to the world below her. She hated waking her, but she needed to talk.

"I am now. What the hell is it?" Her bunkmate didn't sound too pleased.

"You're a real cowgirl," Amy said.

"You woke me up to tell me that?"

"Sort of. I just wanted you to know. I've never met anybody like you. You can do anything. You even know how to birth a horse. I couldn't believe how you helped get that baby out. You went right in there. You did great."

Amy thought back to the first weeks when she'd watched in amazement as this country-bred girl did it all — fed, watered, groomed, saddled, broke and trained all the horses on Jess's ranch. She handled everything except the rodeo stock, the jug-headed broncs born just to serve the stock contractors and cowboys. They ran free in a forty-acre pasture and had just enough human contact to be hauled in for vaccinating now and then. A few had worn a halter and could be tied. Most were just wily and mean.

"Ashley, you think that foal is going to be okay?"

"Oh yeah, sure. Go to sleep."

"No, really," Amy continued. "I mean, he's so skinny. And small. I thought they were bigger than that. Ashley, how'd you know what to do? You had your hands all the way up inside her . . ."

"Amy, go to sleep. I'm bushed. Please."

"I can't sleep. I need to tell you something. You're the real thing. You're somebody. With a job you know how to do. Jess respects you. He relies on you. You know just who you are."

"G'night, Amy."

"How'd you get there, Ash? Huh? You're only a couple of years older than me. How is it possible that Jess McLain looks up to you as an equal and not through you, huh, Ashley?"

Amy was afraid to hear the answer. She was sure she'd gone a step too far. But Ashley was somebody Jess trusted and Amy was nobody, at least here on this godforsaken place. She was just one more problem Jess had taken on, and Amy couldn't figure out why.

No sound. Ashley had dropped back off to sleep and left Amy in the dark to ponder the difference. Then again, maybe she could ask in the morning.

Amy lay back against her pillow and stared up at the darkness, then closed her eyes. Could all this possibly be for real? Five weeks, and she'd finally stopped counting. Five weeks and something. Maybe three days, maybe four. Did it matter any more?

All she knew was she missed Terry Ann like a motherless child. And she feared Jess McLain like a prisoner fears a warden. And then again, there was something else. She adored him. The way he commanded respect, his politeness and then his temper when he lost it. She liked the way he moved. Quiet, composed, like a gunfighter, with a kind of balanced stealth. She loved to watch him. No matter what he did, he never wasted a gesture or a breath, always seemed to account for everything. Must have been from his training as a Ranger, she supposed. The other hands talked about him like he was some kind of Green Beret or American hero. She guessed in a war, your life could depend on knowing how to move. Knowing where to be and when.

Next to Jess, she secretly worshipped Ashley, a woman so sure and confident, she moved through the ranch like she owned it. And she was patient and gentle, with people and with horses. She felt like a sister, something Amy had never had.

Amy had endured the first three weeks in a kind of withdrawal, with a constant feeling of nausea. She yearned for a drag on a cigarette. Miraculously, she found some chewing tobacco in Larry's cupboard in the kitchen and whenever she was on dinner or breakfast detail, she would take a pinch and secretly chew it.

Larry must have noticed, but he never said a word. She was desperate too for a swig of gin or a cold bottle of beer. In fact, until she came to the J-Bar-M, she didn't realize how having a drink now and then had become a daily habit, a day-long habit. And sometimes, a nighttime habit as well — the only way to get to sleep. As a substitute, she drank so many cans of Mountain Dew and Coke in the first few weeks, she thought she'd have to chain herself to the outhouse near the barn, but it was the only way. Her brain hurt, felt clogged and slow, and she woke up most days with a headache. She was glad she didn't have to think much.

Mostly she forked hay, raked manure, loaded feed and cleaned the cabin. She worked hard at the most menial tasks and did them without complaint. It was just easier. Besides, there was no one to complain to.

Amy loved to banter with Double D, and by the end of the first month, she felt somehow like his kin. He was a loner, too. He knew who all his brothers and sisters were, but never did meet his daddy. He told her how his mom couldn't even get her white lover to lay claim on his half-breed son long enough to give him a proper identity, but he didn't have to wonder who his daddy was. His mocha-colored skin reminded him every day and it kept other people guessing. He was just dark enough to qualify for a black man's rodeo, but light enough to try for a white man's game as well. Either way, someone would be calling him names by the time it was over. That's the way it always was.

"You're real nice!" Double D used to say to Amy. "And you sing purty too." After dinner, they'd sing together as they put the dishes away. They could harmonize and Amy loved to hear the old Southern work tunes, the way they were meant to be sung, with sorrow, feeling and a touch of the blues. Amy learned to love David Dallas, almost as much as she loved Ash. She tried to go back to sleep.

"Just one more thing, Ashley. Did Jess tell you why I'm here?" Amy whispered, leaning over the bunk.

"No, no, he didn't! Jesus, girl, would you shut up? Lay off! If I let you tell me, will you let me go back to sleep, once and for all?"

"Sorry, Ash." Amy laughed with a low sigh, mostly of relief. "There's nothing to tell. Sorry I woke you up. Really."

Jess McLain, you know more about me than I know about you. Amy tossed and turned, thinking about her boss.

Why do you look at me every morning as if I were the Holy Ghost? Why are you keeping after me so? I see you staring at me, even when you're talking to everybody else. Why did you stop at the barn door the other night when you found your guitar in my hands — me, into your stuff, without asking? Why didn't you cuss me out, like you should have? You just stood there and listened. Then you took that ax out of my hands and put it away, back in the case without saying a single word.

Why do you have to move like that? Like a hunter. Like everything in your path is your prey and it's just a matter of time before you take it down or make it your own. When you said, "Time to turn in, girl. You best be outta here," I froze to the spot. I couldn't even move. You had to help me up. And you did, real gentle-like. You're strong, Jess. I knew you would be. Why do I feel like you own me, damn it? What do you know about me that I don't?

Amy turned over and let her arm drop over the bunk. It dangled free and she rested her hand on the bunk ladder. Jax, sleeping on Ashley's bed, reached up and licked Amy's fingers, a gesture that moved her. The dog was pure love, the one thing Amy couldn't imagine having or holding on to, but wanted so much. She wanted to love somebody, but mostly herself, and just couldn't. She still couldn't stand the thought of herself as a shit-shoveling weakling too drunk to pull off the biggest break of her whole life. Well, that was why she was here. That and some fairy-tale promise about starting over, about coming out of the ground as somebody new. Somebody as real as Ashley Sharpe. In a way, Ashley was like the very people she wanted to sing to. Fans who would see she was a fake.

It was never going to happen. Never. She wished she had a fifth of something to make it all go away.

Chapter Twenty-one

Meeting of the Minds

McLain had thought it a good idea to keep an eye on his newly born colt; therefore, everyone was assigned an hour to watch it once the sun went down. Larry, however, was not. This was a job for the hands. He and Jess appeared to have something better to do, as usual.

Amy shrugged off the fact that she had the last shift, knowing she would also have the coldest one. Jess feared the colt would get pulmonary edema, his fancy word for pneumonia, and wanted it kept warm. Amy felt helpless with the assignment and didn't know what she would do even if the horse were sick. She didn't even know if she could tell.

But colt watching was a break from everything and for everyone it was a chance to relax with God's creation of life and watch what a real mother does — love her offspring. She suited up in her warmest clothes and made her way to the barn shortly after ten. And she brought her guitar, just in case.

When she got to the big stall, she saw there was an army cot inside and a bedroll and blankets that hadn't been used. A radio played in low static volume. Amy put down her guitar, took a seat on the cot, and studied the colt that lay balled up under the heat of the lamp. McLain had given strict instructions for no one to touch the foal, explaining Momma might not like it much and, in defending the young one, kill a hand, or even worse, her own baby.

Amy sat back, noticing the uncanny warmth of the stall. It wasn't hot, but warm enough that she might be able to play guitar and catch up on some writing. Her mind was packed full of material she just didn't know how to put down. She rubbed her fingers together, working out the day's fatigue and proceeded to dabble with a tune. She sang low, knowing Jess was probably upstairs and didn't want to disturb him or be scolded for playing. She knew that feeling, like hiding a habit. How familiar that felt. She sang the only authentic cowgirl tune she knew.

"There's a young man that I know whose age is twenty-one. Comes from down in southern Colorado. Just out of the service, he's lookin' for his fun. *Someday soon, goin' with him, someday soon.*"

"You're off-key and that's a dumb song anyway," Jess said, walking into the stall and closing the door behind him. Amy stopped.

"Sorry. Was I too loud?"

"No, just very off tune. That's worse. Plus, it's cold enough out here you could damage your vocal cords, so here, sip this," he said as he handed her a thermos.

She put down her guitar and took it. Jess said nothing as he sat in the folding chair opposite and took out his own guitar, which he had brought down with him in its well-worn case. The case was not unlike him: scarred and battered. It could tell a million stories. But the bright red crushed velvet interior and cherry-wood, steel-string acoustic guitar inside was a sight. Amy stared, saying nothing, and poured herself a cup of the tea. Jess then handed her a small cellophane bag of yellow potato chips.

"Oh no, thank you. I'm not hungry," she protested.

"They're not for your stomach, Jersey. The oils on those chips act as a lubricant for your vocal cords. The tea keeps them warm," he said as he returned to tuning his guitar.

Then he began to play. The piece he chose was classical and every finger worked

159

diligently to create a flow of beauty. The music seemed as out of place in its surroundings as a three-piece suit at a rodeo. Amy studied Jess as he leaned back and played, his eyes closed. When done, he looked at her, as if waiting. "Well, you going to pick up that thing or just sit there?"

"Oh, sorry." She followed the order promptly, placing her own guitar on her lap.

"Don't be sorry; just give me a G," McLain requested. Amy was self-taught and knew nothing of notes and reading music. She looked at Jess and understood she was to follow his lead. Once she was strumming the way he wanted, he showed her changes and encouraged her to tap her boot along in time with him. Once he felt she had it, he went on to play his own lead.

Then he started to sing. Amy was amazed. A rich, expressive voice poured out a melody. He sang of a cowboy and a broken heart, with a sadness she'd never heard. He sang all about life on the rodeo road and a lost love along the way. Now she knew why everyone wanted him. He sounded convincing and real. From there he went on to sing a song about Wyoming.

Through the gap, down the arroyo,
Cool water and long sweet grass,

Fresh horses, a place to go.
Red wall shines, hot as a fever,
Warm as a mother's love,
On the day that you leave her.

Lonely rider in the mornin' mist,
Hell bent for the rim to the west.
A bowler hat and saddle bag full of
  cash,
And a pistol he rarely used,
Except for the times when he had to
  choose
Between the hole in the wall
And a hole six feet in the ground.

Amy really felt the song; she didn't just hear it. He went on to sing of train robbing and the wild bunch and men camped out by a fire in the moonlight. When he was done, he looked at her and shrugged as if he was done telling his story for the night. She wanted more.

"What's the hole in the wall?" she asked, trying to make small talk.

"It's a place and don't ask me to describe it. You just have to go there." He put down the guitar and leaned back in his chair.

"Who sings it? I haven't heard it on the radio," she asked.

"Jon Chandler, a Colorado cowboy, not

161

one of those flaming wish-they-weres you hear around here. But let's try something you know. How about Terri Clark's 'This Old Heart'? I heard you singing it the other day."

"Yes, I could do that."

"Okay, let's do it together. Come in after the intro."

Amy feared the opportunity and squeaked out the first chorus. *"If this old heart was made like a truck —"*

Jess interrupted, "Whoa! You sang better mucking stalls. I've heard you. Come on, don't jack with me. Close your eyes. Pretend you're in a truck, leaving the love of your life. Got your cowboy hat on and sore from a day's work and rodeo. Now get into it," he said and went on to play.

"But I . . ."

"Sing, don't talk."

Amy closed her eyes. Pretending to be sore was something she didn't have to imagine, that she'd learned all too well. Belting out the tune, Jess coached her and sang along on the chorus.

"This old heart is flesh and bone, when it's in trouble and it cares too much, just hurts so bad, but this old heart ain't made like that."

Amy ended the song and looked for the

first time for approval. Jess nodded and went right into another tune. She only knew the chorus to "Amarillo by Morning," a rodeo song about a life unknown to her. The first rodeo she had ever witnessed was the Friday night Jackpot held at the J-Bar-M. Amy had seen bull riding in Piles Grove, New Jersey, but never bronc or bareback riding. The song spoke to her and when Jess finished, she inquired.

"So, how do you do that? Put such feeling behind your words?" Amy asked.

"I lived it. I know how it feels. You sing what you know. What you've lived. Lie to your audience and you may as well jump on-stage and shoot 'em."

"Okay. So tell me. Who is Chris LeDoux?" she asked, wanting an answer to the question after all these weeks.

"Boy, you are ignorant. Not your fault. Let's just say he's the voice of the rodeo man and the real cowboy. He's everything he sings about. Now stop with the questions and sing me one of your tunes. I'm done for the evening."

Jess placed his guitar back in its red velvet case. Then he got up to check on the mare, who still looked exhausted from birthing. Petting her, he looked back at Amy.

"What?"

"Are you trying to intimidate me? Or do you want me scared of you, because I am." Amy was almost afraid to hear the answer. Jess shook his head and gave a rare smile as he brushed the mare.

"No, I'm not trying to scare you. And if you haven't noticed, I don't particularly give a damn about how people look at me, or what they think. If you're scared, that's your deal. What's the worst that could happen? Kick you off this place? I think you need to relax." Jess leaned over the mare's back, still smiling.

"Well, I know you don't like me and don't want me here and you gave me this chance anyway."

"I didn't give you a thing," Jess interrupted. "You give a day's work for a day's pay and stay. As for liking you, Jersey, what do you care? Four more months and you might be a big-time country star and probably turn into some puke showing way too much chest and leg to get somewhere. But it won't be your fault. No, those conniving life suckers will use you to fill their pockets, then toss you aside. But if you're as good as Bob says, you'll be well on your way."

"Maybe. Why won't you cut a record? The guys in Nashville said you were the perfect example of what I should be. You've got it all, they told me."

"Yeah, I know. That's what they say. Look, I like being who I am and doing what I do, and anyhow, if I cut a record I still wouldn't have what Chris LeDoux has," he said. "Remember, there's always one better."

"What does he have? A recording contract?" she asked, wondering what he meant.

"No, he had the world championship buckle. And I'd rather have that than the recording contract, not to mention he's a legend. So I play for myself. Plus, I like ranching and my horses. It's simple, it's my life," he told her.

"I hear you're an incredible bronc rider," Amy asked, hoping to change the subject but keep Jess talking.

"Really. And what do you know about bronc riding?" he shot back.

"Nothing, but I have ears and everybody says you're the best. I would like to know more about it, but no one tells me anything. And I know if I pound Ashley for more information, she'll most likely hog-tie me and stuff a sock in my mouth."

"You're trying real hard, aren't you?" he asked from left field.

"No, just hard," she retorted, teasing.

"Well, shit, what the hell? I want to ride

again. But I had a wreck my last competition. Oh, and I know that old coot must have told you. He can't keep his trap shut, so you don't have to sit there and act like you don't know what I'm talking about. Anyway, some things didn't heal the way they should have. They say riders sometimes never recover their form after they have one like I did. I don't like not looking my best. Let's say I don't like not winning either. I have no intention of going through life and hearing 'Well, ole Jess never did get it back. Could have been the best, just was never the same.' The way it stands right now, I was the best and everyone knew it. I met my match, that's all. And I can live with that. But you wouldn't understand. It's a cowboy thing, I guess." He leaned back in his chair, crossing his legs, and folded his arms across his chest.

Amy was speechless. She wondered if anyone had ever heard all this before but said nothing in reply.

"My turn," Jess began. "Why do you use Tawny Talbot and not Amy? You embarrassed about your name or what? And while we're there, why did you have to hide in the bottle? What's your big problem?"

Looking at the ground, Amy searched for the answer.

"Hey, look at me. I'm over here. I answered your questions about my demon. Now look me in the eye and tell me yours. If you can't, don't ever ask me anything again."

"Tawny was something my manager came up with. Said it sounded more country. Sexy too, I guess. The bottle? Easy. I'm afraid. Just a coward." She paused, to see his reaction.

"Afraid of people seeing you fail? Afraid to blow it and be laughed at? Does that about sum it up?" He answered for her. She couldn't help but wonder how he had her pegged so well.

"Yes, and I hate it. I feel terrible. I don't want people to —"

"Not like you?" Jess answered for her again.

She only nodded this time.

"Until you can learn not to give a shit about what others think and just do what you do, you're going to want that bottle. Right now it's scary up there, but I know how I can fix that. Tomorrow you're going to start riding Tommy Boy, my competition horse. Next Thursday, you're entered in the Jackpot at the rodeo here at the ranch."

"Oh, I can't do that. I'm barely riding as it is. I can't."

"Amy," Jess interrupted, "don't ever say that word in front of me again. You can and you will. And if you fail, which most likely you will, you'll wake up the next day and see life goes on. You always have next week, the next show — whatever. Your entry fee is paid. And I don't let chickens work for me. Savvy?"

Amy looked doubtful. "I'm scared. I just want to be so much like Ashley, but I'm from the wrong side of the Mississippi, I guess." She paused. "Hey, you never called me Amy before."

"Okay, Amy. Just did it again." He winked. "Tell you what. I'll put my money where my mouth is. If you give me your word you will run next Thursday night, I'll ride in the bronc riding. See, that event is before barrels, so if you blow it you'll have gone back on your word. Can you commit or are you going to tuck tail and run?"

Win or lose, Jess had seen to it that Amy's fate was in her own hands.

"Okay, you have a deal. But if I make more money than you, do you buy dinner?"

"Try to survive first. Now sing me the song, 'Time and Tears.' Bob says you're onto something there." As he reached for her guitar to hand it to her, he put his hand on her shoulder. It was as hard for him to show affection as it was for her to accept it, but his touch did not go unnoticed. Pushing aside her self-consciousness before him, she started to sing. At first Jess just listened, then he offered comments and, finally, some instruction.

"That's good. Push the note harder. Don't be afraid, put tears in your words. Again, I like that. Come on, Becky, sing to me. Now take it to the end . . ."

He made his way to the cot and sat next to her as she sang the last refrain. He sat close enough that she could feel his body against hers and her concentration fell apart. Saying nothing, he looked at the guitar, and moved her hand as he put his on the neck in a bar chord.

"Listen to this change. Just strum and I'll play the notes."

Amy forced herself to concentrate and do as he said. His face was no more than twelve inches away from hers, and she found herself fighting not to get closer. As she listened, she heard a sudden difference in the tune and the awareness of a counter melody in the chords. She'd never imagined playing that way. His guitar work both complemented the piece and ran opposite to it, like a harmony. She continued to sing although she struggled for breath. And she could feel the warmth of his thigh through his jeans.

"Wow. I like that," she said.

"See the difference there? Gives it a sadder sound, kind of more country." Amy then realized her hand was resting on Jess's leg. She held her breath and hoped he hadn't noticed and couldn't tell that her heart was racing. Jess may just have been helping her, but she was transported — in fact, intoxicated — by the intimacy of the lesson. Suddenly, the beauty of the moment was interrupted.

"Jess, I was wondering if you could — oh, sorry! I thought Amy's shift was over. Excuse me . . ." Brenda said, as she opened the stall door.

Amy felt as if she'd been caught with another woman's man.

"No. Jersey's just playing some tunes for me to keep me company. It's late. Let's call it a day. Both of you probably want to turn in."

Brenda's hostility glowered behind her narrowed eyes, and there was a scowl on her face. Saying nothing, she turned and left. She didn't even say good night. Amy began to pick up her things to leave. As she did, she stopped because Jess had something in his outstretched hand.

"What's this?" she said as she took the

book. She read the cover. *Practice Test and Study Guide for the GED Exam.*

"Now, you have no excuse. If you want help, ask. Everyone here can help, just not Brookes. That kid can barely even read."

Jess made his way to the cot and shook out a sleeping bag. He would spend the night there. She looked at the book and tried to contain her emotions. So much, so fast. One question remained before she would leave him.

"Jess, who's Becky?" she asked.

He rolled over to look at her, squinting at the warming light. "What? What did you say?"

"You called me Becky when I was singing. I just didn't know who you were talking about."

McLain rolled to his back and sighed deeply.

"No one important; just someone I use to know. She sang too, only not near as good as you. You have a real gift. G'night, Amy."

"G'night, boss," she ended.

Amy made her way through the dark to her bunkhouse. Stunned by the flow of events, she couldn't stop thinking about the new version of the man she'd met tonight. He surely wasn't the cold-hearted Jess McLain she thought she knew.

Chapter Twenty-two

The Traveled Road

In the spring on Thursday nights, the J-Bar-M arena turned from a hard-core training program for both horse and hand to a rodeo social gathering. The difficult weather that year kept most of those in Purgatory inside or working countless extra hours. McLain's place broke up the cabin fever that was shared by all. If one threw in a little excitement and the chance to make money, it was surprising how many competitors would come out of the woodwork. With rodeo season around the corner, the gathering was a time for both pro and amateur practice as well as for seeing old friends. For those who just came to play, it was a chance to ride and compete with some of the big stars in the game.

For Jess, the rodeo was also time to do business, and for his hands, it was a time to cut loose and show how good they really were. Gary tended always to take home money in the bull riding: for him the games were preparation. This year would be a coming-out party for David Dallas. He had spent the last twelve months getting on every horse Jess would offer him. Ashley, an arena-tested and proven barrel-racing champion, and one of the biggest names there, was favored to take the whole pot. Brenda was not far behind, but had a ways to go. With this year's events, it was any lady's chance since Ashley had decided to sit the competitions out.

For the guys riding that night, they would face a serious test of character. They wouldn't be using McLain's bucking stock. Instead, Ike Sterling, a contractor from a couple hours north up in Montana, was bringing his best string to determine which horses would make the cut to be in his future shows.

Ike was a legend in rodeo, responsible for sending more animals to the National Finals than any other contractor in history. He had relocated his ranch from Cody, Wyoming, to Montana, and helped Jess get started in the process of breeding rodeo stock. All of McLain's horses had come from the great legend's string or been their offspring. Ike had, in fact, taught Jess the rodeo and ranching game and since the first horse he sold him was the infamous mare named Dancing Wind, he felt obliged to help. Many said he was the hardest man on earth, but the best friend a man could have.

With this turn of events, the J-Bar-M crew could enjoy the show and not have to work. The only one who would be working would be Jess, or so they thought.

Trucks and trailers were lined up and parked in the pasture adjacent to the indoor arena. A train of arriving trailers lined the driveway, and within a couple of hours, several acres were occupied. Hands went from that line to one at the entry table set just inside the door in order to pay their entry fee. Larry Goodman played rodeo secretary, chute boss and sometimes flank man. Though they were the hosts, the hands at the J-Bar-M received no special treatment over the rest of the competitors. They had to wait in line and pay the fee just like everyone else, only Jess saw to it that they had ranch money to pay their fees.

The row of people conversed with a warm familiarity. Lots of folks like to say that rodeo is a family, a close-knit group that takes care of its own. The exception that night was a girl with long blond hair who stood in the line alone.

Amy tried to ignore the strange stares and whispers from onlookers wondering who or what she was. Since no one knew, the speculation was broad. Some thought she was a big-time name-newcomer; others, just some green rookie who was about to learn the hard way. Yet the one comment that hurt the most was when she overheard a couple girls mention that she didn't have a J-Bar-M jacket, so she couldn't be one of "them."

Amy felt very alone, and wanted a drink more than ever. The same gut-turning nausea that she felt before she went onstage, usually quashed with a pint, made her want to purge. It was the only time she thanked God for all the hard work she had done because her clothes didn't look so new that she had the appearance of a greenhorn. Not that she rode that well, anyway.

One more cowboy to sign up, then it was her turn. She'd been practicing all week, with Ashley's help. A decent-sized line still formed behind her, and she was relieved to be done with the long wait. Tired of providing the material for other people's gossip, Amy stepped up to the table to register. She wished the event were already over.

She'd worked on barrels every evening with Ashley and ridden extra on her own time, ignoring her guitar for over a week. Everyone on the ranch knew she was riding and seemed supportive, all except Brenda

175

who now spoke to her as little as possible. Ashley had told her it was because Jess was letting her use his best money-winning horse, Tommy Boy, but for some reason Amy knew different.

"Fifty-five dollars, young lass. Fill out the waiver," Larry said with regimental authority.

"Okay, here you go," she answered, handing him the money. Then Larry gave the crowd a taste of what was to come. They may not have known Amy, but they did know her famous mount.

"Riding Tommy Boy tonight, huh? Well then, you may get this money back and then some," Larry said with a smile.

A warm feeling came over Amy at first, followed by more fear, the same fear Jess told her she had to overcome. She filled out her waiver and passed it across. As Larry looked it over, the group of gossipy girls began to grow louder. Amy couldn't tell, but it seemed the attention had shifted away from her. Proof of her thoughts came by the look of subdued joy on Larry's face, caused by the cowboy that walked up behind her.

Jess McLain strode up to the table like a man with a purpose. Amy realized he was wearing his J-Bar-M jacket for the first time. He looked sharp, tough and professional in his brown rough-stock boots, a black felt hat, and a gleaming engraved rodeo buckle that shone like a star. Jess carried his bucking saddle and gear over one shoulder as if it weighed nothing.

Amy was mesmerized by the sight.

"Step on up, boss," Larry said, smiling at Jess. His face reflected concern.

"Don't mind if I do. Since I have some work to do with Ike, I don't think these people will mind if I intrude and pay real fast," Jess said from beneath his hat.

"Uh — no, don't think so. Don't think you need a waiver, either. Anything I need to know?" Larry asked. Goodman's mood shifted from lightness to seriousness, like a sheriff warning an outlaw about stepping out of line in his town.

"Nope. Just that this fee here is for the saddle bronc event."

"Good luck then, bronc rider," Larry said as he took the money. Jess picked up his saddle and adjusted his hat. Then he turned to Amy who'd been watching with amazement.

"Pressure's off you now. No excuses. Do what you came to do and good luck. I expect dinner to be on you."

The outlaw walked away. Amy was floored by the response that the little scene had made. Jess could have registered quietly and people wouldn't have known until it was his time to ride, but he signed in when the girls were harassing her. He didn't do it for attention; he did it to help out a friend.

Larry reinforced her understanding. "Time to ride, girl. He sure wouldn't have done that for anyone else."

Amy smiled and walked away. She tried to tune out the whispers and comments from those wondering who Jess McLain had been talking to and the doubters who couldn't believe he was really riding again.

Amy reviewed all the tips Ashley had taught her in the short time she'd had to ready herself for competition. Her riding lessons had progressed more quickly than anyone had imagined they would, with Amy taking to riding like a natural. She spent every free moment either on horseback or watching Ashley's tapes. She had an innate sense of balance and a light hand and relished everything about the sport, learning to saddle and groom her horse as well. After the initial fear wore off, she found riding very much to her liking and put in extra time in the arena at night after her work was done.

The cloverleaf pattern that Tommy Boy

could run, with or without a rider, was what she needed to focus on. Ashley coached her closely, even during the warm-up time. Amy tried to concentrate, but couldn't help but see Larry, Jess, and a man she could only assume was Ike Sterling, talking near the bucking chutes. Larry did most of the talking. Jess appeared defiant, stern-faced and resistant. If there was an argument, Amy could see that Jess would not be swayed.

The audience spread the news: this rodeo was to see the return of Jess McLain, an unexpected entry. Ashley couldn't resist voicing her displeasure while Gary and Double D were shocked. No one ever imagined that Jess would compete again. After all, that's what he'd always said.

The bareback riding event had ended, followed by the steer wrestling, one of the more popular events. Calf roping was midway through when Ashley tried to help Amy relax. Tommy Boy was an old vet and knew his job. Ashley just wasn't sure if Amy did.

Brenda, sitting with some other local girls, occasionally pointed at Amy or laughed at her. The Wyoming wind was calm for a change, but Amy felt their whispers cut through her as if it blew hard and strong.

"Don't pay attention to them," reassured Ash as they watched the stock horses load into the chutes. "They're a bunch of kids. Little brat clique. They're just jealous because you're on Tommy Boy. Jess would barely let Brenda even feed him, let alone ride him. Besides, he's half mine."

"You own half of Tommy Boy? Why aren't you riding him then? God, Ash, I feel like I am going to vomit. What if I blow it?"

"Then you blow it, Amy. Who cares? You're not doing this to impress the world. Just take a deep seat, shape the turns like I told you around the barrels, and run for yourself. You fail, there's always next week or another show. Big deal. Plus, I told Jess I wanted you to."

"You wanted me to? Why?"

"Because, Amy, you've been killing yourself here. You've been asked to do more than your part and you do because . . . well, I know why. The others don't, but I think you can do this. I know Jess thinks you can, and other than me, he really doesn't support anybody. So bear down and ride, girl."

"Thanks, Ashley, but I've got to ask you something. Now. You've never told me why Jess treats you different than anyone else.

He trusts you. Don't take me wrong, everyone knows you're the best horse trainer around."

"Well, not the best, but I try."

As the calf roping came to an end, Ashley nodded for Amy to follow her to the garage door that doubled as a runway for the entering and exiting barrel racers. Several people lined up in the building around the arena to watch what was about to take place. As they walked in, a couple of girls brushed by Ashley and burst with joy as if seeing an old friend.

"Becky! Oh my God, we thought you would be on the road by now." A blond girl approached to give Ash a hug. She reciprocated by hugging back. Amy found herself floored by the greeting.

"Darla, hey — how was the wedding? God, I was hoping you'd be here," Ashley returned.

"It went well. Hope to see you after the show." Darla made one more comment. "Hey, is McLain really doing this?"

"Yep, but it was news to me. We're going to check it out now. When we're done, I want you to meet my partner here," Ashley said and they parted ways.

Amy could hardly catch her breath. When they got to the fence, she couldn't hold back anymore. They watched as Dallas nodded to the gate man for his ride.

"Ashley, she called you Becky!" Amy said.

"I know she did." Ashley smiled and watched Dallas put on a show when his bronc exploded out of the gate. She waited for his ride to end before she answered.

"Yes, Amy, my full name is Rebecca Ashley Sharpe."

"The other night Jess called me Becky by accident. My God . . . are you two . . ."

"No, we're not, silly. Sharpe was my ex-husband's name. My maiden name is McLain. So don't get all riled up. People don't know. Jess didn't want my career to be hampered in any way because he's my brother. So now I'm trusting you with that secret. Some night over ice cream and your guitar we'll stay up late and talk and I'll tell you all about Marty Heistler, too — hmm? Right now, just do your job."

Amy was somewhat shocked, but even more relieved. Together, they watched the now-infamous saddle bronc event with no further discussion. All was quiet as the next rider readied himself. Only Dallas had made the whistle thus far on the world-class Sterling horses. However, the next rider had the audience quiet and holding their breath.

Jess shouldered down into the chute and looked like the veteran rider that he was. The horse, big and white, had huge feathered hooves that showed traces of draft horse somewhere in her bloodline. With a powerful scream, she called out to the crowd, sending chills down spines. The mare was as wild as they came. Ike and his imported arena crew worked diligently to keep her calm so that Jess could get on safely. After measuring the rein, he placed it in his left hand. Pushing his hat down tight with his free arm, he began to climb over the gate.

"Okay, JM, crotch her. She wasn't rode all last year. You want to make a statement, she'll talk for ya," Ike said. He relieved his flank man for this rider. Jess was too important to leave to anyone else. McLain squinted and he spoke to himself, easing down in the saddle. His jaw clenched and his mouth grew stern as his eyes focused somewhere out in the middle of the arena.

Amy felt herself tremble and watched as Ashley prayed. This pairing of horse and rider was no longer harmless fun: a horse that hadn't been ridden and a rider who should never have been in the arena were a deadly combination. Amy felt a chill as Jess looked out of the chute. Even in the distance, she could feel his steel eyes pierce her. He nodded and went back to work.

"And behold a pale horse and its rider was death; and hell followed him."

McLain often repeated this verse. Today, it took on special meaning. He leaned back in the saddle, lifted on his rein and nodded his head. The gate burst open — nothing less than a detonation device to an explosion of wild horse and rider. The mare reared out high and showed her power by bucking her very next step. McLain's heels with spurs reached up and stuck her in the neck, keeping him in the saddle. She blew up with every lunge and buck. In the air, Jess's feet were ripped back to the saddle and just when it appeared all was lost, they sprang back to the neck. Though his body looked like it was being torn apart with whiplash at every jump, his face was still cold and focused and returned to a controlled expression every time the bronc came back down.

Ashley cheered the loudest and Amy watched in amazement — a man surviving what would kill most mortals. Yet he appeared to be calm throughout the thunderstorm of spur and hide. Gary, Dallas and Brookes sat up on the fence, cheering. Brenda cheered too, calling him pet names that got Ashley's attention. She was quickly halted by a scowl.

Larry and Ike just smiled at his ride, almost as if they expected no less. It all came to an end when the buzzer sounded. Ike's pick-up men rode in to free Jess safely, but he waved them off and performed a flying dismount. Coming down on his feet, the force caused him to go to one knee. The horse continued to buck lightly and run around the arena just to show off. Jess came to his feet again and did something totally uncharacteristic: he smiled faintly as he made his way out of the arena. Unzipping his protective vest through the gate, it was clear the spectacle was over.

"Welcome back, cowboy," Ike Sterling mumbled to Larry, who seemed to share in the sentiment.

McLain made his way around the arena with a few people giving congratulations, none more than the ones he got from Double D, Gary and Brookes. As he made his way to the south end of the arena, he ran straight into Brenda, who congratulated him from the back of her horse.

"Good ride, Jess. I knew you'd win," she said, fawning. She was pleased to see that her friends were watching closely, but when

McLain just nodded and barely looked her way, she felt lost.

He didn't stop until he got to where Ashley and Amy sat. Ashley showed the only sign that they may have been closer than friends, holding up two fingers in a V. Had Amy not been told, she would have never thought anything of it, but the news she'd learned shed a whole new light. Ashley gave her brother a half hug and he gave back what he got.

"Well, how does it feel to be back?" Ashley asked her boss.

"Felt stiff and a little rusty, but my shoulder feels okay. Back's going to be sore, though. That horse liked to jar me loose inside," he said, as he released her. Small talk prevailed and then he focused on Amy. Standing directly next to her, he put his hand on her leg and tried to comfort her, a gesture even Ashley was a little stunned to see.

"You need to relax," he said. "I could see you're a nervous wreck clear across the arena. It doesn't matter. What matters is to give it all up, leave it all out, and go. No matter the outcome, you'll be fine."

"Easy for you to say. You just made a serious dent in our bet. I have to step it up to make more than what you did after that show. That was incredible," Amy told him.

"Yeah, well, you won't be buying just her dinner, buddy. If she wins, it's trainer and rider both!" Ashley said, smiling. Amy tried to ignore her, but Brenda was staring at them, pure outrage on her face.

"Deal. Well, time to go to work, Amy." Jess made a quick exit. Once gone, a couple of hands opened the south side of the arena and barrels were set up in the cloverleaf pattern.

As luck would have it, the running order would put Amy last. No pressure there, she thought. Larry stood just inside the entry with his flag and stopwatch. The first girl started twenty feet from the arena opening and was in full stride when she hit the timing line. Making one turn to the right, then two to the left, she blazed back through the gate. Larry called out her time of 15.9 seconds and then the next girl went. Ashley had a doubtful look on her face that Amy wanted to understand.

"What?" she asked.

"Nothing. That was just really good time," Ashley confirmed. Brenda would be up next and she rode by Amy as she made her way to get started.

"Try not to embarrass us, Jersey. We know you'll screw up. Just try not to look like an idiot."

Ashley exploded, "That's enough, Bowers. You seem to forget you have never won a dime and you're on my horse. So just shut up and go run."

Brenda put a boot to her horse and turned him on a hard angle. She started her run and as she entered the arena, Ashley turned to Amy. "Blow that off. It's just trash talking. She puffs up her chest when I don't enter. When I do she hides because I kick her ass every time."

Together they heard the time of 16.2. Not bad, but only fourth in the running.

The next five went by in a flash and Amy could hardly breathe. She would have sat there all night if her trainer hadn't told her it was time. She exhaled, then took a deep breath and gave a nudge to Tommy Boy, who sprang to life in an instant. He'd reached top speed as he entered the arena. Amy made her way around the first barrel smoothly, then shot across the arena to the other side and took the left-hand turn, setting up for her last left loop. Holding her breath, she held on with a vengeance and, had the saddle horn not been there, would have certainly hit the dirt. Making her last left, she felt as if she was in a tunnel and could hear nothing. Making her way around, she tucked her head and let

Tommy Boy take her out, just like Ashley said he would. Out of the arena she flew. Bringing the horse to a slow stop, she turned and quickly trotted him back to center to hear her score. Ashley met her halfway.

"Not bad. You rode really well, but what did you forget?" Ashley asked.

Amy couldn't place it. As they got back to the arena, her heart sank. As Larry called out her time, she noticed two of the three barrels had been knocked over. Her 15.9 would have been a good third, but for each barrel came a ten-second penalty making it 35.9. She put her head down and held back tears. She'd known she was kidding herself that she could do it. Not letting Ashley say anything, she turned her horse to exit and go cool him down. The pain of losing racked her as she passed Brenda and her gang who taunted with personal shots. Still, she pressed on.

Making her way out, she tried to decipher exactly what this disaster was supposed to teach her, other than how to fail. She already knew how to do that. Riding through the parked trucks, she only wanted to be alone. It didn't take long to come to the end of the parking area. Stopping, she looked up as if to ask God why she failed the tests and then looked around to make sure nobody was there to watch her cry. Then she noticed a bottle of bourbon and a twelve-pack of Coke sitting on the seat of a truck cab. The truck was unlocked. She could remember Terry Ann telling her once, "Temptation is a witch whose spell is powerful." Amy approached the truck and opened the door. The witch surely had her now.

"Hey, where the hell is Amy?" McLain asked. The rodeo had been over for an hour and most everyone was gone. She might never have been missed, except for Tommy Boy, who'd wandered back into the arena, reins dragging on the ground, still saddled. It had been dark for some time and even Ike was on his way home.

"I don't know, boss. I haven't seen her," Russell answered.

"Would someone like to tell me why my horse is loose?"

"I'll get him, boss. Whoa, Tommy Boy. Easy, big man. Don't know, sir," Dallas said as he approached the wanderer. Ashley quickly ran to aid Dallas.

Jess had been looking for Amy. His concern turned to anger and from there to outrage at the sight of his unattended horse. He whistled for Jax, who always seemed to appear out of some hole in the wall to receive orders from his owner.

"Find Amy," he shouted when Jax appeared. The dog bounded before them as they headed out towards the parking lot. Within moments, they all heard something like singing coming from the south end. Through the lights they saw someone wandering in the distance. They all knew it was she.

Puzzled, Ashley thought she better try and save her by calling, only to find out as she came into view, that Amy wasn't herself. Ash saw the bottle she was carrying and the stumbling, hesitant walk. Jess could barely contain himself as his anger rose. It was all he could do to keep from exploding.

Amy mumbled to herself as she struggled to get closer to the group.

Normally, Jess would not reprimand a hand in front of others but this situation seemed to strike a nerve deeper than anyone knew. They gathered around him and knew the situation wasn't good.

Jess stepped out from the group and marched towards Amy, his jaw clenched. It didn't take long for him to reach her and his fury was palpable. "Having a good time, Jersey?" he asked in a steely monotone.

"Sure, wanna drink? Celebrate your great

ride?" Amy answered. Jess rolled his shoulders and Ashley called out to him as if to stop him. He held his hand up to quiet those behind him. Never looking back, he spoke.

"Nope, that's all your call. Tell you what? Why don't you finish it?" he asked, pointing to the bottle.

Amy looked at the bottle in her hand: it still held more than half its contents. Her tolerance had withered on the ranch. She'd learned that quickly, after the first few sips. "No, I'm just . . ."

"Finish it. Now!"

"No way, I can't do —"

Jess confronted her, blocking her way.

"You finish it now or I swear I'll kick your ass off this fucking planet. Now drink, damn it!" he bellowed.

With raw courage, she set out to test his will, but booze deludes. She lifted the bottle and started to chug. Not being able to finish, she leaned forward to spill some on the ground, but Jess wouldn't let up.

"Finish!"

She then tried again and guzzled more, leaving some again. She began to feel herself needing to purge. Gagging, she stopped.

Jess pushed the bottle to her face. One last time and she polished off the bottle, only to have most of it come back up. Jess grabbed the bottle and heaved it against the arena wall, exploding it. Amy was bent over now, feeling like more was going to come up, but had no time. Jess grabbed her by the collar, knocking off her hat, and began to drag her, barely keeping her on her feet. Even though Amy vomited on herself along the way, he would not be swayed. The others watched, aghast.

Jess came to a large watering trough that was big enough to hold three feet of water and at least two lengths of a horse. Amy coughed and tried to hold back the heaves. McLain then picked her up and forcefully threw her in. With the water temperature just above freezing, shock set in right away. Amy fought to get to the edge and climb out, sputtering and screaming, only to have Jess push her back in, once even grabbing her by the hair and making sure she was submerged.

Ashley couldn't bear to watch. He was drowning her!

Brenda stood in back, laughing loudly. When the cold had ripped Amy of all her strength, Jess pulled her out and let her flop to the ground. By this time, she had purged anything she had in her stomach and had the dry heaves. Sitting on the ground, she shook and sobbed, but was too cold to speak.

"You having a good time, Jersey? Huh? You're gonna have one now! Get your ass up, go put on dry clothes and get to work! Rake the arena. Then clean the stalls. Move!" He picked her up and pushed her in the right direction. Amy stumbled towards her bunk alone and Jess stood, still fuming, removing his wet jacket.

"Goddamn it, how'd she get that bottle?"

"Don't know, boss, don't know," Dallas said. Jess decided to take care of other business. He walked up to Brenda and stared her down.

"Something wrong?"

"No, why?" Brenda replied.

"Well, you thought all that was so fuckin' funny, didn't you? But you don't seem to be laughing now."

"But I just . . ."

"You don't speak unless I fuckin' ask you to, you get it?" Jess ordered. Brenda nodded.

"We don't talk shit about our own here. And like it or not, she's one of our own. Since you thought it necessary for you and those little bitches you hung around with to make fun of her, this is your fault too. So grab a rake, because you're helping!" Jess demanded.

Brenda, embarrassed, turned and left.

There was nothing left to say.

Jess kicked the dirt hard, sending a rock hurtling. "Damn it! She almost had it licked," his voice now tempered by a tone of compassion.

"Don't give up, son, she needs it," comforted Larry, stepping forward. "If you didn't see that before, I know you do now. The little thing's in a bad way."

"Yeah, I know. And I've got to do something about it. It's not about the money any more."

Chapter Twenty-three

A Legend's End

By one in the morning, the punishment had almost run its course. All but one stall was clean. The longest chore was hand-raking the arena. Usually reserved for the tractor and rookies, Brenda did her best to carp the whole time. Amy was too ill to complain, and even though she had changed into dry clothes, the chill didn't seem to leave her. She finished up and placed her tools back in the tool room and forced herself to head back to the bunk. Brenda seemed to linger, even more upset that Amy wouldn't acknowledge her whining.

"Fine, you bitch! I have to stay up because of you. No problem, Jersey. I'll see to it that you leave." Brenda worked her way around Dancing Wind's stall and deftly tripped the latch open. Placing her tools back in their place, she turned to make a hurried escape.

"Where's Amy?" Ashley asked, appearing unexpectedly at the barn door. Startled, Brenda stumbled through her answer. "The little city girl couldn't handle it and went to bed. I finished the job."

"Really? Well, when I checked earlier she was ahead of you. Maybe a little less complaining and a little more work would help. I don't know what's got into you, but you need to get a hold of yourself, Brenda."

Ashley let Brenda pass, wondering why she seemed so much to want to get away. With that, Ash thought it best to go and check on Amy and see if she really was in bed and taken care of.

The blue roan strolled through the alleyway between the stalls. Finding an open door, the smell of grain overpowered her nostrils. Ranchers everywhere know that a horse is a slave to hunger and its stomach. No horse can resist available feed. The mare poked around the open large trash cans full of grain and sweet mix, sensing instinctively that if she ate she would be warmer. She began to consume her newly discovered feast in the calm Wyoming night.

Jess awoke to the sound of screaming — the cries of an animal in agony. He looked at the clock and saw that it was two in the morning. Nothing could rouse him out of bed faster than the sound of a gunshot or a horse's neigh. The cries came over and over. Since his Army days Jess had kept his boots and a set of clothes for the next day by his bed, so he was dressed and down the stairs in minutes with Jax by his side and his Colt .44 in his hand.

Ashley came running across the yard, obviously hearing the same commotion. "What the hell is that, Jess?"

"I don't know. Take Jax and look in the barn," he said as he took the flashlight he carried in his other hand. He set out to see if some predator had located his new colt. Oh, the price it would pay, he thought, hoping it wasn't so. He searched around the barn and heard Ashley call out to him through the door. "Jess! Dance's stall is open and she's gone!"

"Shit!"

Jess heard the cry again and pinpointed its location. He ran behind the arena with the caution of a man walking into an ambush. He turned the corner. Sweat covered his brow at the sight of his discovery. The blue roan lay on the ground thrashing, foaming and frothing at the mouth. He dropped his pistol. Jess bolted for the barn and Jax followed, barking the whole way. By this time, Dave Dallas was in the barn with Ashley, examining the toppled grain cans. Jess grabbed towels and lariats. He shouted out orders to Dallas and Ashley, pushing aside a feeling of panic, but still in a calm voice.

"Grab a halter and get the vegetable oil, now!"

He bolted back outside. With Gary taking the night off, Dave and Ash were the only hands to answer the rescue call. They knew by what he wanted just what the situation was and it didn't look good. With halter in hand and Dallas in tow with a lead rope and gallon of oil, the crew lined up quickly behind. They came face to face with the horror as they turned the corner and found Wind lying on the ground, writhing in pain, squealing and thrashing.

Jess wrestled at her neck trying to get the halter on her head and not be caught by the flurry of flying hooves. He couldn't do it, and Ashley made a loop in the lead rope and got it around her neck while Jess instructed Dallas to whip the horse's behind. He began to coax her as McLain came to his feet and tried with all he had to pull the horse up. If he could get her to stand, he might be able to save her. Ashley grabbed on to the end of the lead and pulled too, but Wind fought them. Her colic had set in, and hard. There was no telling how long she'd been contorted. Jess pleaded with the horse to get up.

"Come on, baby! Get up! Get up! That's

an order! Goddamn it. Get up!"

By this time, Larry was outside and urging the horse with the whip. She wouldn't budge, and Jess knew time was running out for her life. He gave further orders to give it one last try. It was a long shot, but he'd done it before. Jess called out for Ashley to hold her head. From there Larry and Dallas tackled her hind feet and wrapped a towel around them, putting two lariats over the towel. Jess fought with her front feet to do the same. From there he tossed one to Ashley and gave her the command to let go of the head, grab a lariat end and step back.

They would spread out and pull in opposite directions, rolling the horse from one side to the other, hoping that rocking her back and forth might cause the intestines to untwist. It was risky and hard, but was a last resort. When they pulled opposite Jess's side, he grabbed the bottle of vegetable oil and filled the anal syringe with as much oil as it would hold, injecting it in her anus. He repeated it twice before running back to the rope to pull her back to the other side.

They rocked her back and forth for thirty minutes and her cries began to quiet. With every minute, Jess begged for more time.

"Please, God! Wind, don't die! Come on,

damn it! *Work!*" He pulled with all he had. He coaxed her like a father pleads with a dying child, insistent, fearful. They rolled her back and forth, from side to side, their own strength fading. Tears began to spill down Jess's cheeks.

Larry understood what was going on inside the Ranger's head when he collapsed to his knees and began to try to roll the mare with his two hands, without the lariats. The rest knew she was beyond help, but Jess wouldn't give up. He began to act delirious.

"God, no! Please, Jack, don't. Damn it, Jack, we're almost there. Come on, buddy, we're almost there! Please. Please, please, please!"

Larry had not heard his son's name spoken in a long time. He watched as Jess cradled the horse's head and sobbed uncontrollably. Stroking her, Larry now knew exactly what Jess endured in the Iraqi desert — the feeling of complete helplessness. He longed for his son, but he was relieved that he'd died in a friend's arms. The story that Jess could not tell was now playing itself out before them. Now they needed to save Jess. Larry grabbed Sergeant McLain around the shoulders and pulled him off. Ashley held him, making him look her in the eyes. Jess fought and begged.

"No! Goddamn it. I can save him. He's not gone! Let me go!"

"Jess! Jack is gone! Please, Jess, look at me, at your sister! Please," Ashley pleaded with her brother. Finally, Jess met her eyes.

"Damn it, Jess, you tried. There was nothing you could do," Larry said and held on to his adopted son with all his strength.

"Jess. It's me. I love you and I know you loved this horse, but she's not going to make it!" Ashley told her brother. Jess responded with the deepest pain in his heart, a grimace upon his face. He knew what had to be done. Jess stopped fighting and embraced his sister for the first time since his return. Holding him, she cried with him. "Jess, she's suffering. You know what to do. I'll do it with you. We'll do it together."

"No, no, I need to do this alone. I'll be okay." Larry patted Jess on the back and left him with Ashley.

David Dallas just watched, silent and grief-stricken. He could do nothing more. But he knew one thing: that what happened here and what he saw would always stay at the ranch. He owed it to Jess.

Larry knew that the hardest part was yet to come. He picked up Jess's pistol. With his back turned to him, he discharged the cylinder of the revolver and emptied all six shells into his hand. Then he laced one back in. He couldn't leave anything to chance.

Ashley kissed her brother's forehead and took the gun from Larry, who held it out for him. She handed it to Jess and stood by Larry quietly. Dallas followed as she motioned for them to leave. Rounding the corner, they could hear the strangled breath of the suffering horse as Dancing Wind slipped away.

Making his way to his knees, Jess held the revolver in his hand and wiped his forehead with the other. Then, closing his eyes, he placed his other hand on the pistol and held it to his forehead as if to pray. He crawled over to the horse, who looked at him as if begging for him to end her misery.

"I'm sorry, old girl. Please forgive me. I rode again tonight. Did ya know that? I may try again. It wasn't your fault, I know. I'm gonna miss you." He stroked her head. "I'll see you soon. Tell Jack I'll see him, too."

Jess came to his feet and took a deep breath. The mare glared balefully back at him and grew still. She knew. Jess took a deep breath and took aim.

At the far corner of the barn three people stood together. Dallas had his right arm around Ashley, who sobbed uncontrollably. Larry stood a few steps away. This event was the dark side of cowboy life he'd never imagined.

Ashley mourned, not so much for the horse, but for her brother whom, she realized now, had died a long time ago in a distant land. All three were jolted by the loud explosion of gunfire, followed by a scream that carried pain and darkness over the land. Only the scream was that of a man, not of a horse.

Dallas wrapped both arms around Ashley and comforted her. Larry trembled in silence.

Brenda had made her way out to the barn about the same time Gary pulled back in to the drive. Brookes had already met up with Russell. They could see that Ashley, Dallas and Larry were deeply distraught. Brenda continued on past them, only to be stopped by Larry.

"Don't go back there! Leave him be," Larry ordered.

"But I wanted to see what . . ." Brenda interrupted.

"I don't care what you thought you were going to do, just go back to bed."

Brenda stormed back to the house. Everyone followed except for Ashley, who made her way to her brother to sit with him.

That night the legend died along with the demon that had for so long haunted Jess McLain's existence.

Chapter Twenty-four

Armageddon: Part One

Amy awoke about noon with a crushing headache. She couldn't remember how she'd gotten into Ashley's big sweatshirt, but that's what she had on when she crawled out of her sleeping bag and realized it was well past sunrise. Half the day was gone and no one had come to wake her. Something was wrong. Very wrong. The ranch ran with clockwork precision and when something changed, it was a sure sign something was amiss.

As she pulled on her jeans and boots, her head began to clear and the painful, ugly scene of the afternoon before began to surface: the drinking, the thrashing out by Jess and the near drowning in the horse trough. The utter humiliation and terror of it all. God, how she hated his guts. All because of what? A rodeo event? What triggered the shame, the quick exit into the booze? Why couldn't she stand to fail? Was it worth all this?

Amy's stomach started to heave, and she

choked back the urge to spill her guts out on the ground. Her stomach was empty, but her anger at herself and at Jess McLain set off the gagging as much as anything. She wanted to turn herself inside out and start over, transparent and new. She couldn't stand another day as herself. She ran to the washroom and rinsed her mouth out with water. Nothing would come up. She was grateful for that.

"I've had it," she said aloud as she threw her towel against the wall and sat down on Ashley's bunk.

"Had what?" echoed Ashley, somberly. She had just walked in, tossing her jacket down on the bed.

"Just about everything."

"Well, you haven't had everything yet. Wait until you hear this. You're in some pretty deep crap with the boss right now."

"More? What now? I thought he just about killed me yesterday over my own goddamn business. Wasn't that enough? So I broke a rule, is that so bad? Drank a little booze? It's still my choice, you know. Nobody ever said I could conquer this thing. Well, I've made up my mind. I'm leaving here anyway. I knew all this was never going to work."

Amy's eyes began to fill with tears even as

the words formed in her mouth. She didn't want to leave Purgatory any more than she wanted to go back to New Jersey.

Back to what? To Terry Ann on an oxygen tank in a nursing center? To waiting tables in a bar and singing for peanuts to a cotton-candy audience? To being a nobody in a world that couldn't tolerate anything but the best?

Amy hugged her knees up to her chest and let out a sigh that rocked her shoulders. "Okay, I give up. I can't. I can't go anywhere. I can't do what they want. I can't do anything. I don't fit in."

"Yeah, well, whether or not any of that is true, you may not have a choice as to whether or not you leave," Ashley, said, sitting down on the bunk next to Amy. She tapped the toes of her boots together nonchalantly, watching the dust and dirt crumble on the floor.

"What do you mean?" Amy's eyes widened.

"Amy," Ashley said softly. "Look at me."

She stared at the woman who had become her closest friend in the last few weeks and held back hot tears.

"What?"

"We got trouble. Big trouble. Or at least, you do. Dancing Wind got out last night.

Got into the grain room and got herself real sick. Jess tried most of the night to save her but he couldn't. He had to shoot the poor thing. She was suffering that bad."

"No! No, he didn't!" Amy screamed, and stood up, torn by the thought of the beautiful mare shot by the man who loved her so, Jess's wild Dancing Wind.

"He did. It's been real sad around here. Everybody knows that she was Jess's special horse. Worse thing is, Amy, Brenda says you did it. That you let her out. Is that true?"

Amelia Elizabeth Talbot thought the entire world had suddenly come to an end. Her breath caught in her throat and she made a stifled, choking sound. She sat back down stiffly on the bed, and turned to Ashley, looking her straight in the eyes. Her own narrowed to slits and her mouth set hard.

"Say that again . . ."

"Brenda says you did it, deliberately, to get back at Jess for what he did to you."

"Oh my God. That little bitch! How could she lie like that?"

"I don't know. Even if she's lying or not. Nobody does. She says she's not. But somebody has to answer for what happened, because somehow that horse got out of a stall door that takes two hands to unlatch. Look, there's a hearing tonight at six, in the mess hall. Jess is going to let the whole team decide. You're going to have to defend yourself. Your word against hers. You'd better be there."

"Ashley, you believe me, don't you?"

"I think so. I mean, in my mind, it seems like you couldn't have done it because you pretty much collapsed after you finished your clean-up sentence. Brenda did one end of the arena and you did the other. I found you sitting in the bleachers pretty much passed out after it was done. You sure managed to fill a whole wheelbarrow, though, considering the shape you were in. That was amazing. Anyway, I took you to the bunk practically confused. You were still drunk, shivering and exhausted. But I'll be honest with you, Amy, I don't know what happened during the time you and Brenda had to clean up that arena. I only found you afterwards. And I'm glad I did. You might have spent the night lying on those bleachers."

"Thanks. You're the best person I know."

"Okay. Okay. Look, that's not the point. I want to believe you. But it's not up to you. And all of us need to decide who is guilty here. And if so, who stays or who goes."

"You mean . . ."

"Yes, Jess has announced that whoever violated that one promise, never to touch Wind, is guilty enough to find a new home. So stop worrying about fitting in, because I think you may have just bailed yourself out. I'm sure you didn't mean to, that it was just an accident."

"I didn't do it, Ashley, goddamn it! I didn't. I'd never do anything like that. You have to believe me!" The tears were streaming so fast down Amy's face now she could hardly see straight, pleading with Ashley to believe her.

"Look, I'd lie low if I were you. That's all. No one knows what to think. Everybody's pretty upset. You were excused from your ranch chores today. Jess told me to tell you if you woke up to just stay away from the barn. He's been out digging the hole to bury Dancer in. It's taken most of the day. He doesn't want to see you."

"I can't imagine why."

"Hey, listen, whatever's up, which only you know and I don't, let's change the subject. I'm still your friend. But I do know you got a phone call from that woman called Terry Ann this morning. Don't worry. I didn't say a word about what's going down around here. She wanted to know how things are. I said fine. She said Marty

Heistler says there's a schedule change. Something about moving things up. She said you'd know what it was all about. Do you?"

Before Amy could answer, Ashley continued. "Anyway, I don't care. I don't even want to know what she's talking about. I just wish things were the way they used to be."

"What's that supposed to mean?" Amy asked, bracing herself for another barb.

"Jess. I'm worried about him."

"Well, that's great, everybody's worried about Jess. What about me? Why didn't you wake me up, anyway?"

"I tried. No one could wake you up."

"Sorry. Okay. Ashley, you know what? This is it. This is absolutely it. I am done with this drinking for good. I cannot believe the mess I'm in. Nothing is worth all this. Nothing can matter more than knowing where you are and who you are and staying in control of your life. Ashley, I may have been staggering drunk yesterday and not capable of remembering much, but I never went near that horse's stall. Just to be blamed for it hurts more than anything that's ever happened to me in my whole life. God, you've got to believe that. You've got to stand by me, please!"

"I'm out on this one, Amy. I don't know what to say. Except that I'm really concerned about my brother. I guess I shouldn't say this, but . . . well, over these last few weeks, Jess has really gotten to care for you. I can tell. He's talked to me about it. He wants you to win so bad. He needs you to conquer this thing, for him. As a person who can get back out there, back into a world he once loved. He wanted you to lick this problem and take that beautiful voice of yours and sing, bring your music alive, not just for you, but for him too."

Amy shook her head in disbelief. She couldn't imagine what Ashley was saying was true.

"He used to sing, Amy. He used to have a heart that was so open and full of joy, and then first our brother got killed, then Larry's son, and it's all just taken its toll. He's not the same. Anyway, I think he really cares for you, Amy. And he's really down about all of this."

Amy thought of the secret longings and feeling of closeness she'd been harboring these last few weeks. She relived her desperate wish for Jess's attention, the cherished brush of his hand or savored touch of his shoulder against hers. Once, she was sure he'd put his arm around her in the kitchen. She'd softened against him, realizing that he was probably just reaching around her to pick up something, but she welcomed the wrap of his arm as though it had been a kiss. He held her there for a minute, right in front of everybody. She counted every random moment that she'd come close to him and held on to it, hoping that someday Jess might actually treat her like a real woman, not a hired hand, or some lush drunk, and not his slave. She'd never admit it to anyone, but she realized that she wanted Jess McLain's respect more than anything in the whole world. It was simple. She had slowly begun to fall in love with him, but she had no way to show it, nowhere to put it. Another one of those house rules. Don't get too close to the boss.

And so she wrote. She wrote about him at night and sang about him in her dreams and strummed songs without words on her guitar, but with lyrics she could feel in her heart: struggling, silent hopes for a man she couldn't reach. A man she couldn't even talk about. She couldn't admit to another living soul on the whole ranch that she loved this crazy recluse. Except that yesterday she wanted to kill him, wanted to break every bone in his body for plunging her into that ice-green slime.

"Amy, he cares for you. More than you know. But if you're to blame, there's no way I can stop him. You know he believes in justice, responsibility, and accountability. He can't tolerate people shirking off. He can't stand cracks in his world. Don't ever tell him I said this, but he's barely holding himself together after what happened to him back there in the Gulf. He needs a world where order is predictable, and where life is something he can control. All that's changed now. I'm worried about him, Amy. Just be prepared when you see him tonight. He's on the edge."

Chapter Twenty-five

Trial by Jury

The crew sat around the table after dinner. Jess had been absent for the evening meal. Not much was said, but the tension sat thick. Amy had acquired that disembodied feeling, as if she were somewhere else. No one discussed the recent loss at the J-Bar-M, but it weighed heavily on everyone's heart. Even Dallas must have been affected greatly, for this was the smallest and plainest meal he'd ever prepared.

Larry seemed to be in his own world. He'd made a call to their neighbor shortly after daybreak to ask a favor. Sure, the J-Bar-M had its own tractor, but no one seemed to want to use it to take care of Dancing Wind's remains. The neighbor had come over to reciprocate the many favors McLain had done for him. He dragged the lifeless body of the horse to the hole and waited with Larry to push her in. It took nearly the whole day. McLain could have made fast work digging the large grave with a backhoe, but he seemed to feel the need to do it by hand. After several hours, Larry and the neighbor went out and helped to achieve the proper depth. No one else could watch as they pushed her in, but Jess stood by till the last shovel of dirt was placed over her. He hadn't been seen since.

Amy tried to control her emotions. She wanted justice done, as Jess did, and found it hard to keep herself from jumping over the table to throttle Brenda.

Ashley talked the most, but only with Gary. For the first time, she sat next to Amy at dinner. Though she couldn't voice her support outright, she showed her support by patting Amy's hand and smiling often through silent lips.

Finally, the moment had arrived. The sound of boots on the front deck let everyone know that court was about to begin.

It took only a few minutes for Jess to join them. He entered, grim and tense, as if all hell awaited him. His face bore no emotion; his eyes met no one's. He took his seat and began, asking for everyone's attention, wasting no time getting started.

Leaning back in his chair, he glared at the room as if everyone in it were the enemy, except for Larry and Ashley, of course.

"I'll make this short and sweet. My fifteen-thousand-dollar mare is dead. It takes two hands to unlock the stall she was in. Someone tell me right now who did it." Jess stopped. A long pause followed but no one would talk. On any other occasion, Jess would be screaming. Tonight he had an unholy calm in his voice.

"I'm not going to ask again. Gary was gone last night and is a whole lot smarter than to make such an error. Ashley, Larry, and David are out of the question. So that leaves Brookes, Amy, and Brenda. However, I know that Mr. Brookes, not being confined to the ranch, was spending what I hope was responsible time with young Miss Katy. To whose dad, by the way, I owe thanks for helping out today."

Jess paused, then looked at the remaining two. Brenda and Amy sat quietly. McLain noticed a look of confidence on Amy's face.

"So, that leaves you two. The heckler and the drunk. Now before we go any farther, I believe I know who did it. I spent several weeks in an interrogation school with the Army, so if one of you lies, I'll know it. Lie to me, you're gone, no questions asked."

Brenda erupted. "She was the one that did that side of the barn! She was the one who was so drunk she could barely walk. We all know she did it!"

Amy sat steadfast and looked Jess square

in the eye. "Wait a minute," she interrupted. "Yesterday I made a huge mistake. And when I woke up this morning . . ."

"More like this afternoon," Brenda blurted.

"I'm sorry. Ms. Brenda, did I say you could speak?" Jess interjected. "Continue, Amy."

"I have to live with that," Amy continued. "I felt like I let down the one person who really believed in me. I will never touch the bottle again. It's all I thought about last night while I was working. Jess, I wanted you to be proud of me at the rodeo yesterday. I failed you. I failed myself. But I would never have done anything like that to your horse. I know better."

"You don't get it. I was proud of you. For being afraid and competing anyway. That was the whole point. So you knocked over a barrel. You're not the first and won't be the last. As for Dancing Wind, I believe you," Jess said.

"What?" Brenda stood up. "That's it? You believe that act? What kind of crap is this? She doesn't belong here. She let the horse out!"

"That's enough!" Jess ordered Brenda to be quiet. "Ash, who was last out of the barn last night?"

Ashley stated the facts. "Brenda. Amy had headed up to the bunkhouse."

"Oh, so that means you just assume that it was me because I had to finish her side," hissed Brenda. "I belong here. She doesn't." She grew more angry with every word.

Jess leaned forward with a straight face and tossed a work glove, his ace of spades, on the table.

"Whose is this?" Jess asked.

"It's mine. Why?" Brenda asked.

"One more thing. I gave the opportunity for whoever did this to come forward. The truth was all I asked. Okay then. Jax! Dining room," Jess called out for his dog. Jax scurried in and took his place next to McLain.

"Call the dog, Amy," Jess asked. Not seeing where this tack was going or daring to question, she did. On command, Jax went to her and received a pat on the head. Jess then snapped his fingers and Jax trotted right back to him.

"Brenda, call him," Jess ordered.

Doing what her boss asked, she called the dog.

"Jax, come here."

Jax stood motionless and looked at her. She repeated herself, only this time Jax stood and bared his teeth. A light growl filled his throat. Brenda couldn't understand. She called again only to have him bark at her and remain steadfast next to Jess. Brenda looked at Jess dumbfounded.

"Tell you a little story. Do you know what kind of dog Jax is?" he leaned over to pet his partner. "Jax is a Shiba Inu, a small version of a Japanese fighting dog. They're extremely loyal, but one of the neatest characteristics is that they mate for life. Or have a life partner. Jax here had Jasmine who was my ex's dog. Same kind. Well, when we divorced, she took Jasmine and in his depressed and lonely state, he bonded with Dancing Wind. He slept at her stall a lot. Don't ask me why he chose her, but he did. It's almost freaky how these dogs bond with something." Jess looked at Brenda now and directed his closing argument to her.

"That latch is difficult, a real pain. I installed it that way so it was horse-proof. You've probably all noticed how you have to reach your fingers in through the one side to unhook the first part?" he asked.

"Yeah, damn thing — sorry, boss — it's like a puzzle," Gary Russell commented.

"Yep, that it is. Don't worry about it. I've said worse today. Well, you can't get your fingers in and undo it with gloves on." Jess leaned down, grabbed up the glove and dealt out his card, tossing it on the table in front of Brenda. "Next time you decide you want to do something like that, don't leave your glove wedged in the bars of the stall you're unlocking. It was still there this morning."

Jess gave Brenda a stare that made everyone's blood run cold. Tears formed in her eyes as she looked around the room, seeking some way out. Finally, she burst.

"I didn't mean for her to die, I swear it. I just wanted Amy gone. I thought Wind would just get out. Why can't you believe me? Everything was fine before she came here. And the way you look at her, why can't you look at me that way? I'm the one who loves you! I'm the one that wants you! Don't you think we all see it?" she continued. "You never cheered me on when I rode, you never helped me! Why?"

Brenda spilled out her anger and exposed her young, broken, jealous heart in an emotional admission that none could have ever foreseen. But the hanging judge never lost his look of condemnation. He seemed to be even more determined.

"Don't ask for sympathy from me. You lied to everyone here. You made fun of one of our own. You, of all people! You killed my horse, no matter how you look at it. You let the entire ranch down. Amy never did anything to you. Right now, your personal feelings mean squat to me. You set out to destroy another person here. In the process, you hurt me, and cost this place possibly forty thousand dollars." Jess paused and folded his hands together as if a judge was about to lay down his verdict. Then Gary stepped in.

"Well, boss, do we put it to a vote? Like what we've done in the past?" he asked.

"Yes, but this is the first time we've ever had someone try to destroy from within." Jess looked at Gary and a calm fell over his eyes. Turning to Amy he added, "It was you she lied about, you she tried to run outta here. It's your choice and your choice alone."

Amy paused and looked across the table at a weeping Brenda. In a way she could sympathize with her feelings. She'd felt them when she thought Ashley and Jess were together. Jealousy was an awful thing. Anger burned inside her. She held the fate of Brenda and didn't like it one bit.

"No, it's all our decision, right? Why should it be left up to me?" Amy asked Jess.

"You're wrong, it's really my decision. My horse. But it was your life, which means more than that horse. This isn't up for discussion. You decide whether she stays or goes."

Amy fought her own anger and emotion in an effort to find logic. This wasn't just a decision that would affect her. She held Brenda's fate in her hands. For the first time, she knew what influence McLain had over his ranch hands, and knowing about Larry's son, she now understood why he was so passionate about it. She thought long before she answered.

"When I came here, I was told we have to be able to trust each other. Depend on each other. That we're all we have. Now that trust is broken. Because of it, something very dear to Jess died. Lies and deceit are no way to get the things you want."

Here she paused, looking around the room.

"I came here to get a new start, and I did, in a way. Everyone deserves that, if I do. I think Brenda deserves a new start too." She looked into her lap, struggling to find the right thing to say.

Brenda glared back at her with a suffering expression.

Amy continued. "But she broke the rules that we all have to live by, and those rules say break 'em and you're gone. We all agreed to that. So Brenda deserves a new start, but not here. For her, I think she should go out and find a new home." Amy concluded her verdict but felt sick about doing the right thing.

Brenda sniffled, but knew begging wouldn't help. Then, for a man who typically showed little compassion, Jess somehow found some.

"Brenda, I'll give you time to find a place to move. Brookes, I hope you'll stay here until you're at least done with school. Give your sister a chance to build a life. Brenda, you can stay till you find a situation. I'll make some calls in Cody, see if we can get you a place. You are, however, restricted to the house until that time. You can come back and visit, but you can never live here again. I'm sorry."

The part of the statement that caught everyone the most was the ending. The word "sorry" had never been heard from Jess's lips. The group sat quietly as Brenda walked out of the room, trying to hold her head up. Jess made a final statement.

"She'll be fine. We won't let her set herself up to fail. I appreciate your cooperation, everyone. Now, I'd like a few minutes alone with Amy."

Silence. The room emptied quickly. Larry put his hand on Jess's shoulder as if to say everything would be okay. Once they were alone, McLain walked over to the pantry just inside the dining room.

"Amy, you did that very well. It's not an easy thing when someone's life is in the balance. Not fun at all. You made the right choice for the ranch, but more so for Brenda. Who knows if everyone here would have really ever trusted her again? Me, most likely not."

"Why me? I'm worried, Jess. Now everybody will hate me," she said, trying to hold back her emotions.

"No, they won't. You're going to have to make decisions like that in your career. It won't be easy. This is an example of things to come."

"I don't want to be here anymore. I think it's time to leave. I just don't want any of this," she said.

"That's strange," Jess said.

"What?"

"You don't talk like you're from Jersey anymore. No one would ever know."

Amy smiled. "Really? Whatever, but I still think I need to leave. Things might go back to the way they were."

"I'd like you to stay," Jess said. "I won't act like I don't, but I won't hold you back." He spoke slowly, with tenderness in his voice, searching for words. Finally he found them.

"Well, I was going to wait until next week when it was your birthday. But since you're leaving, you should have this now." He handed her the box and she opened it cautiously. She unfolded the inner wrapper and pulled out an off-white canvas jacket with a leather collar and a monogram. It was the same one all the other hands wore on the J-Bar-M: the same coat that struck fear into all other competitors at the rodeo. The one that only she was without when they all went into town. Amy looked at the front and saw her name embroidered on it with the title "barrel racer" underneath, just like Ashley's.

"Next week you turn twenty-one, Jersey. Old enough to drink legally. No one can stop you then but yourself. Next time you want a drink I hope you're wearing that and it reminds you of what you went through to try and kick it. We'll miss you around here. Well . . . good night."

Jess left the room, leaving Amy alone. She held up the jacket and crushed it to her heart, wishing he had stayed. After all that had been said and done that night, she wanted to know one last thing. "Why couldn't he have just said that he'd miss me?"

Chapter Twenty-six

Armageddon: Part Two

Nothing seemed to fit into Amy's duffel bag like it did when she'd come out four months earlier. She'd added the work boots, the overalls, her denim jacket, T-shirts and jeans, and, finally, tried to roll up the new jacket. But she was shaking for some reason as she packed and couldn't seem to make it small enough. Anyway, it wouldn't fit. She'd have to wear it. No matter, she'd wear half of everything she owned if she had to. She was leaving, that's all there was to it.

Okay. So it was Brenda who'd been asked to find a new home. But no one will miss me around here. I can't possibly stay either.

Amy felt horribly guilty. So full of self-blame. How could things have gotten to this point? Why didn't she see it coming? That "kid sister" she'd encouraged and be-friended all along, had hated her. What she'd mistaken for friendship had been Brenda crowding her, taking possession. Brenda wanting Amy so that Jess couldn't have her. Brenda running interference so Amy wouldn't have to go to Jess with her questions and problems. It all became clear now. Little, smiling, helpful Brenda would have sabotaged Amy's success one way or the other.

She rearranged her clothes in the long, bulky bag. The zipper barely caught. Reluctantly, Amy decided that the sneakers with the holes in them would have to stay. She gave one to Jax who lay at her feet, a worried look on his whiskered face. "That's for you," she said with a half-smile. She wished she had a cigarette so bad she could taste it.

"Thanks a lot," came a curt voice at the doorway. Amy looked up to see Brookes, red-faced and puffed up like a cock at a cockfight. "Thanks for arranging for my sister to get canned. She really needed that."

"Don't be sarcastic," Amy answered back, startled.

"Don't tell me what to say! I'm going to have to leave now, too, you know. Thanks from me, too," Brookes continued.

"You don't have to leave," answered Amy. "Don't be silly. You didn't do anything. You don't have to go."

"That's right, Miss Jersey Hot-Shit. I didn't. But where Brenda goes, I go. We're a team. But you wouldn't know about stuff like that. You're just out for yourself. Well, Brenda and I will find something, somewhere. We're gonna hitch our way out of here and ditch this place. I just came by to say thanks and . . . go to hell, bitch."

"Brookes, it's not my fault. There was a vote, fair and square. I just . . ."

"You just what? Decided Brenda needed to start over? Well, that's what I mean. When you're wherever it is you're supposed to be, I just hope you feel real good getting us thrown out like this."

Brookes's voice began to crack. "Who's supposed to take care of her, anyway? Even if she is my older sister, she's a girl. I'm all she's got. And who's supposed to help me? I can't even drive yet. We have to stay together. Never mind. You wouldn't care anyway."

Amy turned away from the rangy teen who fumed at her. He trembled as he railed, and his eyes glowered from beneath his mop of hair. Amy had really come to like Brookes and secretly admired his romantic crush on the girl next door, as well as his persistence at getting his grades back up. She'd taken to eavesdropping on his nightly homework lessons with Larry, who had taken him gently under his wing. She had listened hard.

Brookes was a junior. He would graduate next year. She followed along with the math and biology, listening, wishing, pretending, and thinking she could be doing those assignments, too. She could be graduating, too.

"Please don't be mad at me. What about school?" She tried to change the subject.

"I'm not finishing school, thanks to you!"

"No, Brookes, don't say that. You have to. You have to stay. Your sister will be all right without you. You have to stay here and graduate."

The boy turned his back and walked away, shaking his head. Then he turned to face her one last time, gave her the finger, and disappeared into the dark.

This is wrong, Amy hissed out loud to herself. *Fucking wrong. Jess and his stupid sense of democracy. He turned me into his jackhammer. First I get set up by a jealous brat, then I get used by the Big Man, and then I get spat on by the only real victim in the whole picture. Brookes has every right to be mad at me. Something's screwed up here. I'm not going to take this. I can't believe what a pawn I've been for them all. Brenda was never honest in the first place. Jess wasn't either. Why couldn't he just accept what happened as a bad accident*

*and let it go? Confront Brenda privately?
Why did he have to crucify her like that?
Reduce her to shreds? And now, Brookes.
He'll probably never finish school. And
why? Why? Because of me?*

Amy began to reel with the reversal of
blame and the new perspective she'd suddenly acquired. She wouldn't leave the J-Bar-M
without letting Jess McLain know that she
wasn't ever going to be used by anybody
again. No matter what Marty had set up for
her out there, she really didn't care. That
was his deal, whatever it was. She'd finish
the job she'd set out to do on her own,
without anybody's support or abuse. By
God, she'd let Jess know that she'd seen into
his game of control and manipulation. He
kept everybody submissive and weak so that
he could be in charge. Well, he wouldn't do
it to her anymore. She was getting out just
in time. She was glad all of this had happened. It opened her eyes to a truth she
hadn't seen before. This whole group of
misfits was nothing but a bunch of sick
losers, and she was tired of playing into their
game. Whatever feelings she had for Jess
had to have been her own emotions playing
tricks on her. He'd done his number on her
like everybody else, just to keep himself on
top. She'd learn how to stand on her own

two feet, but it wouldn't be with his help. He was a parasite.

The light in the loft above the barn was on. Jess was up, even though Amy couldn't hear anything. She set her guitar and duffle bag down by the barn in the dark and climbed the steps slowly toward Jess's quarters. She had on her new jacket, the perfect irony for saying goodbye. She'd get this over with and be on the road soon, hitching a ride if she was lucky, or walking to town.

"Who's there?" Jess wheeled with Ranger-like reflexes the second he heard her steps and stopped short when he realized it was Amy, standing like a ghost, her blond hair tucked into her jacket, her hands clenched by her side.

"Where are you going, dressed like that?"

"I'm leaving. I came to say goodbye."

"I told you I wouldn't hold you back, but I think you're confused. It's Brenda who's supposed to be leaving."

"Wrong. Two with one blow. You got rid of us both, Jess. You didn't really think I could stay on here after what I did tonight? Everybody hates me. I kicked a kid while she was down in the name of your miserable brand of democracy. I'm definitely the ranch hero here now. Big sister Amy, the booze-guzzling troublemaker. It looks like Brenda's brother is leaving too. Wasn't that the whole plan after all? Weren't they both more trouble than they were worth? And me too? You just didn't have the heart to tell them to get out, did you? Brenda made it easy for you. No, I made it easy for you."

"Cut the crap," Jess responded. "If Brookes wants to go, that's his choice. I can't stop him. But what's happened to you? You were sane, fair and agreeable back there when you made a decision on everyone's behalf. No one in the group would have done any differently."

"How do you know? Did you take a poll?"

"What's your problem now? Do you have to be loved by everyone, all of the time, Amy? Can't you even see when you're right? Think about it. A horse is dead. She threw me two great colts and had maybe two more in her. It cost this place a lot of money. You made the right decision."

"Right decision? Can anybody tell me what's right about any of this? I can't take it anymore, Jess. I came here to get better and it looks like I've just made things worse. I've tried. But I haven't succeeded. I didn't need to be your problem. But you took me in because it fit your plan. I see it now. You surround yourself with weak freaks and losers so you feel like a million bucks. You can hide up here among the world's castaways and forgotten, and you don't have to explain anything to anybody. Well, I might look like a half-assed drunk to you, but I'm not. I've promised myself never to drink again. That much I've accomplished with your help, though, for the record, nobody, not anyone, ever, will do to me what you did yesterday in that horse trough. Especially you. If you ever lay a hand on me again, I'll make sure you never forget it. I'm here to tell you that I've given this whole game my best shot and I'm done. And you're the reason I'm leaving."

"Weak freaks? I would have kicked Brenda out of here for saying that about you. Watch your tongue. Plus, you seem to forget I'm the reason you're here!"

Amy leered at Jess and stepped away. "What's that supposed to mean?"

"I'm the reason you got your ass shipped up here, Miss New Jersey. I'm the reason you're not out on the street singing for donations. Marty and Bob knew I was the only one who could strip you of your pretenses, your illusions, and your self-pity. Teach what you really needed to make it. Your voice is good, but it ain't magic. You owe me, the hands here, and this ranch, everything you are up to this minute."

"Oh, come on," Amy spat back. "I don't owe you anything. Marty Heistler thinks he can make money off of me. He gave me a time frame to get cleaned up and figure out the front end of a horse from the back so that I could sing western music like a cowhand. Well, I've done that, thank you very much. That and a whole lot more that has to do with what it takes to survive out here. Or anywhere. Nobody tells you about that stuff. But I don't owe you anything, especially after today. Brenda and her brother are going to be homeless and folks around here are going to say it's my fault. Well, I won't own that one, Jess McLain. You can have that one all to yourself."

Amy began to circle around Jess as she spoke to him, baiting him with her attack. His simple loft was spacious, only a desk with a small lamp giving a dim glow in the dark room, a bulletin board above it covered with pictures, and a bookcase. A twin bed was shoved against the outside wall, neatly made with a Mexican blanket and his guitar sat in its case by the door. Jess's boots were parked by the side of his bed. Wearing jeans and a T-shirt, he had almost been ready to retire when Amy walked in.

"I used to think you were like some kind

of a god around here," Amy continued. "Just look at you. You live like a hermit. Like you're hiding from the whole world. Well, nice going. Keep it up. I won't stop you from the hole you're digging for yourself. I'm getting out while I can."

"Now just shut up for a minute, would you, and stay where you are," Jess responded, moving toward her. An insistent tone in his voice almost sounded like pleading, but Amy couldn't be sure.

"You can't insult me," Jess went on. "That was a nice try. But it takes more than that. Look who's talking. Why don't you sit down and listen? If you knew the whole truth, you might just find you're not as smart as you think."

"Why don't *you* listen?" Amy interrupted. "I think I've learned everything I need to know about life in the West from you and your loyal unit. Just tell Larry I'll miss his Copenhagen. It held me over just fine."

"Why, you little . . ." Jess grabbed Amy's arm. "You were stealing from Larry?"

"No. He knew I was taking it. He let me. Leave me alone." With that Amy raised her right hand and swung her arm back to slap Jess's face with all the strength she could muster. He caught her wrist in mid-air and twisted her arm behind her back.

"I don't think so, Jersey. Not today!" he said slowly, and then, pulling up with expert pressure, dropped Amy to her knees, her right arm grotesquely twisted behind her.

"Don't hurt me. Please."

Amy looked up at Jess with eyes brimming with tears, supplicant, now held before her captor and her liberator, and in so many ways, her one true friend. The intensity of his grip on her arm, the feel of his body pressed against her face, and her own helplessness was too much. She trembled before him, feeling a mixture of terror and desire.

"Go ahead. Break my arm."

"Oh quit. I'm not going to hurt you. Get up."

But Jess didn't release her. Slowly Amy rose, her body hard against him. He held her tight, forcing her to come eye to eye with him. Amy's pounding heart pressed against Jess's chest. He looked into her eyes, exasperated, angry, tired. He had no more stomach for anything.

"If you have something to say, I want to hear it with respect. You may not be a lady, but at least act like one. Just what the hell do you want?"

"Respect?" Amy answered, raising her

chin and tilting it back so she could defy him. "You kidding? You're the biggest coward I've ever met. You've got everybody here so intimidated no one dares open their mouth. You give everybody here free room and board as long as they obey every word you bark and in return you ask for their sweat and blood. You've got your very own detention camp, Jess McLain, slave labor for an ex-cowboy with a big chip on his shoulder. And you used me! Just like everybody else! You were too chicken to handle Brenda, so you put it on me. Sure, you made me look like a real hero for a few minutes there at your trial and I actually fell for it. Now, Brenda's hitting the highway and I have to lie awake nights wondering what's to become of her. I've been there, Jess. It sucks! It hurts bad not to have any friends or family or someone to love. It hurts. Like this."

Amy managed to wriggle her wrist free from his grip and this time succeeded in slapping him squarely on the right cheek, her anger rising out of her like a steaming geyser, forging its way into violence, into a strike that would leave him with the pain of her fury.

"The first one is for free," Jess stated. "Now don't you ever do that again." At the same instant, he swept his foot behind her knee and buckled her legs again, this time causing her to collapse before him. He caught her with both arms, and in an instant crossed them, wrapping them around her body, holding her fast. Amy didn't struggle but stood still, trembling in his grasp.

"Listen to me. Don't you dare accuse me of using you or anyone else here! Do you know how you got here? Do you? They dumped you here! It's that simple. So thanks for nothing. Yes, Marty saw you had a gift, but he put you on a plane out here before he ever even asked me. I told him no! Not only no, but fuck no! Bobby Dall saved your ass, because I was going to put you right back on the bus. I was sure you couldn't hack it. But I was wrong. I put you through everything hard I could think of and you made it. And I take back what I said about your voice. It is a gift! But a gift can be a curse when you're too immature to honor it!"

He was holding Amy and threw her down on the edge of the bed. "I don't ever want to hear you accuse me of using you," he continued. "Nothing could be further from the truth. I probably believe in you more than anyone. Why else would I have trusted you with a twenty-thousand-dollar horse? You leave now, it will be just like everything else in your life, a failure. Don't you see it? My sister will never leave here. Rodeo doesn't pay that well and I'm all she's got. And she knows that if it hadn't been for her, I would have taken a bullet a long time ago. Old Larry is dug in here till he dies. Everyone else, I don't know. But you — you have it. Bob Dall saw it and I felt it when you sang that night in the stall. Fact is, I haven't stopped feeling it. You have the talent. You just don't have the guts and balls to make it, to keep them from fucking up your life. My time is over, but you . . . everything's ahead of you, if you can just get there. Why can't you see it?" Jess shouted, turning loose emotions normally reserved for himself.

"See what?" Amy asked.

"That you can make it. And, that I want you to. And that I don't want you to go." Jess sat down next to her, surprised by what he'd just said.

Amy then reached out to hold his hand, moved by his confession. Pulling his arm around her, she leaned toward him and found comfort that he didn't pull away. Amy laid her head on his shoulder and Jess released a painful sigh that had lain buried within him ever since the horse had been lowered into the ground that day. The pain in his chest had heaved and bucked, but wouldn't come out. Not then. Now it struggled to free itself against the thin body of an angry girl who had become a lifeboat to a man floating in a sea of forgetfulness and self-hatred.

Jess couldn't take another loss. Everything he'd ever loved had managed to slip away, to leave him, without his permission. And although his sister had come back, all the people and things that were part of his dreams were gone. And somehow, he realized, he'd been gone too. He'd shut down until the night he'd heard Amy sing.

Amy cut the weight from his heart when she'd encouraged him to put his arm around her, inviting him in, while showing she wanted to be there. She'd awakened something in him he couldn't name but could still feel. And until the sound of the bullet firing into Dancing Wind's head had ricocheted deep into his own heart, he didn't realize how isolated he'd felt. And how scared. Not afraid of dying, but of dying alone. And of never loving again, of never celebrating life.

"I need you," Jess said gently, pulling Amy down onto the bed. "I love you. I wish you could understand how much." He untied the drawstring from the jacket and slipped it off her shoulders, then lay her down against his single pillow. "Trust me, Amy, there's a world out there waiting for you. And I just want to see you fly. Fly, and then come back to me."

Amy lay still, Jess's arms around her. She listened to every word, incredulous that she could be thus, holding on to this elusive man who was now opening the door to his own heart.

"You've been the brightest spot on this ranch and in my life," said Jess, with surprising tenderness. "Like you, I came to Purgatory to start over. Never knew what was ahead, how long I would stay. It was all starting to blur, seem so meaningless. Then you came."

Amy wanted to say that she wouldn't leave, that she didn't know how she could have even thought about it, that she didn't realize how he felt. And that she was sorry that she'd doubted him and that she adored him and felt confused. But before she could say another word, Jess touched his lips to hers and took all the words away with a kiss, the kind that seals the questions and the doubts and the fear with a heat-searing simplicity.

Amy kissed him back, full of all the gratefulness and joy that came from being wanted. She reveled in the warm hold of his arms and the warmth of his lips. She closed her eyes, savoring the closeness she felt alongside him. Then, they lay side by side, quietly, her arm around his waist, breathing in perfect rhythm alongside him. Just a kiss, nothing more, and him, holding her close, her body next to his.

Amy shivered as Jess touched his hand to her cheek. *How could I have hurt him?* she thought. *Gotten so angry? How could I have done this? Almost left him when he needed me?*

Overwhelmed with emotion, Amy mused, *Jess is finally behaving like a man, not a boss, treating me like a woman, at last. Why did it have to take what it did to get to this point? Why did there have to be so much pain?* She wondered if there was possibly any way he could still hurt her more. Softly, she dared ask, "Why did you humiliate me so badly the other night? If you love me, why the punishment in the horse trough?"

Jess turned away and took a deep breath. "Well, you may as well know it all. You and I are a lot alike, more than I would probably have ever admitted. Do you know why I owned Dancing Wind? No, of course not. It's important that you know. When I came back, I couldn't deal with Jack's death and how the Army had hung me out to dry. So I turned to the bottle, and like you, needed to take the edge off before I rode, before I did anything where I had to put myself on the line. And you know what happens when you have alcohol in your system and you're badly injured?"

"No, what?"

"They can't give you anything for the pain. So after Wind and I wrecked and my body was all broken up, I had to sit and endure the agony while they tried to put me back together. I felt every second of it, Amy. That's what you call hitting bottom. I couldn't bear to see you get anywhere near where I was. Me dunking you the other night was my fear of you going down the tubes and my shame because I'd made the same mistake once. Anyhow, Wind was always my reminder to stay away. Now she's gone."

Jess finished what he had to say. They lay quietly in an uncomfortable silence.

Amy began to search for her own answers. "Why, Jess? Why did you do it at all? Why did you finally agree with Bobby to take me in the first place? You didn't need me here. What was in it for you?"

"God, I was hoping you wouldn't ask.

You're not going to like this, Amy," Jess said, kissing her forehead. "You're not going to like it at all." He pulled back and propped himself up on his elbow.

"What?" She turned onto her side to face him. She felt that nothing he could say at this point would make a difference. She was where she was supposed to be: next to him. He had allowed her to get close to him, to love him. And she thought that he loved her. That's what all this was about.

"Okay. You have to understand, Amy, I didn't know you then. Marty is a snake. Originally, when he called, I told him no. But he just dumped you on a plane without asking, or so he said. Anyway, all I heard was the bad stuff. Bob Dall called me and made a deal that I really couldn't turn down. I've barely been keeping this place afloat for the last couple of years and I needed the money. If I go under, everyone here is homeless. Bobby offered me a lot of money and twenty-five percent of his new company, which now owns Marty Heistler, who, I believe, owns you. I bet you didn't know that, either."

"You mean you were paid? Paid to put up with me? Oh, my God," Amy moaned, staring at Jess, her eyes wide. "That's just what I wanted to hear!"

"Look, I didn't know you. And yes, I made a deal with Dall, but I also made him give me his word that he wouldn't let Heistler ruin your life. I'm sorry. I never knew this would happen, but it doesn't make any difference."

Jess's answer tore through Amy's gut like a knife as she fought back the urge to scream. She stood up and paced the room, wishing he hadn't told her. Wishing she were dead. She'd been paid for. What could his affection mean now, after all?

"Look, the money doesn't mean anything," said Jess. "I haven't spent a dime. I want you here because you're you, can you believe that? I want you here enough to give it back."

"You mean that? Do you really mean that?" Amy said, incredulously.

"Hell, yes," said Jess. "Do I have to say it again? Yes. I love you. So, now are you gonna put that coat back on and head into town, or are you staying?" Jess asked.

"I guess I'm staying," Amy answered, defeated, looking at her coat crumpled on Jess's bed. She put her arms around Jess and kissed him again.

"All right, then." He smiled. "Now put that thing on and wear it straight back to your bunk." Amy walked back to the bed to pick it up and Jess put it around her shoulders, tenderly. "And listen, I never want to go through another day or night like this one again. And I never want you to doubt me. Understand?"

Chapter Twenty-seven

An Insight

Jax stood wagging his tail at the bottom of the steps and began to scramble around playfully as Amy approached, vying for her attention. She kneeled to pet him, then picked up her guitar and pack and headed back toward the bunkhouse, the dog gently teasing her ankles at every step. Midway, she noticed lights in the main ranch house and stopped. Who could be up at such a late hour, she wondered, and decided to find out. She had Jess on her mind and wasn't ready to sleep.

Larry raised his cup of coffee to her as she entered. "To the winner," he said, and set the cup down again.

"That's not funny," Amy said, scowling. "Please. Don't ever say that again. That really hurts. What are you doing up so late?"

"I might ask you the same question," he replied, eyeing her coat. "You going somewhere?"

"No, you might say I just came back. I'm not going anywhere at all. It's all I can do to stay right here."

"Take it easy, little girl," Larry said gently. "If it makes you feel any better, you can forget the guilt. They're not out on the road or homeless. Brookes's English teacher heard all about what happened by evening. News travels fast around here. The school doesn't want to lose him. A few phone calls and believe it or not, he's got a new home already. His girlfriend's family arranged for him to stay with the young lady's grandparents, and Brenda's going to live with the owners of the feed store in town. Just till the end of the year. That way, Brenda can keep her job in town and Brookes can graduate, hopefully. They were picked up about an hour ago. It's over."

Amy blinked hard. Hot tears welled up, still feeling a sense of shame over what transpired.

"Hey, I said relax. You didn't do nothin' wrong. Things have a way of going their own way all by themselves. Life is like that. You did what you had to do. But frankly, Miss Amy, you walked right into this one, I'd say. A pot simmering to a slow boil. Jealousy is a bad thing, no matter where you are. It was bound to spoil something here, somehow. Don't you go blaming yourself, now. No way. The horse is gone. That won't change. Brenda's gone, too. And you're going to get through this just fine. You just listen to me. Now come here . . ."

Larry held open both his arms and Amy fell into them. The hug was warm and reassuring and said everything she wanted to hear.

"So, what about you?" Larry inquired, placing his elbows on the big table and folding his hands. "You want a snuff of Copenhagen?" He nodded toward the can of chewing tobacco on the counter.

"No, I'm off that. I'm off everything. I swear, Larry, all I want to do is be free of being hooked on anything. Ever. Ever again. I just want to sing and be successful. And make Jess proud of me."

"Oh Jess, is it now? Have we added him to the stew? What's going on there? Somethin' I need to know?"

"I think I love him, Larry. He's the most honest man I ever met. Mostly, I need him to respect me. That's all there is to it."

Larry looked at Amy for a few seconds and pushed his chair back. He cleared his throat and looked hard at the girl sitting before him.

"Don't get carried away, Amy Talbot. Let me tell you about Jess McLain. You best be careful. He's all I got. My last boy, so to speak. He's every bit the man my son was and maybe more. I can never forget what he did in Iraq and what he's done for me since then, and right up to right now. The woman who loves Jess, or better, the woman he chooses to love, had better be ready to walk the line. That man's life is an open book and when he bleeds, we bleed. Every one of us. Why, ain't one of us here wouldn't lay down everything we got for him. I don't know what you intend to make of your life, young lady, but when it comes to Jess, there's no room for maybe. No ifs, ands or buts. He needs honesty, integrity, and plenty of room. Anyhow, the party here is just about over. I'm not saying you're not good enough for my boy or that he's off limits, I'm just saying you best not be underestimating the man or what he deserves. He's the real thing."

"I understand," Amy said, deciding to keep all the rest to herself. Larry already knew what she was beginning to learn. Only she had to learn it the hard way. And that was that Jess would never take second rate.

"Truth is, Miss Amy, and it's not my place to be giving advice, but I hope you've found whatever it is you were looking for. No one can give it to you. And time's running out here, anyways. Another six months and Jess might have to rewrite the payroll. In fact, he might have to find a whole new address to park this gang. He makes light of the money problems here, but it ain't no joking matter. The well is about dry. The buyout from his ex-wife broke the bank. But you just keep all this to yourself for the moment, you hear? Ain't nobody's business right now. I just thought it might help you make some plans."

"Yes, sir," Amy answered. "I'm so sorry." She was honored that Larry would confide in her, and wondered what he could do.

"Not a word to anybody, now. At least till after the roundup. Jess needs to stay focused on the job. Before I forget, there's a letter for you. Came today." Larry walked over to the phone where he'd stuck the long envelope under the box. He handed her a knife to slit it open.

"It's from Marty Heistler," she said. "I wonder what he wants." Amy scanned the first few paragraphs and then stopped in the middle.

And the good news is that we've committed Bobby's musicians for a July show in Cheyenne. Frontier Days, no less, opening act for Mr. Willie Nelson. Sure hope you'll be ready to peel out of there and make yourself presentable in a week or two. We expect fresh material, a stand-up performance, and you, in the best shape you've ever been, back in Nashville by the middle of May. We'll need four full weeks to rehearse and cut a CD. Confirm you're ready.

Amy read the letter aloud to Larry and sat down. "Oh crap. I'm not ready to leave."

"Yes, you are."

"I'm not. Besides, I'm going on the roundup. How long will that take?"

"A week, maybe ten days. And," added Larry, turning out the lights as he did, "if you're not ready for the world after that, it's my guess you ain't never gonna be."

Chapter Twenty-eight

Return to Sanctuary

Late spring brought the small rural community together like a family reunion. The ranchers had decided on cooperatively sharing the land instead of sectioning it off to each private landowner. Each owner had some area fenced, but for the most part it remained open range. Keeping the terrain open allowed for each specific area to be used in a manner that promoted the growth and survival of each ranch's stock animals. Then, turned out to the open land in October, the livestock were free to roam and graze wherever they could. During the hard months, the ranchers all shared duties, dumping hay and making sure the ice was broken at strategically placed watering tanks.

Cooperating did one of two things. For one, it gave the best opportunity for stock to survive the harsh winters of Purgatory. Second, and sometimes more importantly, it built partnerships. If one rancher had a bad year and was low on his winter feed supply, the others saw to it that his stock was taken care of.

The first two years Jess was there, three of the locals had a tough time and McLain dipped into his supply until he was just about in as bad shape himself, but everything worked out. The past year it had become his turn to receive a hand, only he wouldn't take it for free. None of them did. Early mornings in the saddle, and sometimes an entire day could be spent checking on stock and making sure that water in water tanks was accessible. The community behaved like a family and family takes care of its own.

The rolling plains rose in great arid swells in this region. Most were dotted with rocky outcrops, eroded gullies, and wind-shaped, twisted mesquite. The Grey Bull River that ran from Meeteetse, through the backside of Purgatory, all the way up through Fenton into Burlington, flowed through several different types of terrain. It was typical of the rugged beauty of Wyoming, ridgelines with rocky hills outlining this important water source. The river, both a blessing and a curse, made for difficult herding at times. Water created several nooks and crannies that stock would wander up into and hide.

Ike Sterling still kept livestock there and used both the J-Bar-M and the Deville place, since they backed up to each other. He added feed storage to both places as payment, which most of the time gave ranch owners the better end of the deal. His very seasoned hands would start in Meeteetse and work northeast toward Purgatory, closing in as they went. Donny Deville, Katy's dad and McLain's closest neighbor, would trailer their hands and horses up to Fenton and work south toward Sale's place, then try to create a swing door, angling back up north. While there, they would hook up with John Raven.

John was an Arapahoe Indian rancher from the Wind River Reservation. He knew the land like a scout, and his men were as seasoned and rugged as the Wyoming landscape itself. They would start a day or two before the others, down south at Gooseberry Creek, and work their way up, looking for stragglers and mavericks. Usually, the only horses he found were those feral animals that either caught the smell of their own saddle horses and approached out of curiosity, or had wandered south almost all winter. Still, on occasion he found a horse or two belonging to Sterling or McLain.

Jess and Ike were the only ones who

turned out horses to the open land. These usually found their way to a plateau almost a half-day's ride to the south. Ike kept his studs at his place and Jess had his tucked away on a heavily fenced area back of his ranch. McLain always worried that some vigorous young stud might get the urge and bolt through the fence to chase down a mare in heat. The geldings, mares and colts, however, were turned completely free, grazing along the branches of the Grey Bull and wintering around the plateau.

The plateau was a favorite retreat for Jess. Only Ashley had accompanied him there on occasion. Larry had been there once, too, but Jess always said that he wanted the horses to live as long as they could without the smell or taint of humans. He said it made them better buckers, but Ashley knew it was because he envied them, the simplicity of their lives and the traditional western magic they embodied. Jess felt that watching a couple hundred wild horses on a plateau in front of a Wyoming sunrise was nothing less than spiritual.

Larry and Dallas had set out a day before with packhorses to set up the base camp. The camp sat in the heart of the triangle linking Meeteetse, Fenton and Sale's place. Roundups like this were thought by some to be old-fashioned, but to Jess they were just another way to hold on to the old ways — a time for hands to pay homage to those who came before them.

Larry would have it no other way. His hobby was keeping the old chuck wagon in top shape. A master of prairie cooking, there wasn't anything he couldn't whip up over a fire or bake in a Dutch oven. When he first got to Purgatory he had never even sat in the driver's seat of a wagon, let alone hook one up to two mules. But this had become his relaxation. If rodeo was a way for an overgrown boy to still play cowboy, then being a mess cook on a roundup was a way for an old man to feel like a kid. The rest of the crew would meet up with him the following night with their strays and lost horses.

Among the five stock owners, the ranchers would easily have seventy-five to a hundred head of horses to separate. Once driven in to the J-Bar-M, an ideal point because it was the farthest south into the range and the closest to a holding pen, the sorting, relocating and branding of the animals would follow.

Jess, Ashley, Gary and Amy rode out early like a sheriff's posse. Ashley rode her prized paint that, as she liked to brag, was so willing it would climb a tree if she told it to. Jess rode his favorite cow horse, Sergeant Major, just Major for short, a tall, thick, muscular gray with soft black eyes. Gary and Amy rode two sorrels, good seasoned trail horses. They mounted up in full gear, including slickers and chaps. Even Amy had donned a pair of dark brown shotgun chaps to protect her from the brush. They headed out upon the open plain along the branches of the river, with Jess and Ashley out front.

Jess still wore a canvas duster to fend off the morning chill. He reached into its pocket and pulled out the old tin tobacco box that only saw use a couple times a year. Then he neatly pulled a hand-rolled cigarette and lit it with a white-tipped match.

"Still can't give that up completely, can you?" Ashley asked her brother.

"Oh, here we go."

"Nope, just nice to see you can admit you have a weakness." She laughed.

"Uh-huh, let's see what happens when we get home and I toss out that half-gallon of mint chocolate chip ice cream in the fridge. Then let's talk about weakness," he shot back, ribbing his sister with brotherly sarcasm.

"Okay, point taken. You ain't that tough,

Ranger," she said, as they made their way toward a plateau in the distance.

"Hooah," Jess answered, echoing his Army days.

"Hey, did you know your little sweetheart filled out a permit application to ride?" Ashley asked.

"Really? You think she could handle pro rodeo? I mean, she ain't doing half bad, but I think that has to do with her trainer. By the way, thanks for putting up with all this. And I know I haven't said it, but I'm really glad you're here."

"Wow, you get a lady friend and your whole attitude changes," Ashley said, dodging the subject. "Been kinda nice. What are you going to do when she leaves?"

"Don't ask. I hope she comes back. Right now, just enjoy my time. I know someone else who renewed his card to ride this year too," he added, knowing his sister would be surprised.

"You? Now that's a shock. Seriously?"

"Yeah, been feeling good in the saddle. Plus, you and I never rodeoed together. Figure we could hit some shows."

"Excuse me?" Ashley couldn't hide her surprise.

"Okay, give it a rest. I've been telling Amy to go for it and preaching to everyone else for years. Figured it was time to put up or shut up. Plus, that's something we haven't done, so why the hell not?" Jess answered.

"Nice to have you back, Jessie, been a long time. I just hope when she's gone, you don't slip." Ashley winked at her brother.

"Wait here. I don't want to spend too much time, but I want to take a couple of horses back with us. Catch 'em when I drive 'em on down." With that, he kicked his horse, who responded with a spurt up the hill.

"So, Gary, how long we going to be in the saddle today?" Amy asked, riding up alongside him.

"Oh, about all day. Make it to camp late this afternoon before dark, depending on how many we find. You having fun yet?" he asked.

"Oh my God, yes. Past month has been a hoot."

"Did you say hoot? You been here way too long," Gary said, laughing. "But it's kinda nice to see the boss in a good mood. You guys look good together."

"Thanks. I don't want to leave, that's for sure. First place I've ever felt at home."

"Hey, I know you were pretty upset about it, but you made the right decision back there with Brenda and all. For what it's worth, McLain was spending way too much time baby-sitting those two. I know it was rough, but things have been a little easier around the place. A little more work, but at least we know it's getting done now."

"I was worried that not everybody felt that way."

"Anyone else would have done the same thing. Now just enjoy the roundup. It's a good time." They came upon Ashley, waiting on them. "Hey, where's he going anyway?" Gary asked, watching Jess head up the hill.

Jess disappeared out of sight. They could all hear hooves in the distance. Only Ashley knew what the others were about to see.

"Okay, spread out and make sure that when he comes down, no horse bolts. Make a net," Ashley ordered.

Gary turned his mount, helping to mark a large triangle. Amy stayed put, but maneuvered closer to Ashley. They sat and waited, listening to the sounds and commotion that flowed over the ridge. Amy heard the distant rumble and bit her lip, wanting to know what was happening. Gary hid his anticipation better, but not well enough.

"It's killing you, isn't it? Okay, look, do it real carefully, but ride up to the ridgeline so you can just see over. Don't let him see you. You'll know why," Ashley instructed the pair. "But only take a peek and then get back down here!"

Gary and Amy kicked gut and their mounts shot up the incline. It was steep enough that Amy needed to use her saddle horn. Fifty or more feet to the top and they both stopped short so the ridgeline was at eye level. There, heaven smiled upon them and the word that Jess had sometimes used regarding his horses rang in Amy's head: "Sanctuary."

Before them, hundreds of horses scattered across the plateau. A rainbow of hide thundered over the land. The sounds of hooves and neighing and snorting were much clearer at this level. Gary thought folks could probably hear the rumble of the herd all the way to Cody and Powder River. Mares and colts ran together and geldings jumped and bucked as if happy to see their savior. After all, only thanks to Jess McLain was this spectacle of wild beauty possible.

Amy found Jess in the midst of the herd, some horses drawing closer to come in for a sniff. It was as if they knew him or accepted him as one of their own. Jess had singled out a few and used Major to cut them away from the herd.

Once he was done, Gary motioned for Amy to ride back. As they made their way down, she realized that the way was much steeper than she had thought and her horse's back feet slid now and then. She hoped they wouldn't fall.

"You ever seen anything like it?" Gary asked as they made their way.

"No, and I probably never will again," Amy confirmed.

Ash awaited them at the bottom of the hill. " 'Nothing short of heaven,' as Jess likes to say. Okay, let's make a net when he comes down. The horses may be a little spooked. Amy, don't be afraid of them if they come at you a little. They're wild and most likely will act skittish. You'll be fine. We'll use the hill here to contain 'em. Ready?" Ashley asked as they looked up the hill in anticipation.

"Yep."

"Good, you're about to see something really neat."

The sound grew closer and five horses thundered over the ridge line. At full gallop, they charged down the hill. Amy could spot a couple of paints and two black horses, though one actually looked more blue. Just behind them, McLain and Major jumped over the ridge in hot pursuit. Major continued down the hill with Jess steadfast in the saddle, never grabbing the reins with both hands or the saddle horn. Amy felt it was as though God had let a cowboy of the old frontier return, if for only a few seconds.

Poised against the clouds that rose behind the hill, Jess leaned back in the saddle, his black duster flowing like tails in the wind. He held his free hand up and behind him, the same way he did when he rode broncs in the arena. Amy watched spellbound, but listened to Ashley recite.

"And behold a pale horse, and he who atop him was death . . ." she finished in sync with Gary who had heard the words spoken by Jess when he mounted wild broncs in the chute.

". . . and hell followed him." They ended aloud together, watching the show.

"God, I love it when he does that. Always has to make a spectacle out of everything," Ashley added.

The horses reached the bottom of the hill, sweating and spooked and full of fire. A big brown-and-white paint made a break from the group but was cut off from escape by Gary. Amy and Ashley cut their horses back and forth to keep the cluster together. Jess rode around the outside and took the only empty spot in the net, freeing Gary from doing more work than he needed. Then Jess stopped and held out his hand.

"Whoa, easy," he said repeatedly, trying to settle the string down. A young blue roan continued to pace, snapping her rear hooves at the wind on occasion. Jess admired her.

"Just like your momma — all bitch. Ease down now, girl. Whoa, now." And with that the horse charged at an angle up the hill to get around them, and made a break for open country. Outflanking the net, she took off.

To everyone's surprise, Amy shouted, "I'll get her!" and cut her horse a hard left, bolting out through the river to cut the runaway off. McLain looked puzzled. Amy?

"I'll help her, boss!" Gary said.

"No, let her go. I think she can handle it. Keep 'em together. They'll calm down with Little Wind gone."

They watched over their shoulders as Amy on her sorrel streaked across the landscape. She had the right angle and cut in front of the escapee. The horse wouldn't go easy and made halfback moves to try and fake her. With her free arm, Amy reached down for her rope slung over the horn. Clutching it in the rein hand, she started to let out a loop, not wanting to rope the horse, only to direct it. Twirling it over her head, she cut her sorrel back and forth until the wily roan agreed to make its way back. Gary, Ash and Jess watched with smiles on their faces. Jess was dazzled by Amy's unexpected performance with the rope. He turned to Gary.

"When the hell did she learn that?" he asked.

Gary just shrugged his shoulders, smiling.

"What'd you think? We only run barrels all day?" Ashley responded. "Gets kinda boring after a while. She can tie a calf pretty well, too."

Amy made her way back into the circle. The roan had bolted back to the group as if she was in charge, darting to avoid any of the other hands. Amy rolled her rope back up and put it over the saddle horn. Jess and Gary remained silent but their stares pinned Amy on her horse. She blushed.

"What?" Amy said finally, acknowledging them. Gary chuckled and put his head down with his hands folded over the horn. Jess leaned into his saddle with a big smile.

"Nothin', cowgirl. Nothin' at all. Nice work, that's all. Anything else you can do in the saddle I should know about?" he asked.

"Nothing I'll confess in the daylight," Amy answered, causing the whole group to erupt in laughter. Jess's red cheeks showed her victory.

"Okay, well, this could turn out to be one hell of a day," Jess said, pulling down his hat, trying to shake off the embarrassment. The high-five between Ashley and Amy iced the moment.

"Nothing to say to that, boss," Gary added, with a wide smile.

Jess tried to regain his composure. "Anyway, when we get home, put her in her mother's holding pen. I have a feeling she's going to buck just like her momma." He urged Major forward, then Amy interrupted him.

"Momma? Whose momma?"

"Why, that's Little Wind," he answered in a cowboy kind of drawl. "The first mare colt of Dancer. Look at her. She looks just like her. She was pregnant with this foal when I got her. Time to see if she'll be a world champ like her mother. Lord, I can see that she's just as mean."

The big roan, so blue she looked as if she were made of iron, stood close to seventeen hands and had feathered hooves, or "cowboy killers" as Jess called them. Amy studied her. If she was what her mother was before the accident, then Amy knew why she was so special.

Creating a half-circle, they began to push the horses on. The group rode slowly, keeping the animals together. Jess lit another cigarette and rode the far left flank. Ashley sidled up closer to him as they got farther and farther away from Sanctuary.

"She's quite the cowhand, ain't she?" Ashley said to her brother.

"Yep. Quite the woman. I must say I'm impressed," Jess answered, never looking back.

Behind them, Gary called out, "Hey, stop! Would ya look at that . . ."

The group turned. Jess circled his horse to catch a full view. There in the distance, all along the ridgeline, the wild ones crowded the edge of the plateau to look out at them. It was as if they were saying goodbye to those that would now return to the J-Bar-M.

"What are they doing?" Amy asked.

Jess reached up and waved. Slowly they all disappeared back over the ridgeline from whence they'd come.

"Bidding us a safe journey, and saying goodbye to those who won't return," Jess answered. He turned his horse and resumed his spot at the flank. The rest of the group followed. Amy turned to Ashley before returning to her place on the right.

"You ever seen anything like that before?" she asked.

"No, probably no one has but Jess. That's why he fights so hard to save this place."

In all her wildest dreams, Amy had never imagined seeing such a mystical sight. The power of it left her speechless. Even Jess was quiet, alone with his thoughts.

Amy considered her own horse under her and wondered about its origin, if it had once been free and wild. No matter, it had a comfortable life now at the J-Bar-M and would never want for food or shelter. It had Jess to look after it. The wild horses of Sanctuary were different, destined to struggle and triumph and prosper. They represented all that Jess held dear. They were free, and something more, proud in spirit, unbroken. They were and would always be a part of the West's inheritance, a living history. For Amy, this exciting immersion in the herd, the culling of the few, and now, this unexpected farewell, became the turning point in an evolution that had until then been only partial. On this day, the West had claimed her. It had finally made her its own.

Wyoming itself had slowly gotten under Amy's skin: the wind and dust, the smell of rain, the vivid sunsets and sunrises. But here, in Sanctuary, in the midst of the horses, she was finally touched by the grace of the land and the magic of the wild herd.

In one afternoon, thanks to Jess McLain, she had found her very soul. She truly believed that he'd been saving it for her.

Chapter Twenty-nine

Roundup

Day two of the roundup came with early morning laughter from David and Larry. They were up before the sun, stoking a fire, trying to create a hot-enough coal bed for the Dutch oven. Larry would do his usual overfeeding of all the hands, but according to him, they wouldn't eat until that night, so it had to stick. His lead-ball pancakes usually did just that, and then some. With an assortment of eggs, biscuits, bacon, the famous griddlecakes and his infamous rotgut cowboy coffee, one definitely would not need to eat again anytime soon.

The J-Bar-M crew pretty much worked and slept at the same time. However, a ranch hand from each outfit would sit up and watch for a couple of hours each night. The first night out was easy and most got a good night's sleep, except for the J-Bar-M's head man. With his duster on and his rifle cradled like he was holding a child, McLain had stood watch all night long, never moving. Larry was dismayed when he rose and still saw him there. He made sure he got the boss a hot cup of coffee as fast as he could. The sun would poke up in less than an hour and the day would begin.

"Morning, Ranger." Goodman strolled over and spoke to Jess, who stared straight ahead.

Taking the cup he answered, "Hooah."

"So, did you stay up all night to freak everyone out, or you just got a lot on your mind, cowboy?" Larry said, sipping from his own cup. The stoking of the fire in the background by Double D was the only other sound that could be heard.

"No, I can't really sleep these days too much," Jess admitted.

"I'd ask, but I have a good notion," Larry said. "How much ya short?" knowing full well the situation.

"Hell, Larry, I ain't even close. Even with what I got now, I'm still shy eighteen grand. That only catches me up, though, even if I get caught up. I might just be in the same spot next year. I'm tired and don't have too much fight left in me, Captain. Shit, if I unload some horses I'll make it, but it comes down to this. I need to get out from under the note or I won't ever get the place to make it."

"So is that why you're mounting broncs

again? The money?" Larry wanted an answer to a question he'd wanted to ask long ago.

"No, you don't do it to get rich. I want that gold buckle, is what it comes down to. Wait until you see me ride a bareback horse. I ain't finished, not by a long shot. Well, anyway we'll figure it out, Captain. Now go rustle me up some vittles," Jess commanded in a mocking tone.

"Roger that," Larry replied and returned to his cooking.

Amy tried to fight off the morning chill by staying deep under her sleeping bag, only to have Gary prod her with a stick to wake her up. Dressing as fast as she could, she made her way to the fire, trying to look alert.

Ashley crouched, shivering by the blaze, talking with Gary. She acted as if the cold didn't faze her, but her red nose gave away that she wasn't totally immune to the elements.

"He stayed there all night? Does he do that just to give people the willies, or is that really just how he is? He hasn't moved," Gary asked, kneeling by the fire.

"No, that's just how he is. Dad use to say that he was born about a hundred years too late," Ashley explained. The comment caught Gary off guard and even Dallas leaned closer to hear.

Gary investigated, watching as Jess made his way to the fire. "Dad? You knew the boss's old man?"

Ashley would have kept the secret until she died. She wanted to kick herself for not paying attention and letting the remark slip out. Jess, on the other hand, had come to terms with issues, and this was no longer one.

"Yeah, she knew my dad," Jess answered, having overheard the exchange. "Because he was her old man, too. What, can't you see the family resemblance?" He leaned over and picked up the pot of coffee to refresh his cup and pour some for Johnny Raven who had appeared at the fire out of nowhere.

"You're brother and sister?" Gary looked completely puzzled. "I thought you all were, well like, oh . . . so that's why Ashley didn't get riled when you and Amy started."

"Started what, Russell? Sometimes you're not the brightest bulb, are ya? What the hell did you think was going on?" Jess asked. Ashley loved the fact that for the first time since she had come home to Wyoming, McLain seemed proud to be her brother.

"I don't know, a harem or something," Gary said playfully, only to have Ashley and

Amy simultaneously smack him on the back of his head.

"Well, I think that answers your question." Jess chuckled and left the group with Raven who only chuckled, typically short on words, at least around those he didn't know.

"So, my shadow friend, your outfit didn't know Ashley was your sister?" John Raven began.

"Oh, quit the western-movie Indian voice, would ya? You do that when you're making fun of people. And call me Shadow? What about you?" Jess said, as the two strolled around the herd.

"We've been friends since we were kids, Jess. Grandpa called you Shadow, now it's my turn. Show me this horse you keep bragging about."

"I don't brag. She's really gonna be something," Jess said.

Breakfast brought the groups together: Sterling's men, the J-Bar-M crew and Raven's hands. Deville's crew had not made it the night before, but it wasn't a cause for worry. They usually didn't show until the third day anyway. Most all were tired from the night before, so conversation was brief, but whiskey and tobacco seemed to flow. Each outfit would leave one or two hands behind to watch over the accumulation, while the rest would go out and try to find anything they had missed. Several small tucked-away places found over the years still needed to be checked. One more night at camp, then the drive back should suffice.

Several cows among the beef stock had calves attached to them, so for all intents, it was a good roundup. The numbers were up. No one really paid attention yet to any of the brands. There would be time enough for that when they got back and sorted them at the J-Bar-M.

Gary stayed behind with Larry. Two cowboys from Sterling's and one of Raven's hands made up those who would watch over the thirty or more head they'd found so far. Sterling took Dallas and the last Raven hand and set out west, while Raven, Jess, Ashley and Amy headed east. Once again, all intended to make a big circle, meet in the middle and get back in time for supper.

As the day progressed, stragglers here and there were found. Amy enjoyed the riding and she enjoyed the stories John told about Jess in his younger days more. If Johnny wasn't making them up, one thing was for sure: Jess and Ashley got into their share of trouble when they were young.

Noon rolled around and the crew announced a break. Everyone dismounted but Jess. Something had been bothering him for a couple of miles, and the only other one who seemed curious was Raven. While everyone stretched out and walked out the saddle soreness, Jess poked his spurs and took off up the ridge above the dry streambed. Once on top, he disappeared for a short time, then returned and pulled up next to Raven.

"Well, what do you think, my white friend with good nose?" Johnny asked, never wasting an opportunity to tease.

"Would you knock it off before you're my friend with my boot up his ass? I think I can smell it, big time. Feeling it, too. And those are some seriously nasty clouds moving in. I think you better take a look, Chief Running Mouth. I'm a little concerned." Jess stepped down from his saddle. Raven mounted his horse and followed the same path as Jess.

"So, you two going to hold out on us or do you feel like sharing?" Ashley asked.

"Trust your senses, grasshopper. What do you smell and what do you feel?" Jess asked.

Ashley knew the answer but just couldn't place her finger on it. "Feels like weather," she finally answered.

"What kind?" Jess retorted.

"Smells like snow. The temperature has been going down for a couple of hours now. Thought it was just me. You feel it, the air?"

"I figured I was just not used to being out here and that's why it felt so cold," Amy added.

John came back down the hill with a worried expression. "Good nose, white man. I got a bad feeling on this one. The wind is starting to pick up. Your call, Sergeant."

"We need to hightail it and find Ike. Leave the stragglers here. I can come back, but something don't feel right. How 'bout you, chief?" Jess climbed back into his saddle.

Amy and Ashley didn't question the issue and mounted up.

"I think we're about to be hit with a hard one," John answered. "Anyway, I think we better move quick."

It only took an hour to hook up with Sterling and his riders. In that time the might and power of the northern Wyoming wind had risen and the calm landscape had turned into a howling, bitter hell, filled with wet spring snow. The group rode as hard as they could against winds that had begun to gust over sixty miles an hour. Amy couldn't help but think how it looked like it was snowing sideways, only she couldn't open her eyes long enough to really nail it down.

The prairie began to collect the snow, which hid the few landmarks they usually relied on for reference. Jess had been there in the same conditions before and now relied on the land navigation he learned in the service, as well as his compass, to keep them on the right trail. Not even the horses could see and had to be prodded to keep going. The blowing snow felt like tiny razor blades of ice hitting the skin. Amy hid her face in her jacket, trying to hold her gloved hand over her eyes, peeking out every now and then, making sure she didn't get left behind. The whiteout made it nearly impossible even to see the top of her horse's head. She could feel her clothes getting wet and freezing.

A blizzard in May? This can't be good, she thought, worried. Hours began to feel like days in the saddle with the relentless cold and snow until, finally, a lull in the wind showed that they were next to camp, slowly making their way down into a ravine.

The hands that had stayed back must have seen the storm coming long before the riders did. Everything had been moved down into the ravine. Two pack tents had been secured to the walls of dirt and the wind seemed to blow over the top of them.

Saddles were hurriedly taken off mounts, Jess's crew gathered their things quickly into the tents to join the others in a warm, dry area. Amy followed Jess and noticed how much easier it was to breathe where the wind didn't seem to steal every breath. Inside, the tents were connected and the area was surprisingly spacious. Ike, John and all the rest piled in. Amy took a spot close to Larry who brushed the snow off her hair, laughing heartily.

"Having fun yet, cowgirl?" he asked.

"No, I'm not."

"Good. Well, write a song about this, because this storm may be the worst I've ever seen. Especially in the spring." Larry laughed again, echoed by Dallas.

Jess left the tent briefly, then barged back in with a look of horror on his face. He shook the snowflakes off his hat and out of his eyes and asked in a steely voice, "Where's Ash?"

Chapter Thirty

Trial by Storm

Jess rushed out with his saddle in his hands and found Sergeant Major standing alert, as though he knew he was being called up for duty. Jax had left the security of the tent as well, and joined Jess, who began to saddle up. It was somewhat difficult with wet latigos and blankets, but he managed.

Gary and Dallas ran to the top of the hill to scout the area and see if Ash was just slow returning. The howling wind told the story: she had to be somewhere out on the plain, lost in the sea of white in an area that, if hell did freeze over, probably did so just to re-create Purgatory's open range.

Larry brought Jess a filled canteen and placed it in his saddlebag. The hot water had been boiled over a set of coals kept burning in the middle of the large tent. Not a big fire, just enough to heat the place and create a little smoke that made its way out the hole in the center. Ike and John came out to join him.

"How long you think we rode with Ashley

missing?" Ike called over the wind, hoping to be heard.

"I don't know. Could have been up to an hour," Jess said. Ike and Raven knew the country and knew it well. Was it dangerous to go and try and find her, they wondered.

Yes. Deadly. Would they let Jess do it alone? Never.

"We'll ride out in a star pattern for an hour, go hard inside and try and meet in the middle. If we don't hook up, make back north to here," Raven said. All nodded in agreement.

Gary and Dallas made their way down the hill, scrambling toward Jess. McLain tied a scarf tightly around his neck and watched Amy leave the tent, but found himself side-tracked by Russell and David. "Boss, you can't see four feet in front of you! She'll make it back. If we go out, then we could get lost, too, and then we'd all be in a pickle," Gary warned.

"Boss, should we go or stay here? I mean, is there anything we can do for her now?" Dallas asked.

McLain paused and looked at his two ranch hands, shaking his head in disbelief. He climbed aboard Major and called out to Jax who sprinted up the hill and disappeared into the swirling blanket of white.

"What's the mark of the man, boys?" Jess called, watching Amy emerge from the tent from his side view.

"I don't know, boss!" Gary answered.

"You're right, you don't! Come on, Major, let's go!" Jess gut hooked Sergeant Major who bolted up the hill. Gary and Dallas stood dumbfounded in the snow, trying to figure out what McLain meant, only to see Amy, shrouded in Larry's oilskin duster, her hat pulled down tight, mount up on her sorrel and urge her horse up alongside him.

Larry stood at the opening of the tent, stunned. David and Russell made their way into the safety of the canvas walls and stopped before Larry as they entered.

"Learn the mark of the man, boys," Larry said, watching Amy disappear over the top of the ridge.

"What is it, what does that have to do with finding Ashley?" Gary asked.

"The mark of the man is to be afraid, but to find the courage to go anyway. It's what separates heroes and warriors from the rest. He'll find her. Rangers never leave a man behind." Larry shut the tent flap behind them.

Atop the hill, Ike, Raven and Jess huddled together on horseback, talking over their strategy to find their lost party. Amy rode up next to Jess. All three looked through the blowing snow at her. No one else had volunteered. This mission was dangerous enough that no one would be ordered to go; they had to volunteer on their own accord.

"Where do you think you're going?" Jess asked.

"Don't leave people behind, that's what you always say," answered Amy. "So, what's the plan?" She struggled to get her breath while the wind fought to steal it from her.

"This isn't a game, Amy! We don't exactly have a team of volunteers here!"

"Ashley is like family, Jess. You gonna get going or sit here and argue with me?" Amy asked, squinting her eyes from the snow.

"Ride next to me, not behind me. I don't need two lost people," Jess replied. Amy lost track of the conversation as Ike and Raven got instructions from Jess and then took off. Jess started moving. Amy nudged her horse up next to him and, in no more than a couple of seconds, Ike and Raven had disappeared from sight.

Minutes seemed like hours as they progressed. Every step their mounts took felt like a fight. The blizzard, Wyoming's secret force, was running wild over the land as though the wind of Hades had ripped through man and horse and would not quit. The former beauty of the land was now covered by an inferno of white, blinding the eye. Freezing snow became glass shards that seemed to pierce the skin, even through the leather chaps that covered each searcher's legs. Standing up to the weather, the fear, and the sheer pain of cold bearing down on them with pure, wicked force, Jess seemed unfazed by the storm, as did his horse. But each step was a physical and mental struggle for Amy, fighting to go on. Fear and apprehension flowed through her body as she struggled to say upright and abreast of Jess.

Amy feared dying, the horrifying possibility of not finding Ashley, or worse, finding her dead. She raged against the land. She thanked God for that, because her anger gave her the strength to take another step.

McLain had moved ahead of her by a length but never lost sight. When she did catch him looking back, she couldn't see his face, just a black scarf and darkness where his eyes should be. She heard Jax bark on occasion and knew that he and Jess were talking to each other. Finally, after what felt like hours, he stopped and motioned for her to come up next to him.

"How are you holding together?"

"My ass is frozen to the saddle, my fingers are numb. Otherwise, okay. How long have we been riding?" she asked, bending her head to avoid the wind.

"Three hours, but with the wind and snow, we most likely only made up the time of two."

"I thought you told Ike an hour and a half?" she asked for confirmation.

"I did. But, Jax was running with us and now I can't find him!" Jess called out.

"What does that mean? Oh Jess, I feel like I'm going to die!"

"Stop. Fear is in the mind. Pain is weakness leaving your body!" he said as if trying to encourage her.

"You believe that?"

"No, not really. But I figure if I keep telling myself that, sooner or later I'll believe it. Look, I won't lie. It's getting worse out here by the minute!"

"What do we do?" Amy yelled. She'd never heard Jess sound worried. Now she feared death.

"Ride straight to your left and count the horse's steps to fifty. Pay attention to the ground. At fifty, turn around and ride back!"

"What if I get lost?"

"Don't be afraid! Fear is for those pussies that stayed behind! Do exactly what I said! Suck it up, cowgirl! Move out!" he ordered her.

Amy struggled to find some strength and knew she had to rally. Jess's next words cut deeper than the wind.

"Damn it! I know Ash is out here! That's why Jax took off. We're her only shot at making it. And I know you're scared and tired. Right now it might seem easier to quit. But I carried a dead friend once. I won't carry a dead sister. Now trust your horse and trust yourself. Count fifty —"

Jess was interrupted by the bark of a dog.

Quieted by it, he listened. Jax barked louder. Jess and Amy turned their mounts in the direction the sound came from. Jax seemed to be prodding them toward something. Only a few more minutes passed and they came upon a rock ledge that had a dark mass, a huddled body, beneath it, hiding from the wind.

Ashley was covered by her duster and a blanket of windswept snow. Her horse was nowhere to be found. But her saddle and reins were tucked under the rock. Jess knew she had done the right thing, unsaddling her horse, turning it loose, and then staying put. But she'd been in the weather for a long time. He was worried.

Amy and Jess quickly dismounted. Jess handed Amy the reins and reached under the rock, calling out to Ash.

Ash was weak, but pulled the duster off her face. Her face was red with cold and she shivered violently. Jess held her to his body. "Hey, Ash, it's me. It's okay. I got ya, I got ya." He tried to reassure her.

"Oh Jess, thank God you're here. I got lost and wandered for a while. I turned my horse loose but I belled him first. Jess, I can't feel my feet."

McLain looked at his sister and knew things were serious and getting worse by the minute. There was no way to start a fire, no place to take shelter. Conditions were deadly. The immortal cold would only get colder.

A strong gust of wind bore down upon them. Amy's sorrel suddenly spooked and reared in the wind, ripping the reins from her hands. Major only flinched slightly. Calling Jess for help, Amy searched around on the ground for the reins. Nothing. Jess came running from the shallow ledge that hid his sister. Amy still scrounged for the reins, trying to force her eyes open, but the faint sound of hooves leaving in the distance told her the truth.

Jess picked her up from the ground.

"I can't find them! Where is he?" Amy cried, trying to find a horse that wasn't there.

"He's gone, damn it. Get up!" Jess said, dragging Amy back to the hill. Holding on to Major's reins, he returned to the hole. Amy now felt fear like never before.

"Oh my God, Jess, I'm sorry I didn't —"

"You didn't do anything wrong. We're lucky he didn't break while riding out here."

"God, Jess, what are we going to do? We're going to die!" Amy cried. Ashley was too weak to say anything.

"Goddamn it, don't quit on me now! Look, Ashley has been exposed to the weather way too long. She's soaking wet. We have to get her back to camp or she won't make it."

Ashley seemed to be somewhat coherent and started shaking her head. "No, Jess, no!" she protested.

Amy tried to think clearly, even though a sense of panic had set in.

"Ash, listen to me," Jess began. "Major can't carry us all out. He won't make it. But he can carry out the two lightest." Jess spoke the truth.

Ashley, overcome with cold and trembling violently, shook her head. "No, no, no. No, not like this!"

She was interrupted by Jess, clasping her face with both hands to calm her. "Ashley, listen to me! I need you to do this! I need you to hang in there! Okay?"

Jess's words seemed to calm his sister. Finally, she nodded her head yes. McLain grabbed Amy by the hand and dragged her to where Major stood. Amy fought her fear. Everything was moving so fast.

"Look, you have to get Ashley back. She's fading," he said as he started to adjust the stirrups on his saddle to fit a shorter person.

"Jess, I can't —"

McLain wouldn't have it. He bellowed at her to get hold of the situation. "You don't have a choice! What the fuck did you come out here for? I need you to get my sister back to camp or she's going to die. Do you get it? Only you can do this. It has to be this way. Major can't carry three, you understand?" Jess spoke in such a deliberate tone it was as though he had even calmed the wind for a moment.

Amy now saw through it all. She saw what he had done for Larry's son. She saw now what he would do for her and his sister. He had always spoken about how when your time is called, true heroes rise to the occasion. Her time was now.

"Okay, what do I do?" she asked.

Jess pulled out his compass and pulled her close. He adjusted it so when he stood facing north the red line and arrow on the glass pointed the way he wanted. "Ever seen one of these?" he asked.

"No."

"Good, then you can't screw up by thinking too much. Keep the black line on the red line and you will make it to camp. You have to keep looking at it every twenty steps or so. In the wind even Major will get off track. There's a thing called natural drift, and it's usually to the left. Right-handed people have a stronger right side so they drift left because their left side is weaker. Horses are the same. You have to keep these lines lined up because Major will drift. Too much, and you'll make a big circle and end up back here, or worse. You got it?"

Amy paid attention and nodded. "Now climb in the saddle and I'll bring her out," he said, as he left her. Amy struggled to get in the saddle. Once there, she looked at the compass, fiddling with it and trying to make it out in the snow. The problem now was that the day was coming to an end and soon it would be dark. Then what would she do?

"Ashley, Amy is going to take you back to

camp. Come on." He helped his sister to her feet.

Walking out, she pleaded with him. "No, Jess, please don't, please don't do this!" She fought to stay upright.

Jess got her to the horse and the wind picked up and blew harder. "Ashley Sharpe! Get up in the saddle now! You have to make it to camp, you understand?" He held his sister's shoulders and pulled down his scarf. "I love you!" he shouted over the wind.

She clutched him, trying to fight her emotions. "My name is Ashley McLain!" she yelled, holding the brother who had finally come home.

Jess forced her away and lifted her weak body into the saddle. Amy helped as much as she could. "Okay, now get going. Do exactly what I said!"

"But it's getting dark. What happens when it's dark?" she asked, tightening the leather strap that now tied Ashley's hands around her waist.

"It glows! You'll be fine. Amy, listen to me! You're my only hope of getting my sister back! Do you understand?"

Tears poured from Amy's eyes, freezing to her face. She reached out for his hand and squeezed it, through their stiff and frozen gloves. Leaning down in the saddle, she wanted to kiss him. With his scarf down, he let her. Holding his hand, she straightened up and asked the question all three of them feared. "What about you?"

There was a calming peace in his voice. "What *about* me? Now move out."

"Jess, no, please —" Ashley pleaded.

"Move now. Night is coming. I love you both. Get going!"

Amy fought to say something, for she knew deep down Jess wouldn't be coming back. Major would save two lives, depending on Amy keeping him straight, but that was his limit. How could things have gone this way? Amy searched for answers. She needed to let Jess know that if he were to die, his sister would make it back. She would see to it. Looking back at him, she saluted.

"Hooah, Sergeant!"

He saluted in return. "Get going!" He smiled.

Amy felt sad that she couldn't see McLain's eyes. Raven's name for him came to her: Shadow. With that, she turned Major and took off. Within four or five lengths they vanished in a wave of white.

Jess stood watching, knowing full well he had seen his sister for the last time. Jax found his way next to him and barked.

"Home team ain't gonna make it, buddy. You better go with 'em!"

Jax only barked and remained at his side. Jess looked down at him, covered with snow, and started to laugh.

"Okay, Jack. Jax Goodman! Let's watch the sunset, shall we?" Lifting his face to the wind he whispered, "Get them back, God, please. Tell Jack and my brother I'm coming."

A howling gust engulfed the area and the snow fell even thicker than before.

Ashley held on with numb fingers while Amy fought the terrain on Major to keep the horse going. She struggled to see the compass and received the only pleasant surprise of the whole cursed day: to her astonishment, it was easier to make out the needles on the compass the darker it got. Major only had to be correct, even in the dark.

Amy tried to talk to Ashley as much as she could. It took her mind off how cold she was and how much her body ached. The wind had not let up, nor the snow, but still she pressed on. Ashley talked about memories of her brothers. She had always been closest to Jess. She wondered how she would go on without him. He'd always been there to pick her up when she fell. Now, only his voice rang in the wind. Amy let her speak, even though the words hurt her heart. She knew that as long as Ashley was talking, she was okay.

Time passed heavily with every step the horse took. Every minute was a factor in determining their life or death. In a short time, total darkness had set in. Amy began to fight her own demons within her mind. She kept telling herself not to think too much with the compass. Just do exactly what Jess said. Ice began to form around her eyes and she struggled to keep them open. Her only reason for keeping on was the promise to herself that if Jess had to die, he would do so knowing his sister had made it.

Fear was interrupted by terror. Over a small hill, Major stumbled and fell, struggling to regain his balance. He slid and scrambled in the snow, almost dislodging Ashley as he did. Fatigue could be felt in his weary steps. Amy was so cold she could barely sense Ashley's grip around her waist any longer. She checked the straps and pulled them tight. Ashley, losing her strength, was definitely weakening her hold on Amy, too. Amy did all she could to help Ashley stay on.

The night grew colder as they pressed forward; Amy hadn't heard any sounds from

Ash in some time. The situation seemed to be growing bleaker by the second. She raised her head to look at the snow-covered compass, blowing the flakes off its glass face, when she heard a horse's faint whinny. Sergeant Major called back with a powerful neigh and his step seemed to quicken. Amy let him have his head and released her trust to him. Twenty paces and they were there. The camp horses standing huddled in the snow were an island of hope in the darkness. She called out to get someone's attention. Larry and Ike ran out to help.

Ashley almost fell out of the saddle into Larry's arms. Then Ike helped Amy pry her own frozen body from the saddle. By this time, Raven had Sergeant Major's reins and Ike asked, "Where's McLain? Why are you riding Sergeant Major?"

Ashley sobbed as they struggled to the tent and Amy did the same. Larry, Ike and Raven all stared at each other. They knew; they didn't need an explanation. Larry and Ike helped the girls in, almost carrying them. Raven followed shortly behind. The small fire still burned with hot coals and they wrestled to get as many wet things as they could off them behind the cover of a canvas. With that done, they were wrapped in blankets by the fire and given hot coffee.

Amy, returning to life, glared at Gary and David. No words were needed, her stare was enough to invoke the shame they now felt.

Larry asked, knowing what the answer would be, "What happened? Where's Jess?"

Amy told about the search to find Ashley, how bad off she was when they found her, of how the horse spooked, and how they were left with only one mount.

Ashley rocked back and forth, saying she shouldn't have turned her horse loose even though everyone knew she'd done the right thing. She told of how, when she rode off, McLain seemed to vanish. She fought back her tears.

"Do we try it, John?" Ike asked in a ponderous tone.

John took a long time to answer. He spoke into the fire, more serious than ever. "He sent back his sister, his woman, and his horse. His dog stayed with him. There is a message. He knew they all wouldn't make it. My friend the shadow is prepared to make his journey to the other side. Jax will keep him company until he goes. He knew what he was doing. It was the only thing to do. We all know if we go now, we'll join him on his journey," Raven said, and all the hands were quiet.

Ashley leaned heavily on Amy's shoulder,

spent. They both felt Johnny Raven's words cut like a knife, spearing deep, where emotion was tied to the heart. They briefly touched hands.

Larry swallowed hard, pushing back the lump in his throat. Gary and Dallas sat in grief. Ike stared at the ground, almost in anger. Raven began to speak, slowly, and all listened without making a sound. "Great Spirit," he began, "tonight my friend, Ashley's brother, Amy's man, Larry's only remaining son, and Ike's friend, my grandfather's shadow, is coming to take his place with you. He is a great warrior and a great man. Give him a good horse so he may ride the green plains of your land in the sky. Let him know our hearts will be sad without him. Tell him his sister made it. Tell my friend I will see him soon. But Great Spirit, I warn you, he is a rough man and a strong warrior. If he refuses to come and take his place with you, then show him the way home."

Johnny knelt by the fire. He seemed to cup a handful of smoke and pull it over his head like water. It spiraled into the dark and disappeared without a trace. When he was done, he sat back with the rest and they all huddled together in the darkness, heads bowed, listening to the wind.

Chapter Thirty-one

Silence

Wyoming is a lady, heart and soul. When she's angry she'll storm and rage and make everything in her path feel her wrath. Legend says then it's best to stay away, for her winds can destroy and kill. Afterwards, she'll grow calm again and peace over the land is beyond serene.

The harsh wind stopped just before sunrise. Not too many people slept well, if at all, in the snow-covered tent. Ashley had collapsed from sheer exhaustion, her night interrupted by nightmares and the pain of her loss. Amy had stayed by her side.

Most of the hands tried to sleep except for Raven. He stayed by the fire and seemed to mumble to himself all night. Amy faded in and out of sleep only to see Raven still at his vigil.

It was agreed that at first light that the hands would ride out and try to find McLain's body. Gary and Dallas were told to stay with the stock that hadn't wandered off. Larry started cooking early to feed the searchers before they left. Not much was said and, after the bitterly cold night, there was little room for hope.

The sun rose in a clear sky but offered scant warmth to the ranch hands stirring around the fire. Amy never felt like she warmed up at all, just got less cold, but she was dry and that was good enough.

The crew began to haul their rigs outside to saddle up the horses. Amy replaced her now dry clothes and put Larry's duster back on. Only Ash seemed unable to move. She'd suffered the shakes most of the night and Amy wondered if she would ever get warm. Reluctantly, she went out to tend to Jess's horse.

Larry stopped her. "Cowgirl, you did good out there. He'd be proud of you," Larry said, hugging her shoulder.

"I feel like I failed him, though."

"Now, you know what he lived with every day of his life. I'm proud of you. You don't have to go back out. No one would hold it against you."

Amy put on the leather gloves and hat that had somehow stayed on her head the night before. Dragging McLain's rig out to Major, she felt the aches and pains of her ordeal flow through her body. She couldn't help but notice how barren the land looked as she struggled to saddle Major. The beast looked like he'd had a rough night, too.

Hints of snow piled around the bushes, but for the most part, patches of bare ground could be seen everywhere. One would never know about the huge storm that had blown through if they hadn't been in it.

Amy fed the steel bit into Major's mouth. She had kept it by the fire and stored it under her arm, just as she'd watched Jess do the day before. He told her it was rude to jam a cold piece of steel into your partner's mouth early in the morning. He even poured some hot coffee on it so Major could at least enjoy it for a second or two. Amy tried not to let emotion control her. She fought tears, and everyone could see she was struggling.

A strange sense of calm pervaded the scene. Each of the hands getting ready to ride out and bring back Jess's remains patted her on the back saying "Good job" or "You did real fine, cowgirl." How she wished Jess could hear that she'd earned the respect of her peers. Even John Raven shook her hand. Ike gave her a wink and a nod, which, for the toughest man on earth, was a heartfelt gesture.

The crew began to saddle up and collect

in a circle. The only words spoken were to discuss the plan. Amy forced her sore body up in the saddle. Major seemed to help by leaning toward her slightly. She scoped the land, which was so quiet it felt foreboding, almost sinister. No wind and no birds. Clouds made the morning a dirty gray, but they loomed heavy and still, a cheerless blanket. The land was graveyard calm.

Ashley walked out of the tent dragging a rig. Gary tried to dissuade her, pleading for her to stay. Finding one of the J-Bar-M horses, she started to saddle him anyway. Ike had his own thoughts on the issue.

"You sure you feel up to ride, Ms. Sharpe?" Ike asked.

"It's McLain, and yes, I earned the right. It's my brother's body. I'm bringing it back." She stared at the group as if to dare anyone to cross her.

"I have no doubt of that, Ashley, I was just going to offer one of my horses," Ike said, proving his confidence in the younger McLain. Amy turned Major and walked him toward Ash. Shielding her from the rest of the group, she leaned close to talk.

"We'll bring him back together."

Ashley looked up with tears in her eyes. Fighting to be strong, she struggled for words. "Thank you. Thank you for saving me. Help me bring him back. He said if anything ever happened to him, he wanted to be buried on top of Sanctuary. I can't do it alone." She tried to get a hold of the moment. With a deep sigh, she said, "I never told him I loved him." She closed her eyes and braced her head against the saddle. Amy put her arm around her shoulders.

Finally, Ash was ready to mount up. It was then that a couple of horses whinnied loudly. No one paid attention, and then they whinnied again. Raven held up his hand for everyone to remain quiet. He listened carefully.

Nothing.

Ike and his men had discussed how they would try to find their lost party. Larry, listening in, tried to cope with the situation, already grieving over his loss. They could all see Ashley's hurt, but knew she would go anyway.

Raven excused himself from the group and took his horse up over the hill. Amy joined them, giving Ash a moment to compose herself. Ike moved over to welcome her in. With hands folded over the saddle horn, he gave her a welcome nod.

Silence.

Raven then reappeared atop the hill overlooking the camp. He called to the group to join him.

"I think you all better come up here," he said and turned his spotted horse. The group urged their mounts up the hill. They gathered around Raven, looking south over the landscape. Still nothing.

"What, John?" Ike asked, trying to figure out what Raven was talking about.

"Listen. The bell tolls," Raven said.

Confused, all listened. Studying the landscape, they wanted to hear what John did.

"What is it, John? I can't hear squat," one of Ike's men asked. Then they heard it. Amy did too. Something unknown, but a faint sound, uneven. Ike smiled for the first time since the storm. Amy couldn't understand. Then she heard it again. A cowbell. They waited and it grew more frequent. Ashley had joined the group and when she heard the ring, she knew what it was. The bell grew more distinct, and everyone's prayers were answered with the sharp bark of a dog.

Over the horizon walked an impressive sight. A figure off in the distance guiding two horses toward camp, one tied to the other. It took some time to see clearly, but as he grew closer, they could see Ashley's paint horse tied to Amy's sorrel. Walking in front of them was a man and, not a few feet away, a bounding dog.

"The bell tolls," said Raven.

Jess McLain walked with two horses in tow. Why he wasn't riding, only he knew, but as he came nearer, Ashley struggled to believe her eyes.

"Can you believe it?" said Ike. "Only him."

Jess grew closer and the horses called out to the camp. Ashley's horse whinnied to her. The younger McLain dismounted her horse and began to walk out. Amy almost followed, but Ike stopped her.

"Let him come to you. He came this far. Trust me." He winked at her.

She wanted to rush out to him but knew Ike was right. Ashley had been blaming herself all night, and for the last several hours everybody had been preparing to return Jess's body. Ashley's walk turned into a run. McLain waved, as if he were on a morning stroll, and Jax trotted around sniffing and surveying the land, leaving a scent here and there. Ashley made her way to her brother. As she embraced him, he stopped and scooped her up.

"Dear God, thank you, thank you," Ash whispered.

"What? Didn't write off your brother, now did you?" Jess said behind a cold, red face.

Ash cried and hung on.

Jess had been out all night, though it wasn't the first time, and this experience would be chocked up as another story for the ranch hands to tell in front of the fire.

"I love you!" she said, not letting go.

Jess now helped her detach. "I know you do. Now do me a favor and get in the saddle of this paint, would ya? Been a pain in my ass since I found him. Dear Lord, I hope there's some coffee on." Jess helped her mount up. She rode alongside him until they both joined the group.

Ike spoke first, relief in his voice. "Nice night?" he asked.

"Well, it got a little chilly but we made it," Jess said, tipping his hat back while still holding on to Amy's horse.

"I figured you were just too mean to die. How ya feeling, Shadow?" John asked.

"I could use some coffee. And some dry socks," Jess said, laughing. Jax barked as if to say "Hey, what about me?"

The group shook their heads in disbelief.

"Maybe something to eat too. Then, I figure we got work to do."

The group turned their mounts and made their way back down the hill, except for Amy who remained on Major. She dismounted and walked toward Jess.

"Well, you made it, cowgirl," he said. "Looks like I owe you one. Here, this is your horse. We better trade. I can't let ole Major here see me riding anything else. He may get jealous." He handed Amy the reins.

She hugged him hard when he got close, then had to give him a kiss.

"Well, that's a nice return," he said, smiling.

"I prayed you'd come back. We didn't think you would. How did you?"

"Can I answer that over breakfast? I need to sit down for a while. I can only act tough for so long, hmm?" They turned and walked down the hill.

Larry shook his head as if he'd known it all along. Gary and Dallas made their way over.

Amy left him and took her horse to unsaddle.

"You just go in and eat. I know you're still smoked from last night. By the way, you did good," Jess said.

"Unsaddle these horses," he ordered Gary and Dallas. "We'll need fresh ones to finish rounding up." He handed the reins of both to Gary.

"Glad to see you back, boss. Be good to ride with ya today," Gary said, as he took the reins.

Jess stopped and looked at them.

Gary spoke again. "Sorry, boss."

Dallas nodded his head, saying the same.

"Well, I needed my best hands out there last night, so don't worry about it," he said and turned to walk away. Then he added, "Oh, speaking of that, put Ashley's and Amy's saddles on your horses. They'll need fresh ones. We got some catch-up work to do today, plus we need to go find Deville and make sure they weathered that storm last night. I need my best hands out there, that being Ashley and Amy. You two won't mind staying here and putting camp back together?"

Gary and Dallas said nothing; they knew they'd failed.

"I didn't think so," Jess added and made his way in to the tent.

Breakfast took a little longer than usual, as everyone wanted to hear the story. Jess told of how he and Jax had dug in and prepared for the worst. Hours went by and he thought they might not make it until he heard the cowbell tied around Ashley's paint as it wandered by.

He and Jax decided to try and make it back, late in the night. Along the way they found Amy's sorrel stuck in some bushes, and after unhooking the reins wrapped in the branches, he set out with the horses in tow. A few wrong turns reminded him of when he took the Ranger test. Then he finally got a break in the weather. He said he knew as long as they kept moving, they might make it. Complaining that his feet hadn't hurt that much since his service days, his mood was high. Amy sat close to him and smiled in surprise when he kissed her cheek after she poured him more coffee.

After an hour or so, he said he was ready to get the day started. With dry socks and boots on his feet, he claimed he felt like a new man.

While readying the horses, Deville and his three hands rode up with ten head. After they put them in with the rest that hadn't wandered off over the night, they too joined the group for some food and coffee. Their night had been much easier than it had been for the rest of the group. Deville had seen the storm coming and dug into a dry creek bed, enabling him to have a fire shelter. Jess made a joke that he should have tried to find them last night — they might have fared a little better.

They all saddled up, understanding the day's agenda. The same groups would go out, only Gary and Dallas were now under Larry's employ. He commanded them both with a smile. Back on Major, Jess rode with Amy by his side as they started out.

"So, between you and me, did you think you would be okay? I mean did you do some Ranger magic or something?" Amy asked under her breath so only Jess could hear. He leaned close to her to answer.

"Honest? It sucked. I didn't think ole Jax and me would make it, but I can't let them know that, now can I? Now let's go and get some work done."

That night the weather was calm and the temperature had risen. Stories poured out around the campfire from everyone, but McLain kept to himself. A few nips of liquor were shared, and the gathering was enjoyed by all. Only Gary and Dallas were assigned more chores to do. Their punishment wouldn't last forever, but such was the price of letting down your brand.

In the morning, they would take the stock into the J-Bar-M and take a day to do the sorting. The roundup had come to an end. It was an experience none of them would forget. For Amy, the weeklong adventure had meant even more: the coming of age for one hell of a special hand.

Chapter Thirty-two

Confluence

The sharp Wyoming wind blew briskly as the roundup returned, a string of many riders spread out under flat-bottomed clouds billowing over the gray and yellow hills. The overnight storm had faded into nothing but a memory that had left the riders with wet tents and a bad scare. On the rutted ranch roads, dust devils swirled up where the trail was most worn, while overhead, the sky gleamed a bright azure blue. At the lower elevations, it appeared as if there'd never been any snow at all, and the ground was still hard and dry, begging for spring's much needed rain.

Jess led the way, keeping an eye on Ashley, whose ordeal in the elements had left her muscles weary but her spirit unbroken, her fingers slightly numb, and her cheeks red and chapped, the only visible testaments to her near catastrophe. That, plus a certain quiet, a deep stillness about her. She'd been that way ever since the rescue, ever since they warmed her and got her talking and moving again. She came to life with intensity when Jess returned the next day, but then withdrew to some deeper place once the ride home began. It had been two days since the incident and she was still moody and pensive.

"Leave her alone," said Raven, knowingly. "When the soul has been spoken to by the Great Father, it is always followed by silence."

Local ranchers split into groups. Leading the way ahead of them all were Gary and Dave, Jess, Amy and Ashley, a somber crew of the J-Bar-M. Larry and his mules brought up the rear.

Raven decided to make another small circle with his men, stopping short of the J-Bar-M.

"See you tomorrow," he said, pulling up his horse. Then, before turning away, he urged his pony next to Amy and reached out to her. He held up her own gloved hand to his and clasped the fingers in a grip of friendship for one brief moment, nodding his head. "To my new sister. For lending her spirit to another to survive the dark storm. For bringing my shadow friend home."

Amy could only shake her head and smile, flooded with emotion at Raven's gesture.

The Indian had credited her with Ashley's safe return.

No one expected Bobby Dall to be leaning against his big black Lincoln when they rounded the bend of the ranch road. Jess realized who the man was the second he saw him in his familiar wrap-around shades, designer jeans, and alligator boots. Jess whistled like a banshee. Gary and Dallas dismounted, taking Major from Jess's hands as the boss leapt off. They knew what they were expected to do.

"Son of a bitch, Bobby! What brings you here?" Jess grabbed the other man's hand and smiled. "It's good to see you. What's up? Don't tell me you drove all this way for a beer and a guitar session."

"Nope," said Bobby. "You got that right. We got plenty to talk about. You, Miss Talbot, and me. I didn't want to do it over the phone."

Jess exchanged glances with him and saw the expression in his eyes. "Gotcha. Let me put a few things away. I'll meet you in the main house."

Amy dismounted and began to remove her tack in order to walk her mount. Jess had taught her always to cool your horse, even if it's just sweating lightly, and returning from a week in the open country was no exception. Slowly walking her mare in her faded Wranglers, dust-covered J-Bar-M coat, and her cowboy hat pulled down low, she looked like any one of the J-Bar hands. Only her long blond hair gave her away. Bobby studied her for a moment, drawn by the shapely way she filled out her jeans and the pretty picture she cut with a horse, and seemed puzzled.

"Well, I'll be damned, what do we have here? Or, better, who? Amy, you look like a cowgirl!" Bobby cheered. "Honey, you are lookin' good!"

"She more than just looks like a cowgirl, Bob," Larry cut in. "She is one. Don't be messing with her. She's a good hand."

He punctuated his last remark with a wink, reassuring everyone around him that he meant what he said, but was in no way disparaging any of the others. Nonetheless, David Dallas and Gary didn't smile.

"Thanks, Bob. Yeah. I'm just a ranch hand around here at this point," answered Amy. "And you'll have to excuse me. I've got work to do. And then I'm heading for a shower."

"Well, don't be going too far. Or for too long. What I got to talk about concerns you. But wait, before we get down to business, somebody wants to say hello."

Before Amy could say her name, Terry Ann Hill stepped out from the passenger side of the luxury vehicle, its dark glass windows previously hiding her from view.

"Oh my God, it's my little girl," Terry said, holding her arms open. Then, instead of coming forward, she just stood, leaning against the car, her breath shallow, her balance uneven. "For the love of Pete," she said, her voice almost a whisper. "Just look at you! Come here and let me have a hug."

Amy was shocked by the wisp of a woman who stood by the car. The bleached blond hair and harsh makeup were the same, but the sassy Terry Ann she used to know had faded as sure as the sand-washed skinny denims she wore, topped with a big overshirt, something she'd put on to hide how much weight she had lost.

Amy handed her horse's reins to Ashley and walked over to Terry without speaking.

"Oh my God. It *is* you," Amy said, wrapping her arms around Terry Ann's bony shoulders, tears squeezing out of her eyes as she tried to remember the woman she'd left behind. She hugged Terry Ann harder and felt as though she could almost pick her up, as if her weightless body was in some kind of fragile shell.

317

"Terry Ann," Amy said again, as she held this strange imposter in her arms. "I can't believe it."

Jess decided anything they needed to talk about would include Larry Goodman. He gave instructions to put the coffee on. Larry pulled some biscuits out of the freezer and set out plates for Jess, Bobby and himself.

"Things have started to heat up, Jess," Bobby began, his feet propped up on the old wooden table. "Don't quite know where to begin. While Heistler was waiting for Amy to get back out on the road and structure her management, I released a CD sampler of the work we taped in Nashville. I tried a couple dozen stations down South, across Texas and Oklahoma and up here, just to see what the DJs thought. We saved the best material from her last rehearsal, added the takes we made of her two originals, and mixed the rest in studio. Released it by artist Amy Talbot. It's been pretty well received. In fact," he turned and smiled at Terry Ann, "damned if we didn't hear airplay on the road to Purgatory, not more than an hour out of here!"

"No kiddin'," said Jess, attentive but wary. "That was a smart move, Bob. I should have known you'd use your head if somebody gave you a chance."

"Marty's been pushing me to get her back onstage by summer. All the bookings we applied for were full except Frontier Days! That seemed good enough for me. In fact, better than anything in Nashville or Texas. A week of concerts in front of a real western audience could make or break a new career. She'll be the warm-up for a big name to make her mark, if she gets it right. I've got the same musicians we used in Dallas: they're ready to try it again, given the right conditions. Meanwhile, Heistler's been on my case about a salary as her road manager or some kind of bullshit. I told him he'd get his share when we have profits, but he thinks I'm making money off the CDs, which isn't the case. He forgets he turned Amy over to me after the Dallas fiasco, and frankly, I think he doesn't like the fact he's only an employee now. But I can handle him. He'll get paid eventually."

"So, what does this have to do with me?" Jess asked.

"To be honest, Jess, we need some cash flow. Everybody has to put in or this isn't going to happen. I was kinda wondering if you have any way of putting into the deal now."

Larry raised his eyebrows in a look of

utter disbelief. "You've got to be kidding."

"No, I'm not," said Bobby, scowling at Goodman. "Look, Jess, I know I promised you a percentage once we cash in, but I've got all kind of costs I hadn't counted on. Whatever you can give me now, I can return with interest if she's any kind of success at all."

"Now this is a switch. I never thought I'd see the day Bobby Dall asked Jess McLain for a loan. Who are you kidding? I never have any money! Tell me who's paying for that black hearse out there? The CDs? The band you've lined up?"

"It's all covered, for another month. I need someone to carry Amy through rehearsals in Nashville and get her back on the stage in Cheyenne come July. My credit line is maxed out. I know you've done more than your share here, but you're not just a shareholder, you know. You're a partner."

"What kinda money you need?"

"Ten grand, at least."

"Get in line," said Larry. "You have some nerve. You have any idea what it costs to run this place?"

"You know, old man, I don't know who you are, but I don't think this is any of your business."

"Hold it right there," Jess said in a clipped

voice. "Talking to Goodman here is just like talking to me. Don't push it, or Marty's ass-beating may fall on you. We got plenty of our own obligations. Ten Gs doesn't shake a stick at what I need to cover expenses this season. But wait. When do you need it by? I don't have it lying around but I've got an idea."

"ASAP," confirmed Bob.

"I don't like the sound of this," Amy said, coming in to the middle of the conversation. She sat down in fresh jeans and a T-shirt, ready to listen. "I'm not sure I'm even ready."

Terry Ann listened without saying a word, just holding Amy's hand.

"Then get ready," said Bobby. "If we can get you back to Nashville for six weeks and on a steady rehearsal schedule, we just might have it made. In that time, I want a complete re-do: hair, clothes, the works. I want a glamour cowgirl come July, or else."

"Hair and clothes, I think she can handle. Bob, relax, you don't need to make what's already there. She's every ounce a cowgirl. When does she have to leave?" asked Jess.

"Tomorrow. When I do. We're just here to say hello and goodbye. Sorry to spring this on you but the vacation is over."

"Wait a minute," Amy interrupted.

"Don't I have anything to say about this?"

"Yeah, sure. Tell me you're dry. That's all that matters," Bobby continued, ignoring her previous question.

"Yes! I am, but . . ."

"But nothing. That's what I wanted to hear. Stay that way. I'm in charge of everything from here on out. I won't let you fail, but we have some serious work to do."

Jess eyed Bobby Dall suspiciously. "I don't like the tone in your voice. You're talking to a lady, not some trick pony. One of my best hands, and I don't mind saying so. Amy has the ability to make a decision for herself. You may be her manager now, but you don't own her. Remember, you said you would take care of her. That's the deal."

Amy looked around the table, uncomfortable with the tension beginning to rise. Like vultures, almost every one of them there had planned on a piece of whatever it was she'd earn. The pressure already felt unbearable, and it hadn't really even begun. She had been at this point before, though, when she laid down the verdict on Brenda. Jess was right. She would have to make decisions down the road just like this one. She just didn't know it would be at the same table.

"I hear you," Bobby retorted, "but I don't

think you really understand, Jess. Miss Amy is a property with a shelf life, and I'm not willing to let her get stale. Her window of opportunity is small. Jess, I wouldn't be here and in this state of crisis if I didn't know this was going to work." He shifted his focus to Amy. "Now, are you going to be ready to leave tomorrow or not?"

"Yes, I guess so," she answered.

"And Jess, can you get the extra bucks for this project or not? I didn't know where else to go but to you. You got my word this is going to explode."

"Yes, I believe I do."

Larry stopped the electric can opener from turning as he attempted to open another can of coffee. His face registered complete surprise. Both he and Amy turned to Jess with questioning eyes.

"Go outside and see if Ike Sterling is handy, Larry," said Jess. "There's an offer I need to discuss with him."

Without warning, a small four-door, covered with dust, peeled into the parking area and rumbled to a halt, brakes squealing.

"Who's that?" asked Larry, looking out the kitchen window.

"Johnny Raven?" Jess answered. "No. That's not his car. Maybe one of the boys from the other outfits. But Ike and Deville's guys shouldn't be here until tomorrow. Hell, I can't tell."

A man in dark glasses, a jean jacket and black Levis got out, lifted a pack from the open pickup, and walked toward the house.

"Oh shit," said Bobby.

"Who is it?" said Jess, squinting, suddenly sensing something familiar about the walk, the build, and the attitude of a man he hadn't seen in years. Last time he'd seen him, he'd left him lying in a pile of dust for betraying a friendship and hurting another. It took years of phone calls to smooth that last fight out.

"Wonderful. Somebody tipped him off that I was heading up here. I see he wasted no time. Must have left just when I did. Might as well just go for it then, head on."

"Who is it?" asked Amy, peering out the window.

"Nashville's current version of the boogeyman. Don't say a word about what we've just discussed. It's between us."

"Why? Who is it?" said Larry, peeved at the unfolding events. He didn't like surprises and didn't like strangers on the ranch either. Jess got up to take a closer look.

"Ah hell," said Jess. "I'm in no mood for this."

"For Christ's sake, who is it?" demanded Larry.

"Marty Heistler," said Bobby. "Couldn't stay away. Had to come pick some bones."

"Howdy, gentlemen." Marty flashed his biggest smile as he burst through the kitchen door and threw his pack down. "Hey, Jess. Long time no see."

"What are you doing here?" asked Dall, glaring at Marty. This was his meeting.

"I thought you'd ask that. I have my reasons."

"Oh yeah, sure, what kind of coincidence is it that you're here? I'm in charge of the rest of this show and you know it."

"Don't flatter yourself, Dall. Why does it always have to be about you? Jess and I go back, way back, way before I ever met you. Last time I got involved with a music deal that had Jess's name on it, things got ugly, out of control. I'm not up here for you at all! I just needed to set the record straight. I didn't want Jess to get in any deeper with you or me or Miss Jersey here without me making sure where we all stand."

Bobby sensed it might be time to bow out. "You want me in here or not?"

"In fact, I don't. But you're going to stay anyway."

Bobby motioned to Amy and Terry to head for the door.

"Don't leave. Stay right where you are. Jess, this is about you and me. And Becky."

This spark ignited a fuse. For years Jess McLain had purposely steered clear of Marty. The incident concerning his sister had been sealed at her request. Until now, Jess had let it die. Heistler's appearance and attitude brought it back.

"I don't recall inviting you in. And I'm frankly not interested. You have ten seconds, asshole, before your life comes to a sudden halt," Jess said, rising in defiance. McLain felt old wounds and memories begin to resurface as Heistler barged in. His aggression could be contained for just so long.

As if on cue, Rebecca Ashley McLain Sharpe entered the kitchen to join the fray. She'd put all the stock away and had come up to relax. The gathering took her by surprise. One look at Marty stopped her in her tracks. "What are you doing here? I thought I told you I never wanted to see you again."

"That's precisely why I'm here. I made some promises to the one man who's never let me down. I'm determined to keep them, this time." Marty lit a cigarette and continued.

"What happened between us, Becky, should have never gone down. I took you on when you wanted to break into the business to give you a chance in a world that had no room for you at the time. I was young as a promoter, inexperienced. We got more involved than we should have. Way more. I never meant to destroy the girl you were, along with your dreams. Your brother's never forgiven me for that. I never counted on you falling in love, or my having to let you down on all fronts. Let's not go over what happened again."

Jess stewed in the boiling lava of Heistler's deceit. Too many times Heistler had stabbed him in the back or come at him with an angle to fill his own pockets. For years Jess had bitten his tongue over what the man had done to his sister. The volcano looked as though the pressure had grown too great; McLain was about to erupt.

"That's it, Heistler: I've had enough." Jess lunged toward him, only to have Larry stop him.

"Wait. The way I see it, we're on the verge of launching another dream," Marty countered. "Another girl who might make it. I may have turned Amy over to Bobby for good reasons; he's got more power than I do, there's no denying it. But I'm going to watch him and the boys and every music pimp in the business to keep Amy Talbot from being used, exploited or run over. I'm here to give you my word. Maybe if I can get this right, you'll realize I never meant to hurt you or Becky."

Marty stared at Jess's sister with deliberation, then turned to Amy. "I've been talking to Larry. I've heard how things are going up here. I'm proud of you, Amy. And of you too, Becky, for teaching her as much as you have. For being her friend."

"You keep blowing that smoke and I swear I'll kick your ass back to Nashville," Jess said, seething.

"You've given this girl shelter, courage, and a road to follow, Jess. We're going to take it from here. Bobby, you may think I'm out of the picture, but you're wrong. I'm here to watch you. All of you, every step of the way. And I came all the way from Nashville just to make sure Jess hears it out of my own mouth. I'm going to get this right. And Amy, you're going to be everything Bob said you could be. With all of our help."

"Hey, take a break, Heistler. You don't have to be a lying asshole all the time," Jess said.

"Look, I just couldn't see all of us going forward on this without clearing the air. For the record, Foxworthy and I have parted company over this one. He doesn't think we owe you anything, but I do. It was a helluva drive to get here, but I wanted Bobby and Amy to hear it from me. And maybe restore some honor, if there's any left."

Ashley listened in disbelief. Marty had once abandoned her and broken her heart. And in the process, he'd destroyed a family because of his lies and greed. She, more sharply than anyone else, watched her brother hold back from seeking justice.

"I don't know what you came for, Marty," interrupted Amy, "but I'm on my way back and I'm going to need all the help I can get. I need you and Bobby both on my side, whatever it takes to show you all who I am. I don't know what happened between you back then, but this is now. And it's my career. I'll be ready to go in the morning."

Bobby stood up and reached across the table to shake Marty's hand. "Goddamn it, man, why didn't you say all this before?" They seemed to have come to some middle ground. But McLain's anger still couldn't be contained. He wouldn't interfere with Amy's career, but he didn't have to stomach Heistler longer than necessary.

"Are you done?" Jess asked.

"I give you my word," Marty said.

Jess swallowed his anger. "Bob, you have to do what you have to do. I trust you. Do what you feel is necessary. I know you'll take care of her. I, on the other hand, don't forget that easily. Marty, you've said your piece. Now get out of my house. I may have to live with the decision, but I don't have to like it," Jess said, backing up to the kitchen door.

Marty knew now that this bridge couldn't be repaired. "Jess, I'm giving you my word."

Jess couldn't see past the wrong done to Ashley or forget that Marty had loaned him money only to try and sucker him into a deal, one that would exploit him. His rage demanded justice.

"Your word isn't worth shit. Everyone can stay here tonight but you. I'll say this only one time. Don't come back, and if you think I'm kidding, try this on. If you do, I'll end your life. Get my drift? You do her wrong, same thing. Bob, I'll find the money, but the check goes straight to you. Now, if you'll excuse me, I have work to do." Jess left the room, slamming the door as he went.

Chapter Thirty-three

The Search

"Ike, if she has a colt, do me a favor, huh? Let me buy it off ya. I really want to fill my string with that blood line."

Jess had cut the deal with Ike a month earlier, but the loss of Dancing Wind's first colt to the stock contractor still tasted sour in Jess's mouth.

"Now, I didn't drive four hours just to refresh your memory," replied Ike. "I already agreed to that. I've brought five of my own and I see you have an entire pen of broncs out there. Just so I have this straight, what exactly is it you plan to do?"

Six bucking chutes held five of Ike's rankest and meanest. Their combined worth was enough to buy the J-Bar-M. Ike didn't make house calls for just any man. Possibly the greatest horseman alive, and famous in bucking stock for pro rodeo, his interest in the deal to buy Little Wind was what brought him to Jess now, friend or not.

"Look, Ike, I've been out of the game for a long time. Cheyenne is in four weeks. A great man told me once that when you get lost, go back to the beginning and start over. Well, you taught me to ride broncs and my riding is lost, so here we are and I'm starting over." McLain began to suit up for battle, starting by spurring his boots.

"But you've been riding for the past couple months. Larry told me he had to tell you to stop entering the Thursday night deals because you kept winning. So what's this going to prove, Jess?" Ike asked.

Ike's pick-up men began to warm up their horses. He wouldn't trust the safety of his stock or McLain to any J-Bar-M hands. The broncs he'd brought were nothing short of man-killers. All five had been to the National Finals and been in the eliminator pen, known for animals that hurt and grounded cowboys.

"I've been riding my stock, Ike. I know my horses. Someone taught me that," McLain said, referring to the education he had acquired from Sterling. "Chances are I could end up riding one of these in Cheyenne. I don't know yours. Help me out. Ike, my head's really messed up. Amy's been gone for a month now, and it ain't a whole lot better. I need your help. Help me find what I lost."

Ike had one question. "Who you doing

this for, or what?"

Jess belted up his chaps and grabbed the protective vest he now wore, black leather with a neck roll attached. No rookie, he wore it to prevent old injuries from coming back to haunt him.

"I want that gold buckle. I'm doing it for me and only for me. I unloaded a horse for money, Ike. My bills are caught up. Is that what you wanted to hear?" Jess asked, putting on the vest and leaving it unzipped. He waited for his mentor's verdict.

"Okay, here's the situation. Your head's in Nashville. We got to bring it back. Do what I tell ya. But we ain't riding these horses first. I'm gonna burn these and bring in six of yours. I want these fresh for when your head's really into it."

Ike whistled for his pick-up men and arena hands to come to the chute.

"Show me the way, Ike, I'll follow."

"It's not going to be the most fun you ever had. But we'll get ya fixed up."

McLain's horses were in the chutes and the first was saddled up. Gary and Dallas didn't argue with Ike when they were instructed to postpone the first five, but keep them in a pen close by for later use. Ashley and Larry watched from inside the arena.

They were startled out of their conversation with the opening of the chute gate.

The first bronc bolted out and took a run before breaking to buck. Once it did, McLain was completely out of time. Five seconds into the ride he hit the dirt. He sprang to his feet angrily, disappointed. Jess marched to the bucking chutes as if the pick-up men didn't exist, chasing the rider-less bronc around, herding it out and un-latching the flank.

Dallas had another bronc saddled and ready with Jess's backup saddle. Ike awaited McLain atop the chute that he'd just exited and proceeded to give Jess instructions.

The second bronc reared out with McLain in the saddle and at first jump, Jess found himself once again hitting dirt. For the next hour, the scene repeated itself in one form or another and in sixty minutes it was broncs — six, Jess McLain — zero. Ashley bit her lip as she watched her brother repeatedly hit the ground like a rookie.

Five years earlier, McLain had been a household name in the rodeo community. At the moment, he was lost and it showed. Each time he hit the ground it took longer for him to come to his feet. The sixth horse tossed him hard enough that he crawled to the fence and remained on his hands and knees for several minutes, dazed and shaken. By that point, Ashley had had enough.

When she walked into the arena, Jess stood alone, uneven. On his feet, he leaned against the fence, obviously trying to compose himself. Ashley headed towards him. "Are you done yet?" she asked, curt and to the point. She didn't get the answer she wanted, but the one she received was the one she'd come to expect.

"Don't start with me. Just don't, all right?" McLain hissed. His breaking point was imminent, but he wasn't quite there yet.

Ashley knew it was a matter of time. She left him to complete his journey, but with a final thought added, "So, this time it's to the morgue instead of the hospital."

McLain said nothing as he headed to the chutes. Ike would tell him when to quit. Only he knew how to help a lost friend find his way home.

Gary Russell turned to Ike on the chutes, hoping to receive insight from a master in the rodeo world he himself had entered. "Why is he doing this? He always tells us to quit when we're havin' a bad day. He'd say quit and think about it and get our head straight. What's this going to do?" he said, spitting a stream of chew out into the arena floor.

"He's not focused," Ike answered. "On top of that, he's dealing with the pressure of being who he is and making a comeback. All eyes will be on him. I would agree with him that walking away most of the time works, but now he has to ride it out. If your head isn't one hundred percent clear, you can't ride. Plain and simple. He has to find something. I don't know what it is. Nobody does, not even him. Only he'll know when he finds it. I just hope he does before this kills him."

Ike made his way to another chute with a bronc ready to go. "Jess, turn loose of that saddle. You're charging like a fat cow. Here's another one. Go ahead and crotch him. Come on!" Ike hollered.

Three more broncs, three more times Jess faltered. The total now: nine broncs and nine wrecks. McLain was in good shape, but no man can handle that type of beating and keep getting up. Number nine was the one that kept him down. Holding a shoulder and limping painfully, he made his way to the fence and held himself up with his riding hand.

Ashley had seen plenty. She marched to Jess with rage in her eyes. The entire arena would hear her wrath.

"What is this going to prove? Are you trying to kill yourself? Damn it, why are you doing this?" Ashley stood before him, her eyes blazing.

Barely able to stand, Jess struggled to compose himself and put the pain aside. He glared at his sister.

Ike saw the showdown and figured out a way to excuse everyone. "Jess! I need to give my pick-men a break. We take a half hour?"

McLain understood no one wanted to listen to him get his ass chewed, so he nodded and said nothing. The crew made their way out discreetly, but with haste.

Once alone in the arena, Ashley again demanded, "What the hell is going on?"

Jess looked at the ground, reeling in pain. "I said leave me be. If you don't want to watch, then leave. I didn't ask for your permission."

His answer didn't satisfy her. "Goddamn it, Jess, that's not fair. Amy's gone. You can't change that. Don't take it out on me." She knew McLain had done to himself in a couple of hours what had taken him ten days to do to a young blonde five months earlier. He'd reduced himself to a place where he needed to ask for help.

"Take what out on you? I don't see you

out here. This has nothing to do with you or her, so back off!" he responded, wincing in pain.

"You're going to end up in the hospital, or worse. What good can possibly come out of this? I almost lost you five years ago, then again in May. I won't sit here and watch you kill yourself. She's gone, Jess, and she may never come back," Ash now pleaded.

He began to walk away. Ashley had touched a nerve, but not the one she assumed. "Don't you walk away from me!"

McLain had reached his limit and broke. "Why not? You walked away from me six years ago! Remember? You have some fuckin' nerve even bringing that up." Jess turned from her and proceeded to limp to the rail.

She stood her ground, not moving. Then she asked. "What did you want me to do? Sit here and watch you die? Ever since you came back in 'ninety-two, you haven't been you. Don't leave me again."

Jess stopped with his back to his sister and folded his arms defiantly across his chest.

"No! I needed your help when I was all broke up and my wife left me. And you took off to chase Heistler and become a wannabe country star! I needed help and you left, so don't tell me about leaving you.

You were no different then than they were. Those assholes leaving me and Jack to die in the desert, only you forget. When Marty dropped you like a bad habit, I took you back! I paid your bills! I gave you a home and a job!"

Ashley felt the pain of her past mistakes and now understood for the first time in her life how her brother felt.

"You think I wanted to come crawling back here?" she said. "All my life, Mom and Dad talked about why their other children couldn't have been more like Jess. I finally had a chance to be something on my own, not live in your shadow."

Years of hurt flowed through both their words. Jess's, however, were filled with anger. "I almost died. Where were you when I was laid up in bed for six months, learning to walk again, huh? Where were you when I came back from the war? The hearing — you never made it to even one. You never even called! Where were you when I buried Jack?"

"I was trying to find you. When you came back you turned the whole world off. I was seventeen, okay? Did you think I could handle that? You forget I was taking care of Mom while you were in the Army. Sure you sent home money, but I was the one taking care of her. What happened out there? Why couldn't you let it go? This has nothing to do with me. It has to do with you. You can't let it go. I know it hurts, but . . ."

Jess had been pushed to the point of combat, now he pulled the trigger. "Don't even act like you know! You don't know a thing! You watch your friends' bodies blown to shreds around you! Your country hangs you out. You have no idea what I went through!"

Ashley interrupted him, shouting over his voice. "Then tell me! Why can't you tell me? I can't read your mind, Jess! You never told me. How was I supposed to be there? I know what Larry told me, but you never trusted me enough to tell me!" Ashley held the lump in her throat.

"What was I supposed to do? You tell me. Come home and tell my sister that I had killed and killed, that it was my job? That I watched men die and looked them in the eye when I finished them off? Tell you what it was like to be left out there to die? Better yet, what it was like to hold my best friend and watch him suffer! Cough up blood and beg for me to help him with no way to? Here's one. Try to tell you what it was like to carry a dead body for days, and afterwards? You feel like you can't wash the smell of dead flesh off your hands."

"Yes! Goddamn it, yes!" cried Ashley. "You don't have to do it alone. You don't have to live with it alone. Don't you see what we see? You would have given your life for Jack. He knew it! Tiffany didn't love you, so she left you, but I do. I'm sorry I let you down. I just wanted you to be proud of me. I wanted to be somebody. I was wrong, but you wouldn't let anyone help you! I never understood. I never saw you for who you are until the roundup. You would have died for the both of us. I never knew you loved me until then! You shouldn't have come to get me, but you did, and I almost lost you again! You're always there for everybody else. Why can't you let me be there for you?"

Jess calmed himself and shook his head. He looked down at the ground, then out to the horizon, anywhere but his sister's eyes.

"I thought I showed you that I loved you by helping you, especially when you came back after Marty left you on the street. I wanted you to be somebody. That's why I said don't use our name when you rode or sang. I wanted you to be you. I'm sorry. I should have told you more."

The years of pain and unanswered questions had been resolved. Now the rest was up to Jess.

341

"Just let me be there. You don't have to die for people to show them that you love them," Ashley said softly.

Her comment cut to the bone. Jess looked her in the eye and nodded.

She still wanted answers. "You still haven't answered me. Why are you doing this? What are you trying to prove? Look, I know selling Little Wind hurt you deeply. But that was a wonderful thing, you paid for Amy to chase her dream, and we all have a place to live for another year. So what is it? Don't say it. I know you miss her —"

Jess interrupted. "This isn't about her. I did what I did knowing full well she probably won't come back. I guess in a way it was my penance for not helping you. I don't know. This is about me. I need to do this for myself." He paused for some minutes and looked at her, then spoke the two words Ashley never thought she would hear from her brother's lips.

"Help me."

"What?"

"I said help me."

"I bet that hurt," Ashley said, quoting her brother.

"No, not really. Not compared to how my body feels right now."

Ashley searched for the right thing to say.

"Okay, how many rides do you have left in you?" she asked, getting down to business.

"I don't know. If you hadn't pissed me off so much, I might not even be standing," Jess said. He made a decision.

"There's three rounds in Cheyenne. You need the three best rides you've had to date, so go with three?" she suggested.

"Deal. I need some athletic tape and two pieces of cardboard, eight by six inches."

They walked back to the chutes side by side. Ashley put her arm around him. "I'll tell them to run in three of Ike's. Anything particular in those five? Let me guess. The rankest?"

He only nodded.

Ashley told Ike the plan. He agreed, cutting out his three meanest animals. Ashley had rounded up the requested athletic tape and cardboard and sent it with Dallas to give to Jess. She asked Ike what it was for.

"It's his thighs," he explained. "That means he's so bruised in his legs from the saddle he can't feel anything. So he'll tape cardboard to his inner thighs under his chaps to give him some grab. The cardboard forms to his saddle. It'll help him make it through three more horses. God knows he'll need it."

"Good idea."

"I didn't teach him that. I told him to just tape two pads of Kotex to his legs. He didn't care for that much."

The first bronc quivered in the chutes, edgy and skittish. The big horse was all power. The paint had a reputation of being trashy and hard to ride and lived up to her name, Copenhagen Cut Throat. Jess shouldered down into the box and the horse gave a slight jump to let the would-be rider know she was alive and ready. Sliding his stirrups on to his boots, Jess sat back.

"Bear down, cowboy," Ashley said. "Let it go."

Jess winked. He nodded to the gatekeeper. The gate slammed open. The sound of the latch let the champion know it was her turn. She reared straight up and slammed back down. She covered twenty feet with each lunge and buck, dropping her head between her legs and grunting with every thrust. Her back hooves fired like cannons with every leap and twist. Jess lifted on the rein and charged his feet. Putting the pain aside, he squeezed with his thighs. Dragging his spur licks back almost to the seat of the saddle and charging them forward, he created a spectacle of rough-stock riding beauty.

Ike spoke to Ashley as they watched the ride. "I don't know what you said to him, but if he covers all three of these horses, maybe you should come train a few of my cowboys. And talk to my teenage son while you're at it, because something you said lit a fire under your brother's butt!"

The whistle blew and the ride came to an end. Jess didn't wait for the pick-up men to free him from the bronc. He took a leap, saving his own life.

"Hey, they get paid all the same. Why don't you use the help?" Ike yelled out to McLain.

Jess made his way back and began to help Dallas finish saddling the next horse with his backup saddle. The horse, Big Foot, was large, even for horses that were part draft. He was so big he rested his head on the top of the sliding gate and appeared bored as he was being saddled. With the bronc halter in place, Big Foot was ready. Ike couldn't believe McLain wasn't taking any kind of break. Ashley knew it was because he didn't have much energy left and if he stopped, he wouldn't complete what he set out to do.

The big bay thundered across the arena. Big Foot was as trashy as they came. He ducked and dove from side to side, not creating any rhythm to his bucking pattern. He

345

also lifted his head with each jump, giving Jess a loose rein and nothing to lift on. Charging with his feet, Jess struggled to stay square in the saddle. His free arm whipped violently, giving proof of the bronc's pure power. Fading, Jess heard the whistle and leapt to the ground, unable to hang on even one-hundredth of a second more.

Jess winced as he hit the dirt and remained on all fours. Ashley put her head down, knowing her brother was on the brink. If fatigue or pain got in the way, he wouldn't last two seconds on the last horse. She intended to climb the fence and help him. Ike put his arm out in front of her. "He has to want it, Ms. Ashley. If he can't make it up here, he has no business getting on that last horse." Ike preached the rodeo gospel.

Ashley called to him instead. "Come on, Jess! Get up once more. That's it!"

They watched as McLain forced himself to his feet and fought to get to the chutes for one last trip. Exhaustion streaked down his face in pain, rivulets of sweat that looked like tears from his soul.

"Ike, what horse is this?" Russell leaned up over the gate and asked. Everyone knew he just looked for clarification.

"Lady Sadie Skoal, why?"

"Bucking bronc of the year at the National Finals two years in a row?" Dallas confirmed. He liked to keep current on the reputation of bucking horses. Ike just nodded. Dallas turned to Gary and told him of the horse's dance card. "She threw Dan Mortenson and Billy Etbauer last year at the finals and Jason Grey scored eighty-eight points on her in the tenth round. It's what won him the all-around. She doesn't just throw you. She tries to kill you."

"You want to give her a shot, Dallas? I hear you ride rank broncs pretty good these days," Ike asked, knowing the answer.

Dallas shook his head politely.

"Well, champions want to ride the rank ones, wannabes want to have ridden them," Ike said.

Dallas smiled, but he knew this horse was out of his league. Her bucking pattern was unlike any he'd ever seen. When she left the ground, she ripped her head forward between her front legs. The way she arched her back and then fired all at the same time sent an explosive wave through her body that ripped most riders, even world-champion riders, right out of their saddles.

McLain climbed down onto the white horse that stood dead calm in the box. He'd taken a short break to gather his energy for this ride. He knew who she was. Earlier that year, Jason Grey, the World All-Around Champion who lived in Cheyenne, had been quoted as saying she was the only horse that made him fear for his life. The big mare had even been a topic of conversation between Jason and Jess when Grey had stopped by shortly after the finals to buy a couple J-Bar-M horses. Jess knew he had to pull both triggers on this ride.

Ike readied himself at the flank as McLain put his game face on. With his rein in hand, he climbed in the saddle and spoke under his breath. Only Ike, Ashley and the gate men, Gary and Dallas could hear.

"And behold a pale horse, and he who atop him was death. And hell followed him."

Slipping on the stirrups, horse and rider waited for the gate to open. Jess eased back in the saddle, his free hand resting on the inside of the gate, his left clutching the bronc rein. Ike gave no pre-ride instructions. This wasn't about a score; it was about making the whistle. Survival. He nodded only once. The gate opened and the horse shot like a bullet across the arena. McLain headed his spurs in the neck, holding his mark out, preparing for her to explode. She didn't disappoint.

Erupting in the middle of the arena, she

put on her signature trip, each buck a violent explosion that rocketed Jess out of the saddle every time. The rides of grace and beauty he had put on the past two horses had vanished. Now he struggled just to stay in the saddle. Out of rhythm and out of time, he fought to charge his feet forward. Out of sync with the horse, he was only successful once out of every third time. The horse had won, but her victory was not complete. When the whistle blew, Jess fired out of the saddle, hitting the ground like a rag doll. He lay flat. The horse ran off, bucking wildly, leaving the spent cowboy in the dirt. Ashley gasped and others held their breath. A few seconds passed and finally Jess appeared to move. First up on all fours, then, in agony, he forced himself to stand. Smiling at Ashley, he unzipped his vest and made his way to the closest fence.

"Well, Ike, he may not be Mortenson, Etbauer, or Jason Grey, but Jess made the whistle. What'd you think?" Ashley asked.

"Jason Grey is five years younger than your brother; he's got some youth left. But excuses won't hold up in Cheyenne. I think he's ready. I have a feeling Jess may surprise a whole lot of people."

Chapter Thirty-four

Countdown in Nashville

By the third week of rehearsals, the rhythm track had been laid down tight: drums, bass, and lead guitar. Amy sang along, off-mike, to keep the musicians in sync with each song. Their goal was to set a foundation to build upon. The drummer, Texas hotshot Taco Short, brought unexpected percussion to each session — Native American drums, congas, the works. Amy learned just how important the drums were: vital to the finished sound. Any other instrument could come back and punch in corrections to mistakes, but not Taco. He had to get it right the first time.

The sound engineer began to record the over-dubs. One instrument at a time would lay down their fills for the verses and choruses, as well as their solos. Marty liked to call them "rides." Slowly and deliberately, each song came together, as each part was laid down upon the next.

Amy spent hours alone in the sound booth recording the vocals. What she wanted to hear was the pure sound of her own voice coming through the headphones, recording over and over the new lyrics that now seemed to have a life of their own. Since her trip to Wyoming, her music had been revitalized. Some of her old songs had changed and new ones took their place. She found new ways to wrap the melodies around the feelings that had surfaced, and the music flowed like a river, out of a deeper place.

At the end of every recording session, she found herself drenched in sweat, exhausted, but also sharp and attentive, her receptors humming. She felt more alive than she'd ever felt, living on passion, Diet Coke and energy bars, as the retakes often lasted for hours. She didn't care. She savored every day, every single hour.

Bobby stayed with her through all the vocal work. He couldn't get enough. Amy's voice had just enough sultry in it to be sexy, and just enough power to rivet the listener with its strength. Her range ran from a full rich alto to soprano, and she used everything she had to interpret the music, but without overkill, without wasted or extra sentiment.

"Could you warm this up a little?" Bobby would ask.

Or, he would listen and pause, and say, "Okay, hon, not bad. Just a little wet. Too soppy for me. Maybe a little less reverb?"

Take after take, day after day, Bobby listened with his earphones on and his eyes closed. He assured Amy that by the time they got it all to the mixing process, she could kick back and enjoy herself. That's where he took over. In the mixing room, the producer and engineer could play with the levels on every instrument and add the equilibrium that was missing to any part. Once that was done, he'd send it off to be mastered and compressed, on its way to a finished product that could become her first complete CD.

As she sang, not needing to play her guitar, Amy learned she could focus on the images behind the words, the harmonies and the kaleidoscope of experiences and feelings that had grown out of those many months in the windy hills of Purgatory.

When she warmed up before each session, she liked to close her eyes and imagine the big sky over Wyoming and the light and the long afternoons. She remembered the evening with its soft violet clouds, and the dawn coming up during those early morning runs with Jess. She especially loved thinking about the sunrise, the bright rose and yellow-streaked glory of those clear mornings on the ranch and the way she felt every day, hopeful and strong, getting up to tackle something new, something bigger than herself. She remembered, too, the awful feelings of coming apart at the beginning, as if she were going to die, when the alcohol was leaving her system and her body had to adjust. She remembered the falling apart and the coming back together again as well. And she remembered Jess, always goading her on. She couldn't stop thinking about Jess McLain and how he saved her, really, from herself.

From the very beginning, she had looked up to him and wanted to be near him, a distant man she both loved and feared. She remembered failing him and losing her resolve and then hating herself and being afraid, knowing that she had nowhere to go, no other self to go to, no other Amy to be. She was afraid he would turn her away, but he never let her down. He asked for more and waited and believed in Amy Talbot just the same.

The world of the J-Bar-M changed the very way Amy saw herself and how she saw others, too, especially Gary, Dallas and Ashley, each with their patience and support. And Jess and dearest Larry — inseparable. Amy looked back on how they'd helped her create the new woman she knew she had to become, and gradually let go of the lonely child that had driven her to drink and fail and be afraid and be rescued, over and over again.

More than anything, Amy had been touched by the magic of the wilderness at Sanctuary Ranch: the land and the horses: the great blue roan, now dead, but bigger than life in her unexpected death; Tommy Boy who rode around the barrels like an athlete; Jess's valiant Sergeant Major, her savior; Ashley's paint, whose loyalty matched that of her owner; and her own patient sorrel mare who carried her on the roundup and back home again. She missed the gentle sway of their gaits and the rich scent of their hide, the sound of their hooves and their manes flying as they rode. She missed the saddles creaking, the clouds of dust and the racing gallops that took your breath away and, of course, Jess, always Jess, somewhere, in the lead.

Jess McLain filled her thoughts and overwhelmed her heart. He stood alone and powerful and far away, but over time, also by her side. He had truly let her in. He'd given her a place to stand and be herself and be seen. He believed in her. And, for just one night, for that brief sweet time, he had opened his heart to her when he'd lain by her side and told her all about Jack and the mare and his demons and his pain. And he'd kissed her. He let her in close enough to think she'd made a difference. Close enough to feel his body and his tears and how human he really was. And close enough for Amy to know that she'd never be the same.

Bobby pulled the musicians back in to try a new piece that Amy wanted them to learn. She hoped there was still time to add it. She'd written the words down and knew that when she did, they were meant for someone besides herself. The rhythm track recording went fairly well the first time. The second time around, Amy stopped them.

"Let's try this one from the top again, guys," she instructed. "Come in with me on the second verse. The first one I do *a capella,* one octave below where you are, solo. Then, on E. Greg, use an open E-tuning if you can. Tommy, give me a snare drum when the bass guitar picks up the beat on the second verse. Stay with me, all of you, through the last verse, and I'll close solo again on the last chorus."

"Hey, you're doing my job, girl!" Bobby

Dall cut in on the talkback. "Who's putting this piece together anyway? You or me?"

"Me," Amy answered.

"Well, okay then!" Bobby smiled and gave her a thumbs-up. That was his girl. The new Amy. He liked it.

The band cut back at the chorus as instructed and Amy closed her eyes, leaning into the mike:

> . . . *And when you're tired of riding*
> *out there all alone,*
> *When it's time to put your saddle*
> *up and finally come on home,*
> *I'll be here waiting for you.*
> *It's a promise that I'll keep, 'cause*
> *I'll be there in your sunset,*
> *When the world goes off to sleep.*

The band trailed into a fadeout and Amy walked out of the recording booth. Bobby Dall stood quietly in a corner of the studio, headphones in his hand. He'd pulled out a handkerchief and proceeded to wipe his eyes.

Nashville seemed like one big land mine after another. Everywhere Amy turned she found temptation, but she didn't give in. Bobby took her out on the town the night after they arrived just to reintroduce her to the music scene. From one club to the next they barhopped. At the Exit/Inn, 12th and Porter, and finally Legends, they muscled their way through the crowds, stood in the smoky bars and drank Cherry Cokes and Perrier while sizing up the bands. Bobby couldn't get over Amy's ability to resist alcohol. She refused, even when Hank Bluestein, VP at Mercury Records, offered her a drink. Coming in on a break at The Backwater, Amy was thrilled to hear her own "Time and Tears" playing over the house system. She'd arrived, somehow or another, and not a soul knew who she was.

"You know, sweetheart," Bobby said, as he brought her home that night, "I wouldn't have believed this if I hadn't seen it with my own eyes. You've lived up to your part of the bargain so far. Now, don't let me down."

"I don't ever want to hear you say those words again," Amy shot back at Bobby. "Don't kid yourself. I'm not doing this for you."

June 10, 2004

Dear Jess,
It sure seems strange to be writing to you and not looking at you across the

kitchen table. I guess I could have called, but I just felt like putting a pen in my hand. Wyoming seems so far away, like another planet from here. Saturday night Bobby is taking me down to Franklin to watch the Jackpot rodeo but it's just not the same.

Things in Nashville are hot and humid and so busy. Bobby's got me booked four mornings a week at the re-cording studio. When you think about it, four weeks isn't much time to pull it all together but we're doing the best we can. He wants a full CD ready to sell by the time I hit Cheyenne. The record-ings go to master in another week, then they tweak it, do the cover, and there it is. Instant music. Well, not exactly, but it sure feels that way.

I like the guys in this band. We're really in sync this time and they seem to respect my new work. I'm learning a lot by reworking some of Terri Clark's songs. And Patsy Cline's, too. We're even doing a Janis Joplin piece. I never dreamed I could sing her music before but it suits me now.

Marty took Terry Ann and me shop-ping the other day. He insisted on dressing me up for the Frontier Days gig, but I think he's got the wrong image completely. Seems kind of trashy to me. The shirt's one of those tight, low-cut, lace-up-the-front things that makes me look like I'm all tits. The jeans are bell-bottom low riders in flash denim, studded with crystals up the sides. My old boots aren't high enough, so we got some new boots with real stacked heels. You wouldn't recognize me, Jess. I'm not sure about any of it. Maybe that's the way it's supposed to be, but I don't like it. But I guess he's the manager. I better not hassle him since he paid for it all. Believe it or not, he tells me I have to pay him back once we start making the money. I can't argue right now, but if I mention your name he backs off a little.

Hey, listen. I need you to know that Terry Ann's pretty sick, much worse than any of us thought. Living with her here and taking care of her like this has shown me just how weak she really is. I'm guessing this summer will probably be her last. She's been a real trouper about everything though and never complains, but she can't do too much. Mostly we watch TV together at night. Chemo treatments have stopped and she's in a wait-and-see mode. None of the doctors have much hope for things ever turning around. We don't talk about it much. I think it's better that way.

One thing: Terry Ann finally opened up to tell me her story. Looks like Nashville didn't treat her too kind. She left in '78 and headed up to the clubs in New York with some guy who promised to marry her and then didn't. Left her broken-hearted and broke. I guess she sang pretty well, but you'd never know it now. Her voice is nearly gone. She's been coaching me, though, on the best framework for each song, and she sure likes the new stuff I'm working on. She's good to come home to, I can say that much.

Hey, guess what? We've discovered the Westerns Channel, old movies and reruns from the TV westerns. I just love them. Funny, Jess, but I don't feel so alone anymore. All those old actors — they're the parents I've been looking for. They've left me their stories to interpret, their music to revive. And I want to know them all. Seems like between Terry Ann and me, I just might. All we've got at night is time. Anyway, *sometimes she falls asleep on my shoulder before a movie is over, just like a kid. Then I put her to bed. God, I'm going to miss her, Jess, all over again.*

Oh, and one more thing. I thought you'd be glad to know that if I ever come back to the J-Bar, I'm one step ahead. When I got to Nashville I decided to enroll in a GED program with the local public school system. Believe it or not, with five hours a day, I can finish that one semester I was missing in just a month. Most afternoons, that's all I do is study. By the time you see me in Cheyenne, I'll have made the grade. Literally. Thanks for making it one of the rules, Jess. I might not have had the courage to try. I'm halfway through already and you know what? It's not so hard. I owe you one, Jess. I guess I owe you everything.

Sending my love,
Amy

"Soften the ending, baby," said Bobby through the microphone that linked him to the sound booth. Two record producers, the sound engineer, himself, and Marty Heistler, all stared at Amy from behind a glass window. She felt like a bug under a microscope or a body in an operating theater, split wide open for everyone to see.

"Trail it, darlin' — don't punch it like that, take it down for me. We can do it electronically, but I want to hear you bury it, quietly. Everybody knows we can digitize you, but I want your live performances to sound just like this CD. Always."

Amy motioned to the sound engineer to repeat the last stanza and closed her eyes. *"And when you're tired of riding out there all alone, when it's time to put your saddle up and finally come on home . . ."*

Once more behind the words came the vision: the wild horses on the ridge traveling in freedom between the ranches of Purgatory, a moving tribute to the landscape. The wild band, milling by the hundreds against the yellow earth and the shale bluffs, at home in the West. And handsome Jess, in his long duster, astride Major in the midst of the wild ones, flying through a tapestry of horseflesh, his own horse deftly cutting off the lead mare and splitting out the herd, the great thunder of the chase. Jess, one of them, a part of them . . .

The lead guitarist fingered the quiet melody again, *"and when you're tired of riding out there all alone . . ."*

And the blizzard. Amy still couldn't put away the nightmare: the bitter, endless storm that had challenged them until finally they found and carried Ashley back, blue with cold, almost unconscious, all the way to safety, only to spend the night mourning for Jess, who had made a quiet plea bargain with death and won.

Amy paused while the lead took the melody up a notch, a poignant modulation that added direction to the music and intensified its reach. She knew without a doubt that Wyoming had become her new love, and Jess her hoped-for lover. She wanted so much to be back. To exchange glances with him from a distance. To brush by him and touch him when no one could see. To be with him in the world he'd created, the ranch where everything was possible. She wanted, too, to inhale the aroma of fresh coffee in Larry's kitchen again and the smell of fresh straw in the barn, to rub Jax's furry ruff and see the love dance in his warm brown eyes, to be one with the wind and the weather and the big sky and never complain. To be at home anywhere on the J-Bar-M. *"And I'll be there waiting for you. It's a promise that I'll keep. Yes, I'll be there in your sunset when the world goes off to sleep."*

Amy closed her eyes and sighed. She motioned to the engineer to cut it and stepped out of the booth. No one had to tell her that Wyoming was where she belonged.

Chapter Thirty-five

Show Time

Cars jammed the parking lot on all sides of the fairgrounds. The constant Wyoming wind had subsided just enough to keep the bright flags fluttering above the grandstands, but leave the rodeo queens' stiff blond hair in place under their high-peaked white hats. Frontier Days 2004 was about to close with as much fanfare as a coronation. The final concert was the one nobody wanted to miss.

"You'd think the president was coming, there's so much security here," commented Bobby, unloading their gear from the van. He and Marty had driven out from Nashville in separate vehicles, just in case one broke down. They wanted to make sure they all got there. Chuck and Ripper Williams drove the truck with the equipment and had no room for passengers. Amy and the rest of the boys rented a six-passenger Ford maxi van, and managed to get everything in or on top of it.

"It's simple," answered Marty. "You've

either got a ticket to this gig or not. The concert has been sold out for weeks. The rodeo events are too. Anybody who tries to sneak in either gets handcuffed or hanged."

"I see. Where's Amy?"

"Still over at the Days Inn. She's wiped. I told her to get some sleep. She's got all of three hours before we get our chance to do a sound check. Then maybe twenty minutes to warm up. That is, if Willie leaves us any time. You think he'll be up there long?"

"Who knows? They've been setting up all morning. His crew started linking the lights and PA system about noon. I was told that he's scheduled to check around five after the rodeo ends, and we're supposed to get some time by six. Hell, the whole shootin' match breaks open at seven. Gates, grandstand seating, the works. That don't leave anybody much time."

"What do you need time for?" asked Marty. "We don't even need to rehearse. She's perfect. The band is perfect. We took this thing to the last second, gave her as much time as we possibly could. She's got this stuff down better than I ever dreamed she would. Don't sweat it."

"I'm not," answered Bobby. "It's just that I have high hopes and big money riding on this one. And so do you."

Marty couldn't believe that Jess McLain had drawn to ride in the last regular rodeo performance that Saturday in saddle bronc. To see the great one return had to be a crowd pleaser. So much for all the years of teasing about getting back in the game. Jess had left so wounded, no one ever dreamed he'd ride rough stock again, much less compete. Marty wondered what bet or dare gave him the guts for a comeback. He would never have bought the rumor at all, but he'd run into Gary Russell who confirmed the news.

"Yep. Boss is going to give it another try," Gary said, obviously excited. He'd never seen the legend bronc rider at his game, at least not in world-class competition. Jess had finally turned into the hero he'd heard about for years, and all in a single weekend.

"Yeah, well. I'll be damned. Let's just hope he doesn't go and get himself killed."

The 107th edition of Cheyenne Frontier Days was nothing less than the Super Bowl of rodeos in the middle of a nonstop western extravaganza. Entertainment had been booked from the first day to the last, with greater and lesser luminaries in the music world packing the grandstands every night. The closing act was always the big finish, the one everybody came to see. Amy couldn't have gotten a better debut. The gift of serving as Willie Nelson's opener was still a miracle Bobby couldn't explain. All he knew was that the regular act, booked nearly a year before, had to cancel, opening the door for Amy Talbot and the Pick-Up Men, a last-minute name for the group that they chose in a hurry.

"Look, Amy," Bobby had explained to her back in Nashville. "Warm-ups are like leftovers. Most people don't want 'em and don't even listen. Audiences are notorious for talking their way through the many unknown voices that take up stage space while latecomers are being seated. But the anticipation is going to be so high here, you can't lose. These are the man's fans, all of them. He's an icon. All that energy out there can't hurt. You can capture some of it. I know you can. You have a chance in a million to make yourself remembered, kid. Don't expect Willie to notice you or thank you for a job well done. He probably won't. Stay out of his way. Just get in there, give it all you've got, and walk off like everybody came to see you perform, okay? No matter what happens."

"Are you trying to be reassuring?" Amy asked. "Because if you are, you're not.

Thanks anyway. I'll figure it out."

Willie's sound check went without incident, except that it ran long. Very long. By the time the Pick-Up Men got their amps, drums, and other equipment hooked up, it was almost six-thirty.

"Shit," said Chucky. "This is exactly what we didn't need. I hate to be rushed. And the goddamn wind's up. I can't seem to get anything balanced." Far to the north, dark clouds loomed on the horizon and westerly winds battered anything that wasn't tied down.

"This is definitely not looking good," said Bobby, eyeing the elements carefully. The grandstands were partially covered but the soundstage on the southeast end of the arena was fairly exposed. They had little protection if the weather changed.

"Just deal with it," answered Bobby. "Do the best you can. Meet you all at the catering truck after we're done. There's barely time to eat. Anybody want a beer?"

Amy shot Bobby a hard look. "Thanks, but no thanks. You're doing it again."

She shook her head with a disgruntled frown, then pulled her guitar out of the case and lifted the strap around her neck. She plugged in her amplifier, strummed a G chord and ran her fingers across the strings.

She was really here at last. Ready to shine in front of 10,000 western music fans in the heart of Wyoming. She was a complete stranger and it didn't even matter. She hummed a bar of "Someday Soon" into the microphone and closed her eyes. When she opened them she was staring into the face of Jess McLain.

"So, can you really play that thing or are you just pretending? Why don't you move this for a second?" Jess lifted the guitar up and around to Amy's back and hugged her, hard.

"Damn, you look good. I'm impressed!" McLain said.

It wasn't that Amy had changed, not physically — but in so many ways, she had grown. She looked as pretty as when he'd first met her, but even more so. Her hair was cut full and layered and streaked more blond than ever. Yet that wasn't it. It was the presence of her in this place, in this arena of the greats that gave Jess the confirmation he was looking for. She fit. She really fit, in her boot-cut jeans and her snap shirt, tied in a tight knot at the waist. He noticed that she'd put on a little weight, somehow in all the right places. Her breasts showed full under the open top snaps of her sleeveless plaid, notched-pocket shirt. Her scuffed boots were the ones she'd worn at the ranch when she rode, as was the laced and carved leather belt, the one he'd bought for her in town. The last time he'd seen her, climbing into Bobby's black rented Lincoln, he wondered if she'd really ever finish the last chapter necessary to write the book of her life, the one that they'd all been banking on to carry her into the future. Jess knew too well that the road to music stardom was littered with kids like Amy who flared briefly and then died out, a cold ash in the grate of success.

"Jess! Oh my God! So good to see you! What are you doing here?" asked Amy, excited to find Jess before her. "I didn't think I'd see you before tomorrow. Congratulations! I heard you made the cut this weekend. And that you're actually riding in the finals tomorrow, for the big money. I'm so proud of you. Man, you look good, too!" She hugged him back, not caring what the band members or the dozen or so cowboys watching from the arena rails thought.

"I was hoping we could talk before the concert," McLain said. "Any chance you could pull away for a minute? Just to catch up. I just want . . . to look at you. But if you're busy it can wait."

Amy put her guitar away and told the

band to do what they had to do. "Are you kidding? I'll meet you all at the catering trailer in ten minutes," she said, and looked at her watch. The faithful would start moving in by then. They'd have to be on-stage by seven-fifteen, just after the opening formalities. The wind still threatened and clouds blotted out what should have been a spectacular sunset.

Amy and Jess headed toward a clearing under the grandstands and stopped. Amy smiled, finally reaching for Jess's hand. "Never believed it, did you?"

"Well, yes, of course I did. Hey, you're really something, I gotta tell you. You made us all look good back there at the ranch. Like we'd really done our job. But you know, things haven't been the same since you left. Dallas's cooking got bad. Jax went nuts. Damn dog tore up your shoes, then the bedding, everything! Hey — you've arrived, cowgirl. I'm proud of you."

"I'm sorry about the dog. Kinda makes me glad, though." She smiled.

"I moved Jax upstairs with me. I think that's kind of what he always wanted anyway. Listen, thanks for the letter. Congratulations on that high-school diploma. I know I didn't answer you, but I've been bronc riding till I can't sit down. This qualifying wasn't easy, but I've done it. A wake-up call, though. I ain't as young as I use to be."

"Don't talk to me about easy," said Amy, looking into Jess's eyes. "I know what is and what isn't. Like watching your best friend die while you're being born all over again. Try that one on for size."

"You forget who you're talking to, pretty lady. Makes you hard, doesn't it? I'm sorry, though," Jess said. "I was going to ask about her. That's a damned shame about Terry Ann. She's that bad, is she?"

"Yes," answered Amy solemnly.

"Hey, Gary and David are here. Ashley, too. Everybody. They all came to see you," Jess changed the subject.

"Oh, come on. I think they came to see you."

"What's the difference? We're both here," Jess said with a grin.

Amy smiled and put her arms around him.

Jess looked out to the darkening sky. "Damn. That's not fair. You need good weather here. Sure hope the wind dies down." Jess's voice trailed off as he turned to look at the girl who had grown into the finest-looking woman he'd known in a long time. Graceful. Confident. Composed.

Ready to touch the audience with her music and her heart.

"I don't need the wind to die down, Jess," Amy whispered. "All I need is you."

Jess put his arms around Amy and kissed her, touching her lips with the thanks, the love and the hope that had brought them to where they both stood. He wanted her to know that he didn't want her to leave again. That he missed her. And that they weren't done. She had everything he wanted in a woman, and always had, and he hadn't even known it until she left. And he hadn't known how to tell her until now. He still didn't. Instead, he just held her tight.

"Hey, Amy! Where've you been?" Chuck called as he intruded on Jess and Amy as they embraced. "Sorry, man, but we've got a concert to play!"

"Oh, my God, what time is it?" replied Amy, frightened that she'd stayed with Jess too long.

"Bobby's just fit to be tied looking for you. We thought you were on the other side. Anyway, it's show time! Get your ass down there. Fast."

"Looks like it's time to nod your head," Jess said. "Go get ya some, cowgirl!" he added, smiling, but his voice was reserved.

Amy gave Jess one more kiss and ran.

He stood looking after her, immobilized, as though pierced by a lance. Seared by his own emotions, a rush of heat and desire and feeling flowed through him, unlike anything he'd felt since Jack died. Without warning, the part of him that had died with Jack came back, raging through his veins, demanding to be known. Jess was himself again. Amy had seen to that. Now, hands on his hips, his hat pulled down low, he watched the woman he loved leave for the second time.

"Ladies and gentlemen, we ask you to bear with us just a few more minutes." The announcer's voice bounced around in the fierce wind and echoed off the grandstands. "We've all had a great week here at the 107th Cheyenne Frontier Days, and we know you'll have a great time tonight!"

Cheers from the audience rose as programs blew and hats skipped across the arena. The concert had been delayed fifteen minutes already, and people could be seen milling about, buttoning jackets, edgy in their seats. The announcer looked nervously their way. It was seven-thirty-five. The band looked back at Bobby Dall: this was what they'd all been waiting for. It was now or never. Bobby motioned for the musicians to get onstage and in their places.

Amy had ducked out to the ladies' room while the wind delayed the start, and when she returned, Bobby was foaming at the mouth.

Marty hustled Amy toward the stage. "This is it! You just have to go on, do it any way you can. Fight your way through the wind. Sing over it if you can. Hey, where's your outfit? Damn it, get dressed! We're outta time!" Heistler pleaded.

"I am dressed," snapped Amy. "This is how I'm going on. And don't you swear at me! Boys, let's go!" She kicked up one boot at Marty to confirm the fact that she was going onstage the way she was. All she'd added was her Wyoming-creased black hat, pressed down snug in case the wind tried to blow it off. No way was she about to lose that.

The band's appearance onstage drew clapping and whistles from the impatient crowd and more remarks from the emcee. "If this wind dies down, we can all say thanks to somebody up there when we're in Cowboy Church in the morning. Tie down your children and say a prayer, folks. They're going to need it."

As the lights went down around the arena and the spots came into focus onstage, some kind of miracle did happen. The wind slowed enough to make those opening notes by Chucky sound clear and crisp. Tents stopped flapping. Flags hung down instead of snapping in the breeze. As if by some pre-ordained stroke of grace, the weather decided to give Amy her chance.

Chucky's powerful instrumental, introducing Amy's single, "Time and Tears," familiar to some, reached into the audience and grabbed every listener with its haunting introduction. The bass followed, and within seconds, a noisy, restless audience had turned toward the unknown band and the slim girl in the black hat standing center stage, waiting for more. The clapping and chants for "Willie, Willie!" had died down to a hush, and as Chucky reached the last note of his melodic instrumental, Amy drew her pick across her guitar in a sweeping brush to join him and her voice broke the night with an incredible wail.

Hands started clapping as music lovers realized the song they were hearing, the very same one that climbed its way up the charts on rural stations all across the West. Clapping increased as people confirmed their approval. As Amy sang and the rest of the instruments joined in, the arena filled with the vibrant joy of a vocalist and her band rocking in perfect harmony. "Tears" put the dance beat into feet already tapping and started people swaying and bouncing in their seats. Those who'd heard the single realized who was onstage, and those who hadn't discovered a brand-new talent that could rival all the ones who'd gone before. Amy could feel it. She had them. She rocked and swiveled with each line, smiling at the band, urging them on. They'd started off high and headed for the sky.

As the lights played across the audience during her second number, Amy could see Jess and Larry and the gang from the J-Bar-M, all together, just a few sections over. Surrounded by family, the rest of the strangers didn't matter. Amy could sing to the people she cared for and, as she moved on from her original music into material borrowed from other writers of the West, she smiled as she dedicated each song to someone she knew. Twenty minutes wasn't a long time to show your best hand to the world, but Amy had picked five numbers to sell her product. Warmed, excited and smiling, she gave credit to Donnie Blanz and Judith and Ed Bruce for their tune, "You Just Can't See Him from the Road," and lead up to it in style.

"Hey there, rodeo lovers! I hope you all got to take in the competition today.

Nothing like watching cowboys do their thing. The real deal is hard to find these days so, when you meet a cowboy, honor him. This one's for you, Jess McLain, and all those others you just can't see from the road."

You don't see him much
On the big screen anymore
Kids don't ride along with Roy and
   Gene.
That ain't really him
With all those feathers in his hat
And some Frenchman's name
   embroidered on his jeans.

He's still out there riding fences
Makin' his living with a rope
As long as there's a sunset
He'll be riding for the brand.
You just can't see him from the road.
Well, he never learned to two-step.
Hell, he barely learned to walk
He's 'wore' a lot of leather off the
   tree.
He's had one or two good horses
He counts among his friends
He never drew a breath that wasn't
   free . . .

The audience joined in as Amy went back to the chorus.

As the set unfolded, each song brought Amy closer to the life the audience led and the world they wanted to live in. And, thanks to Bobby and Jess, she too had tasted it, touched it, and made it her own. She could put it into music by feeling it. Her voice, filled with passion and love for the land and the one man who personified it for her, rose and swelled and reached out across the dark grandstands and the sea of unknown faces. It made itself felt in the hearts of every listener. When the crowd got to their feet after starting with Stan Rood's sweet ode, "Ride to the Sunset," she knew she had them.

Somewhere out west
There's a blue moon a rising,
The sun disappears down below the
  horizon,
A cowboy beds down as the stars
  gather round.
His home for the night is a piece of
  the ground.
The coyotes are howling
A high lonesome sound
And the night is cold and clear.
He's the last of the cowboys,
He rides to the sunset,

Searching for new trails to cross.
And he goes on believing
In the life he's been leading,
Riding, but knowing he's lost . . .

As she repeated the last line to the last verse and gently brought the song home, the audience cheered. And stamped. And clapped. And cheered some more, demanding an encore. Ten thousand fans who'd come to see the great Willie, stamped and hooted and whistled and asked the little cowgirl from Jersey to sing just one more. She could see Willie and his band standing impatiently behind her. She looked at his stage manager over her shoulder, who gave her a thumbs-up, smiling as he did.

"Okay," she said to the audience. "I'd be glad to! And I thank you. Thank you so much." She beamed at the thousands who had risen to their feet in appreciation.

"I'd like to dedicate this last song to someone I love," she added. "Miss Terry Ann Hill," she said softly into the mike. "And to Mr. Willie Nelson, too. You all call him Willie, but when you open for him, I believe it's Mister . . ." she added with a bold wink and a smile.

The band struck up the familiar intro and swung into Ed Bruce's beloved ballad,

"Mamas, Don't Let Your Babies Grow Up to Be Cowboys." The audience exploded and Willie himself stepped up to the mike to join her.

"Way to go kid," he smiled. "You're a hell of an act. A winner." And together they brought the song to life.

Chapter Thirty-six

The Reunion

Nine days spun out like an action-packed movie. The best cowboys from all over the world had come to the rodeo to reach for the big stakes. Playing out the hands they were dealt, the initial competition field of over 1,000 had narrowed down to fifteen in each event. Over $100,000 within the seven events was yet to be made. The game had become serious business.

The arena sat in the heart of Cheyenne, rising above the Wyoming plains, a towering mecca for the American rodeo cowboy. Frontier Days had a hundred years of tradition written in blood, sweat, disappointment, pain, and glory, all etched with spurs on a canvas of hide. "The Daddy of 'Em All" was not only the biggest regular-season rodeo in the West but also the largest outdoor rodeo arena in the world. With ten wood bucking chutes on the east side separated by a turn-back gate, the arena flanked a one-mile racetrack. Three full levels of grandstands cradled the legend. Here, the toughest livestock and the greatest cowboys reunited every year to put on a show that was second to none. This was a place where dreams could come true or a life could be ruined in an eight-second dance. A successful ride could win a cowboy enough money to shoot him into the top fifteen positions in the world and possibly qualify him for the National Finals. Cowboy celebrities and newcomers alike all paid homage to Frontier Days' greatness. For one cowboy on his way back up, the legend Jess McLain, it represented a desperate attempt to return.

The week hadn't been bad for the hands from the J-Bar-M. Gary Russell had been thrown from his first bull the first Sunday out, but bounced back in the second round to take a small check. David Dallas showed that a black man could ride broncs. In the rookie saddle bronc event, he placed a respectable second and fourth on two heads to take home the average win, thus earning his full membership in pro rodeo. The biggest name to come out loud and strong, smoking the competition, was Rebecca Sharpe, now Rebecca Sharpe-McLain, beating her competitors on her acclaimed horse Tommy Boy. She finished with both a first and second in the first and second go. A consistent run in the day's finals would win her the average and a shot at the world title, if she and Tommy Boy could stay healthy for the rest of the season. With Ashley there, the rumors ran hard. Everywhere throughout the arena and hangouts, the whispers flowed that the myth had returned.

The Ranger-cowboy Jess McLain lived up to his reputation. The silent professional sneaked in the back door to the finals and sat in third place. Through his first ride he struggled in the first go-around on a horse that one stock contractor had said was inconsistent and just plain mean.

Jess stayed in the saddle and finished in the top seven. In the second go and the last Saturday performance to qualify for the finals, McLain's comeback proved true after posting an eighty-one-point ride on Sterling Rodeo's Copenhagen Black'n'Tan.

The big paint horse scored the highest of any bronc thus far at the show. Still, it was only second best. Jason Grey, hometown boy of Cheyenne, put on a legendary ride aboard Sterling's Lady Sadie Skoal. Grey and McLain had not run into each other yet, but Jess made it a point to come down a day early to watch. From the stands, he understood why the reigning all-around world champion was on top of the list. On a horse that left him hurting for two weeks, Grey made bronc riding look easy and received eighty-seven points.

The top fifteen lineup of riders boasted names like Etbauer, Mortenson, Johnson, Reeves, and more. Grey sat on top but McLain was eager to challenge the younger superstar.

Sunday brought a reunion. The extended rodeo cowboy family welcomed the return of one of its own and took Jess back with open arms.

McLain made his way to the contestant area underneath the east grandstand. The large area was fenced off by chain link to separate fans and onlookers from the competitors. Security checked everyone coming in to make sure they belonged. Two men in black shirts only said hello to Jess; they knew he was in his rightful place. Inside, contestants had begun to assemble. McLain spotted an open spot, and found himself next to an old friend. Setting down his gear bag and saddle, he took a seat on the edge of the fence. In his white straw hat and freshly starched white Wrangler shirt and pressed jeans, he was hard to miss.

"Good to see you, Jason," he said to a familiar cowboy nearby, extending his hand.

The cowboy grinned and returned the handshake.

"Well hell, looky here. It's not a rumor after all. Good to see you back." Jason Grey greeted his old friend.

Jason wore a black felt hat, creased the same as McLain's, and a bright white shirt. "Haven't seen you since the first of January. How the hell is life treating you?"

"Can't complain, good to be back. Be doing better if I was in the lead, though." Jess winked and began to rummage through his gear bag.

"The day's still young. Did you see that Chris is here? Did you know he ended up losing his ranch down in Eaton? You should go and say hello to Wade Davis. He was asking about you." Jason glanced around to see if he could find any of those mentioned.

"Asking what?" McLain asked.

"If it was true. Had to see it with our own eyes. Should we go hunt 'em down?" asked Jason with a serious look in his eyes.

"Oh, I will. Just want to relax here for a spell. How's your father-in-law?" Jess asked, reminding himself that rodeo was made up of competitors who are extremely close. A family that's hard to break into, but one that's caring and loyal. Jason had weathered a rough year, and Jess knew all too well what he was going through.

"Well, he took it pretty hard when my wife passed, but he should be here today," Grey replied, dropping his tone.

"How 'bout you? You doin' all right?" Jess queried. "Ashley was askin' about you, too."

Jason paused briefly before answering. "Well, it was hard there the first months, but now I just take it one day at a time. Trying to keep my head into my job."

"I been down that road. You should come up to the ranch sometime and we'll have a few brews. Talk about it if you want," Jess said, pulling his chaps from his bag.

"Thanks, Jess. I just may have to do that. Hey, but no matter the outcome, it's good to see you back. Come on, let's go. See who else we can find." Jess and Grey proceeded to seek out old road friends, with hearty handshakes and welcomes all around. McLain had returned, and full circle.

The stands filled quickly. People flooded the stairs trying to find their seats. Even the cheap seats sold out, everyone wanting to see the show beneath the hot afternoon Wyoming sun. The press buzzed about and TV cameramen sought interviews. It wouldn't be long before "The Daddy of 'Em All" would be well underway. The box seats also began to fill with VIPs. Amy had heard that these were the best seats in the house to watch the best rodeo in the world. They were filled with corporate sponsors, rodeo contributors and superstars.

Amy felt strangely inconspicuous as she sat in a VIP box with people she didn't know and didn't care for. Marketing and publicity types all seemed so transparent: she felt like she could see right through them. Adopting the McLain style of diplomacy, she found herself reacting to them sharply, answering questions straight to the point. She quickly acquired a reputation as a hard-nosed cowgirl who tolerated no pretense, and one whose number-one priority was her music and her fans.

The previous night's concert had been a wakeup call for everyone, including her. The single "Time and Tears" had climbed into the top ten since it was released on the first of April, and Amy wasn't an unknown anymore. She discovered that signing autographs and having fans tugging at her, all trying to get a piece, would take some getting used to.

Amy continued to sport a down-home attitude. She wore faded Wranglers bunched up over her worn riding boots and her favorite denim shirt, which had seen its share of saddle time. The straw hat was new but creased, like she belonged on the arena floor. The only things that sparkled were her bright smile when she let it and the gold buckle given to her by Ashley. She wondered how Jess had stayed away from rodeo for five years. She had only been there a short time and was already under its spell.

"Hey, there are some comp tickets for fifth row up from the chutes. You more interested in seeing this from there?" asked Marty. "It's in the sun, but . . ."

"Yes!" Amy interrupted. "Let's go." She stood up, grabbing the worn J-Bar-M coat, which, if it didn't rain or get cloudy, would be way too hot to wear. But unlike the buckle, it was something she had earned.

"Where are you going?"

The new publicist he'd hired, Natalie Rose, a recent college grad from Chicago, was determined to shadow Amy wherever she went.

"Natalie or me should go with you. After last night you're liable to get mobbed," Marty said.

"We don't want any of these hicks making a scene," Natalie added.

"Hey, the only thing that will cause a scene is you. Remember, you work for a hick. Let's go, Bob. Take me to a rodeo!"

Bobby followed her out, assuring Marty that she'd be fine. Heistler tried not to chuckle over how Amy put the other girl in her place.

As they walked down the back stairs, some people gazed and whispered as Amy passed, but she ignored them. Looking over to her left, she peered through the chain-link fence. It only took a few seconds to see that this was the contestants' corner. Cowboys filled the area, readying themselves for battle. They weren't anything like the part-timers and weekend warriors that sometimes rode on Thursday nights at the J-Bar-M. These were the elite, the ones who traveled full time and made a living doing so.

"Well, there he is," Bobby pointed to Jess. "The prodigal son has returned. Damned if it isn't the great one."

Amy looked over and saw Jess McLain being mobbed by other riders. Surrounded, he was smiling at his fans. He appeared to finally be at home. She also saw one of the men standing with him who seemed familiar. Although she had only been around rodeo for a short time, his image and his reputation preceded him. One man, poking fun at Jess, just laughing along, also looked like someone she knew from the media.

"Aren't those two guys Jason Grey and Wade Davis?"

"I think so. I've only seen their faces on the tube, but I think that's them. Funny, Grey looks bigger on TV," Bob said as they made their way to the bottom step.

"Is there anyone Jess doesn't know?" Amy asked.

"You know, no matter how Jess may have ended up, Amy, there was a time when he was really special in that saddle. I hope he finds it there again," Bob said as they made their way along the walk to a concession stand.

Watching people, Amy started to feel more comfortable around them. Since she could pick out a wannabe or a "buckle bunny" in a blink, she felt more experienced, as if she almost belonged. Some younger people passed by and said her name. When she turned, she knew they had her. Amy signed a few autographs and had her picture taken with the group, then cut it short when she sighted a tall cowboy. Excusing herself, she sought him out.

"Ike?" she called out. Instead of a hug, Ike shook her hand.

"Well, Miss Talbot, you look great! Want you to know, my daughter likes your music. Pretty classy," he said.

Amy had always been in awe of Ike, who now treated her like an equal. In Wyoming and especially at Frontier Days, he was the true star.

"Well, please tell her thanks. I'll send her an autographed CD. It's good to see you."

"You too. Can't stay long. I have the draw sheet here and I need to get it up on the wall," he told her.

"What horses do you have up today?" she asked.

"Well, they're half mine and half other stock. I have Lady Sadie, Big Foot, Painted Wagon, and a few you may not know like Crazy Eighties and the new bronc-riding nightmare, Fire'n'Lace, or at least that's what we been calling her."

"Fire'n'Lace? I assume she's a mare?" she asked, knowing he was in a hurry.

"Yep."

"So who did Jess draw in the finals?"

"He drew one of my new horses. Should be a good ride to watch. Look me up when the show is over. I need to get this sheet up," Ike said, heading toward the pens.

"Thanks for the info," called Amy. "Tell Jess good luck if you see him." *Oh God, please don't let him get hurt,* Amy thought as Ike walked away.

She returned to Bob Dall who had grown

tired of waiting and was standing in a concession line. "So, who was that?" he said, as they moved up one spot.

"Ike Sterling."

"You're not kidding? And you were asking who doesn't Jess know? Even I know who Ike Sterling is — the living legend of rodeo and stock contractors."

"Wish I could see Jess before he rides," Amy said wistfully. "But that wouldn't be fair."

He could see through her cover-up. "You should find him after the show's over. Don't let it wait."

Interrupted by more teens clamoring for autographs. Amy was able to leave the thought behind briefly. Suddenly, before her stood a young man with a familiar smile.

He spoke first. "Hi, Jersey," Brookes Bowers said shyly.

He was the same Brookes that Amy remembered, but just not as scruffy — more clean-cut than when up at the ranch. She tried to get a handle on the moment. "Brookes Bowers, how the heck are you?"

"Oh, doing okay. Living in Cody with one of my teachers," he answered.

Bob could tell Amy felt uncomfortable, but he stayed out of the way.

"Good. Glad to hear you're back in

school. And your sister?" Amy asked bluntly.

"She's okay. She's living in Casper. Starting at Casper College this month. Working for a bank down there," Brookes said, putting his hands in his pockets.

Amy didn't let up. "What brings you all the way down here?"

"I came down with some friends early this morning. Wanted to see Gary and Dallas ride." Brookes fumbled with his words.

Amy was seasoned enough to know what a day sheet was and who had made it and who hadn't. She called him out.

"Brookes, I hate to disappoint you, but Gary didn't make the finals and you know that the rookie saddle bronc event is only two rounds with no finals. If you came down here to see them ride, it looks like you may be out of luck," she informed him politely.

Brookes struggled, his eyes filled with disappointment. Bob stepped forward to order for them both, allowing Amy to talk to the young boy. Brookes continued, "Well, uh, I was thinking I would run into Jess here."

"Really?" Amy was amazed by his confession.

"I kinda wanted to apologize for how I left. I didn't really have it that bad at the ranch. Guess I was just pissed. I miss being there. I mean, where I'm staying at now is okay, but I don't have a dog or horses and anyone to hang out with. I would rather clean stalls than sit and watch the tube all the time. Anyway, I have to get going." He could spill no more.

"I see you still have the manners Jess taught you," Amy answered brightly, coming back with a reassuring smile. "It's nice to see a gentleman. Maybe someday you can go back. Good luck, Brookes, and say hello to Brenda. Tell her I miss you both." Amy planted a kiss on Brookes's cheek, raising a crimson blush on his sunburned face.

Brookes returned to his friends who assailed him with questions as to how he knew Amy Talbot. He waved to her when he went to his group. She waved back.

"You keep up being who you are, Amy, you're going to be just fine," said Bob. "Back in February, I would have never guessed you'd be here. You're on your way." They made their way back to the stairs en route to their seats. Amy looked and saw Jess signing autographs for a group of young cowboys and cowgirls with their parents in tow.

"Maybe, but will I be alone at the top?" she asked, watching while Jess was engulfed by mobs of children. Bob looked in Jess's direction.

"Yep, but broken hearts sing the best country music. Why don't you just tell him? You may be hiding it from him, but you sure aren't good at hiding it from me," he added.

"No, not now anyway. He's back where he belongs."

"Maybe you belong with him. Ever think of that?"

"Maybe. Let's go sit down."

Amy watched Jess from a distance as he shook a young boy's hand and signed the kid's program. Two worlds apart, these kinds of fans were something new to her. Handling them was something McLain clearly had done for a long time.

"Aren't we a pair, rodeo man," she sang to herself. "Aren't we a pair?"

Chapter Thirty-seven

The Reckoning

"Ah shit. Just what I need — colt-riding practice." Jess walked away from the recently posted day sheet. It didn't take a study session to know he had drawn an unknown bronc in a string of world champions being ridden by world champions. It looked bleak in the winning department.

Grey, Mortenson, all three Etbauer brothers and Ronnie Dixx had all drawn deep: horses with résumés like prizefighters. Jess fought not to let disappointment set in. Grey looked more optimistic at McLain's draw.

"Hey, at least it's a Sterling horse. You still have a shot. Should see the nag of his I drew in Bares. Damn. Well, I drew good in the bulls. Hell, could have a good day with all three. Don't sweat it, old man. I'm sure you still have some magic in those golden spurs."

Jess nodded and knew it could be worse. He envied the younger competitor, though he wouldn't admit he, too, wished he were in more than one event.

They both returned to their places and proceeded to ready themselves for the war that lay ahead. Jess took his time putting on his spurs and taping his wrists. The vest and chaps would come before show time, no need to give the Cheyenne sun more ammunition to drain a man. Jess looked over at Grey. With a neck roll on his vest, a hinged brace covered by at least a full roll of athletic tape, and a shin guard substituted to a forearm guard, he looked like a gladiator.

"Christ! When did you start wearing all that?" McLain said.

He watched Grey stand up and grab his bareback rig from the ground. Grey grinned as the sound of wild horses being run in the loading chutes sounded behind them.

"When I started winning world titles," he said and winked.

McLain knew Grey to be one of the humblest riders around. He wasn't bragging. His confidence came from demonstrated ability. "Quit grinding your teeth over your pony and come help me win some money."

McLain shook his head and smiled back. Both made their way through the narrow gate under the stands to the backside of the bucking chutes. Once outside, the bright noonday sun poured over them and they were engulfed in the sounds of the crowd watching the opening act.

A wave of mounted riders began to make its way along the track. Flanked by beautiful ladies with bright white hats and colorful flags, the guest of honor rode, waving to the crowd. A sea of red, white and blue poured down the path separating the west arena stands from the arena floor and east tiers. Waving and smiling, the participants continued to file along the dirt to the sounds of patriotic tunes. Several members of the armed forces sat in wagons and waved to the cheering crowd. It was a salute to the military on the last day of Frontier Days and they pulled out all the stops. Servicemen and women packed the audience.

Over a dozen American flags made their way in the arena on horseback during the parade. The cowgirls who carried them rode around the arena in patterns, with Old Glory flying in their wake. The announcer gave thanks to the men and women who had fought and died for their country and explained that they were the true reason why all the fans could enjoy the rodeo on that hot Wyoming Sunday afternoon in the greatest nation in the world. When they came to a stop, the announcer asked for a moment of silence in remembrance of those who had given their lives for this great land.

Jess and Grey had just finished putting the bareback rig on Jason's draw. The horse had stood like an old vet, and now the rest would be up to a good flank man, along with a little luck.

The two waited on the platform of the chute, gazing across the arena. Both stood and listened to the announcer talk about America and those who had heeded her call and not returned. Jess milled about and paid attention to his own world. Grey couldn't help but notice his uneasiness. Just as he did, a Marine honor guard standing on the concrete platform at the other end of the arena began to play taps, paying homage to those who had lost their lives. Jess snapped straight up and stared across the field, now deathly still. Holding his hat over his chest, Jason leaned over and spoke under his breath, "You all right?"

Jess stared at the flag, his gaze steadfast. "Yeah. Funny, I haven't heard taps on the bugle since I handed Larry his son's flag."

Wrestling with memories, he remained at attention. When the bugler had finished, he did an about-face in proper military style and rejoined the other members of the honor guard made up of a representative from each branch of the service. From there, the national anthem engulfed the stadium. McLain studied the audience on the other side of the arena and noted several representatives had assembled for the opening ceremony. Most wore head covers of the U.S. Army.

He saw a green beret and it reminded him of how loyal those brethren were to each other and also to him. The sight took him back to the trial and how the Green Berets who made it back to the mainland stood up for him, even if it meant their careers. According to them, Jess and Jack had saved lives, making sure no man was left behind. He saw sand-colored berets and remembered when Rangers had worn black. Still, they reminded him of the colors he'd worn and how proud his family was the day he was awarded his Ranger tab for graduating. They reminded him too of how angry he'd felt the day he packed away his uniform and black beret and how he'd struggled to be proud of what he had done in the midst of blame and scapegoating.

The announcer's voice came back after the anthem had finished and gave one last request to the audience.

"Ladies and gentlemen, as you sit and

enjoy the rodeo today, keep our soldiers in your thoughts, and if you're sitting next to one of those veterans, shake his hand and thank him for the great sacrifice he paid for our great nation. Now, let's ride some bareback horses!"

Jess replaced his hat and watched Jason Grey climb up the chute. Sitting on the top rung, Jason pulled his white and metallic purple chaps back so they hung over the sides of his knees. He rested his right foot on the horse's back, just to let it know he was there and keep it calm while other horses began to buck out clear on the other end. With his bareback glove taped on at the wrist, he adjusted his hat. Then he reached across his chest with his free hand and extended it to Jess. McLain watched and looked puzzled.

"What, you won't shake my hand, old man?" asked Jason.

"Normally, you shake a man's hand and thank him for his help after you're done riding, Skippy," Jess said with a smile, referencing Jason's comment that he was younger than he. Still, he shook his hand.

"I'll thank you for that when I win here. Thanks, though," he said as he released his grip.

"For what?"

"For serving. You used to be one of those guys over there in uniform. Just thought I would say thanks, war hero."

Grey might have been twenty-six years old, but he sounded like a wise older man. They looked out into the arena and watched the first horse blow out of the chute.

Jess savored the moment. A man thanking him for giving four years of his life to protect his country. He tipped his hat, nodding his head. As they watched the first rider make the whistle, he finally spoke. "Interesting. That's the first time anyone's ever thanked me. Not like I asked for it, but it's odd. Takes on a whole new meaning."

"Well, pard, then it was long overdue. The battle's in the arena today. Let's earn some money."

Jess collected his thoughts. He didn't come to rodeo to receive an award. Still, for the first time since putting away his Army greens, he felt proud. It helped put to bed the shameful demons of the past. All he could do was smile.

Chapter Thirty-eight

Ghost Rider

Saddle bronc horses thundered in to the loading chutes. Grunts and squeals came from impatient mares and geldings kicking the gates that separated them. The turn-back alley separated the ten bucking chutes, five per side. And wild rage quivered inside every box. On occasion, a horse would rear or buck inside the holding area. A wealth of hide had poured in and now awaited saddling. Outweighing the competitors, most well over 1,100 pounds, the broncs impatiently awaited a chance to test a cowboy's nerve, skill, and their ultimate threshold of pain.

Cowboys suited up for battle and conversations stopped. The chute director helped to point out the stock brand numbers to the cowboys. Those in the front scurried to get their equipment on the right side if their horse happened to be on the other side of the alley. This was an interesting feat in itself because it required a cowboy to climb over the loading chutes, over already unhappy broncs, and into the alleyway. Then, up the opposite side, over another horse and the inside of the loading area. Scurrying over horses and chute walls in chaps is a trick. Carrying a bronc saddle, halter and bronc rein on top of that is even more difficult, to say the least.

Jason Grey's horse would buck out first. Grey and McLain made their ways out to the loading chutes to get Grey's horse saddled up. The chute director called out a series of numbers in a hectic pace while cowboys scrambled. McLain's brand hadn't been called, so that told him he would be close to last.

Grey climbed up on to the chute and began to put the halter around the bay's nose. Silver Tongue Skoal stood there as if utterly bored. All the while, Grey talked to the horse like it was a child, using soothing words and giving it an occasional scratch at the shoulder. The bronc rocked his head on occasion just to be difficult, but in a short time the halter was on.

McLain handed up the saddle and Grey eased it onto the horse's back. Holding the saddle, quickly Jess reached through the gate with a long metal hook and gingerly pulled the cinch to his side. Feeding the latigos through the strings, McLain had the back cinch loosely buckled. Since Grey was first, he tightened up everything right away. In a flash, he tucked the excess latigos underneath the seat, buckled the back cinch, and all was ready. McLain eased up to the platform in Chute Number Nine and held the horse's head. Grey pulled the bronc rein tightly to the swells of the saddle, past his fist that rested up against the middle, measured it, and let off. Tying a piece of leather at the mark, he waited for the chute.

Ike made his way to Chute Number Nine. Sterling was old school; he flanked his own horses. Standing on the second to top rung, he got hold of the leather tail that was hooked between two D-rings on the flank strap. The horse would kick it loose by the end of the ride and be unlatched by the pick-up men, but its application could determine how much the animal would perform. Sitting on the top rung, Grey swept his chaps aside, the bronc-rein firmly in his grip foot, resting on the seat of the saddle. Ike told him to get ready.

"Okay, Jay, crotch him!"

It was a command that Grey had never heard and he started to chuckle. The announcer had made a big deal about Grey and how the reigning All-Around World Champion was on a world-class bucking horse. Shouldering in, Silver gave him no fuss. Feet in the stirrups, Grey leaned back and nodded his head.

With an excited crowd sparked by the opening of the gate, the large bay took a run out of the chute. Ike jerked up on the flank, tightening the belt, and then the horse broke.

Violent lunges and bucks lifted her with every jump. Grey's head and body remained calm and still in the saddle. His only movement was that of his feet. They spurred back with every jump, only to charge to the front of the horse's shoulders and beat the bronc's front hooves to the ground. Throwing his free arm back, he lifted on the rein every time the horse tried to bury its head between the plunging front legs. The whistle blew and eight seconds were over. Grey rode two more jumps, leaving nothing for the judges to guess about. He didn't wait for the pick-up men and leapt from the saddle. Coming to his feet, he tipped his hat to the horse and waved to the crowd.

Making his way back to the fence, the announcer called out a score of seventy-nine points. Good time, obviously putting him in first for the moment, but a score that could be toppled. He had already come up short in the bareback event, but shooting for three wins was his objective and he just smiled big as he made his way back.

"Damn, Ike, that guy can ride," Jess said. Ike just smiled.

"For one, the kid is bigger than you, and last year he didn't make the top fifteen, so don't give it to him yet. You haven't rode." He didn't want to downplay the younger hand's talent but he knew his friend needed some confidence.

"So, Ike, I have to ask. The horse I drew, Fire'n'Lace? I never heard of her. What can I do to get a few more points out of her?" Jess followed Ike to the next bucking chute.

Ike took a short second to convey a message he had planned to wait on. "Well, cover her. Nobody's made eight seconds yet. You've ridden rank broncs before. Just keep a deep seat and give her a double on the rein: she buries her head."

Jess assumed he was done and turned to walk away. Ike called McLain back. "Jess, one more thing. No matter what happens, no matter what you see — and I mean it — no matter what you see, just ride. Savvy?"

"You're the man, Ike. Sounds like a plan." Jess winked and made his way back to the chutes.

Standing by his saddle, Grey joined McLain, grinning from ear to ear. He unzipped his protective vest and slapped Jess on the back. A small group of people were within earshot and heard Grey say, "Boys, you could wear Kotex and win money at this show," getting a laugh from everyone but McLain, who just smirked.

"Classy, Jay. Real classy."

Grey leaned closer and whispered, "Hey, I have to get into these guys' heads somehow. That score didn't secure shit for me. I need all the help I can get. Don't tell me that you never played mind games, old man."

Jess nodded and knew he had done the same in the past. He was just glad there were no women there to hear the sexist comment. Then the chute coordinator's voice carried out: "Last horse is J23, Fire'n'Lace. Saddle her up."

Jess grabbed his saddle and walked around the corner. He could hear a horse fighting the chute, screaming loudly. The kicking of hooves sounded like lightning crashing through the alleyway. Jess made his way back through the narrow loading area with Grey in tow. Finding his place, he stopped dead when he saw what stood before him.

The large horse was thick and muscled. She sported a long, tangled mane and big, feathered hooves and must have stood close to 1,400 pounds. Every ounce was mean, every ounce wild. And her color: the satin, blue-speckled roan ranged from pure indigo to charcoal black, and was so lustrous, she even shimmered in the shade. Jess stood studying the horse, who eyed him nervously. The colt of Dancing Wind, now called Fire'n'Lace, held Jess McLain's fate in the minutes to come. No one could get within four feet of the mare without her coming apart. Rearing and kicking, she seemed so mean that even the flank man stayed away. Grey moved with a hook at the ready behind Jess.

"Okay, so what's the plan?"

Not answering, Jess handed him the saddle and slowly crept up the chute. The mare stood still, quivering violently and stomping her hooves on occasion to let everyone know she was pissed. She had been kept by herself, away from the other broncs, because she was so aggressive. Now the arena hands and rodeo workers watched as this man appeared to use magic to get up close. Standing on the rungs of the loading chute, he gently rubbed her neck. An arena hand came over on the other side with a six-foot rope and proceeded to try and toss it over the horse's neck. Normally, tying a crazed horse's head in was okay, but not today. Jess caught the rope in the air and threw it back in the young hand's face.

"Hey! We have to tie her in, bud," the hand said.

"The hell you do. Now step back. She won't fight me." Jess proceeded to halter her. She shook but didn't fight.

"How do you know she won't fight you?" the hand shot back.

"Because I helped birth her. Now go away," McLain said.

"Oh, there he is!" Amy said as she sat up in her seat. Bob stayed relaxed. They both watched as Jess walked down in front of the chute area. His horse ran in and Amy watched him climb the chute with another cowboy. Studying the horse, she sat back and waited. She could see it suddenly, plain as day. "Why is he riding his own horse? How does that work?"

"It's not his horse anymore," Bobby said, sipping his Coke. He tried to leave the booze behind, at least in Amy's presence. Amy turned and looked hard at Bobby Dall.

"What do you mean? That's Dance's colt. He wouldn't sell that horse," she said.

"Oh, I guess you didn't know."

"Didn't know what, Bob?"

"Well, how do you think you had such a nice apartment for yourself and Terry Ann to stay in? All your food and the rental car? Costs big bucks. When I came to get you, I asked if Jess had some money. He gave back the check for ten Gs and sold that horse to Ike for fifteen grand or something." He paused. "I thought you knew."

"But that money was supposed to bail out the ranch. Bob, how could you let him do it? Damn it." She sat back and watched Jess ready his horse.

"I didn't ask. He offered. Don't ever think nobody believes in you. Don't worry. I wouldn't let him take his name off the company. He'll get it back soon."

She breathed a little easier, and the crowd roared as they watched the horse rear up and try to climb over the chute wall. Jess and Jason Grey got her back under control, but it didn't look like it was going to be easy to get the mare out.

"He better, Bob. Promise me."

"Got my word, Amy."

Ike made his way over and climbed up the chute. Jess sat on the rung, gripping the bronc rein, his inside foot in the saddle. Buckskin and white chaps draped over his knees and a thick black vest protected his chest. Ike readied the flank.

"You never wore a vest before. When did you start wearing a vest?" Grey asked, staying away from the horse's head.

Jess just smiled and looked at him. "When I decided to start trying to beat world champions."

"Touché, smart ass. Well, just beat my seventy-nine and you're a daisy," Grey replied.

Ike gave Jess the okay to shoulder down. Jess leaned down and spoke to the gate men first.

"Hey, pay attention, because I want to get her out quick. The second my ass touches the seat, I'll be nodding," Jess instructed. The gate men nodded in return.

Shouldering down gently, Fire'n'Lace began to quiver even more. Sweat ran down her sides and the blue roan glistened. Jess was true to his word. In one motion he slipped his feet into both stirrups and brought his butt to the seat, then nodded his head.

The gate was flung open and caught the mare off guard. For a split second, she hesitated, then Jason Grey pushed her head out. Instead of taking a run at the arena, she reared straight up on her hind legs, turning to an angle when she came down.

Jess lifted on the rein, hugging the saddle and reaching up with his spurs, turning himself almost completely upside down. The force from her slamming back down to the ground would have sent most riders right over the front, but McLain leaned back and took the shock of the first plunge in stride. As he remained steadfast in the saddle, she exploded with the glowing power of a Wyoming sunrise, her front hooves alone rising three feet off the ground. Floating like a demon in the camera flashes, she would have lit up the stands if the show had been at night. Dropping her head between her legs as she descended to the earth, she made a powerful landing on all fours.

Jess's spurs made it to her shoulders before her feet could hit the ground. She exploded time and time again in a wild display of violent eruptions, ragged but edged with grace. In mid-ride, Jess appeared to fly out of the saddle. Those at the chute gate could hear his spurs click together over the seat and beneath him. The mare slammed to the ground, now ducking and diving with her head, dropping like a boulder from the sky to the dirt. A miracle occurred at every landing. Jess stayed on, time and time again.

With each jump that sent him out of the saddle, Jess managed to come back to his seat, his free arm reaching behind, picture perfect. Fans stood up in their seats in disbelief, hooting and hollering for more.

The stands on all sides were flooded with cheers and screams, none louder than those coming from a beaming blonde in the fifth row. Amy prayed Jess would triumph and not get hurt. Cowboys watched in awe as the magician and the blue roan leaped and danced. The usually reserved Ike Sterling cheered and coached at every jump. With each takeoff of the horse, each ripple of sheer power that rolled through her body, McLain returned to the saddle. When all appeared lost and a buck-off inevitable, still he stayed.

The buzzer sounded at last, and with one more jump that left the horse airborne, McLain reached his spurs to the front one more time, so high that the moment felt frozen in time. Jess double-grabbed, but in vain. Fire'n'Lace got her wish and rocketed the cowboy to the ground, only she was a second too late.

McLain rolled through the dirt, visibly shaken. He came up slowly, but he did come up. Even those not in the rodeo world knew he had accomplished the impossible and survived. Walking back to the chutes, slowly and with a small limp, he held his hat up to the audience. Standing at the chute, the score clinched the drama of that brilliant, unforgettable afternoon.

"The great one returns, folks!" the announcer cheered. "You saw it here today — my, oh my! And the judges say, 'Eighty-five points'! Your Cheyenne Frontier Days Saddle Bronc Champion, Jess McLain! Let him know you liked what you saw!"

The flag girl approached with another horse in pony. Jess shook out the dust and waved at the crowd. The winner's lap would be taken by him: a short gallop around the arena to thank the fans, to stand up and be recognized. Stopping by the chute where Ike and Jason stood, he extended his hand to Ike, who accepted and shook it.

"Okay, old man. Take your lap. And take your time. You earned it. Just wish my money wasn't attached to it," Jason laughed.

Jess mounted up, but instead of bringing his horse to a lope around the arena, he held his hat in his hand and walked the animal. Not normal protocol, but he'd returned, and in a big way. He wanted to savor every second. The horse even pranced, seeming to feed off the moment.

"Damn, the check would have been nice," Jason said. "Looks like my luck ain't too hot today, Ike. Two second places."

Sterling answered, "Maybe, but you have another ride coming, and that was worth the money. McLain truly has a gift. That was nothing short of magic. You think you could have rode that horse?"

Grey paused, spat in the dirt and said, "I would have given it one hell of a go, but that's one mean bronc."

"You think she's rank? You should have seen her mother. She was special."

Amy sat back and watched Jess make his way slowly around the arena. The fans adored him. Then the announcer joined in, telling of the accident that had kept the magician from riding for four years. Only a few people knew that the horse that had just carried him to victory was the direct descendent of the one that almost killed him.

"Larry was right," Amy said aloud, speaking for the first time since McLain had exploded out of the gate.

"Right about what?" Bobby asked.

"He said Jess was one in a million. He's right. I wonder what he'll do now?"

"I would venture to say he'll shoot for Vegas. For the top money, the rodeo finals. That's a hard row to hoe this late in the season but I think he's on his way."

Thinking about the past seven months and what had transpired, Amy could only agree. She looked over the crowd and noticed four young ladies that called out McLain's name as though they knew him. Halter-topped and heavily made up, they screamed like cheerleaders. Amy just shook her head as the love of her life finished up his victory lap.

"Buckle bunnies. God, I can't stand 'em."

Chapter Thirty-nine

Sunset

The day ended in glory. Months of anticipation, only to fly by, left competitors wishing for more. Wyoming's legendary show was over for another year and, like the setting sun, it had brightened an unforgettable week in the American West.

Fans poured out almost as fast as they had poured in after the award ceremony. Even the relentless Wyoming wind took time off to acknowledge the champions. It had been a day of coming out, of returning, and a day of reckoning.

The bull riding saw Jason Grey bucked off. With two second places he clinched the All-Around. But the focus that day was not on the modern-day legends like Sandvick, Mortenson or Hancock. One cowboy, the conqueror, Jess McLain, had received a standing ovation and had added Cheyenne Frontier Days to his list of conquests.

The press hadn't even let his spurs cool before they were in his face, asking for more. Question after question rolled by and

Jess answered like the celebrity he was, yet with humility. It was all he could do to get back and round up his gear. The contestant area had cleared except for fans, who flocked around the gated area, waiting to get a piece of the winners. Only Jess and Jason Grey remained while the other cowboys fought through the crowd. Jason had cut his interviews short and sweet. Jess, on the other hand, had obliged everyone with a program and a pen. The two sat and joked about the day, hoping they could get away sometime soon.

Amy and Bobby made their way back up to the VIP box only to see those inside pacing feverishly. Something important was obviously happening and conversations flew. Everyone seemed to be on cell phones. Marty was almost hysterical, and the PR girl gabbed wildly to someone on her line. Marty finally put an end to the chaos, shouting, "Everybody shut up!" He pocketed his phone. Turning to Bob and Amy, he asked, "You want the good news or the great news?"

"Either. Just spill it," said Amy, holding her breath.

"Okay, I can't believe this. All right, all right . . ."

"Come on, Marty, just say it," Bob insisted.

"As of today, Amy Talbot and 'Time and Tears' hit number one on the Billboard top-fifty country singles! Albums are being preordered!"

Everyone in the room began to cheer and clap. Amy had officially arrived. Stunned, she exhaled and collapsed in the nearest chair. She closed her eyes and smiled for the second time that day. Jess would have loved to hear this. Bob patted her on the back and just winked. She wanted to celebrate but stayed grounded. Like the true professional she had become, she quieted the group.

"Okay, Marty, just so I can only have one heart attack, what's the other news?"

"Oh, no big deal. Only that Willie-boy loved you so much, he wants you to continue. You're now booked through December as the opener for him. What'd I tell ya? What'd I tell ya? We leave in three hours. You have another show day after tomorrow in Jacksonville, Mississippi. You're on your way, girl!"

"Oh my God, I can't believe this!" Amy tried to take it all in. Suddenly, her dream had come true. Now, instead of playing for pieces, she'd be playing real venues. She savored the moment but kept her head, knowing the real work lay ahead. Long nights on the road, different towns every other day, and during it all, trying to come up with a follow-up album. It was almost overwhelming.

Natalie intruded, breaking into her thoughts. "We already have two radio station interviews in Jacksonville on Tuesday morning. Wow!"

"Let the party begin," urged Bobby. "Okay, folks, good change of events. We need to get the vans loaded up. Road trip."

The group dispersed. Amy pulled Bob aside as everyone filtered out. "But, Bob, I kinda wanted to head up to Purgatory for a day. I mean this fast? Just like that?" She felt confused.

"Welcome to the big time. We have to be on the road in a short while. If you have any business you want to take care of, hon, I suggest you do it now. Good job, kid. I know he'll be proud."

With that, Bobby left. Amy sat in the VIP room with her publicist waiting outside. It was strange how alone she felt.

"Hey, old man, you pack slower than a schoolgirl. So what's your plan?" Grey asked, observing that the crowds were dying a little but they would still get no clean escape.

Zipping up his bag, Jess leaned back and

adjusted his hat. "Well, I took a gamble and entered a couple of shows, so with this win I think I'm going to hit 'em. How about you, Tiger?"

"Oh, I didn't think I had it in me this year, losing the wife and all, but I think I'm going to try for a repeat. So I have to ask — who're you going down the road with?"

Jess took a second to grasp the question. How long it had been, but how welcome it felt. "No one, right now. This show was my deciding point. Why? You traveling with anybody?"

"On occasion I go with Wade and my brother, but if I'm going to keep this party going and try to repeat it, I need to really hit it. I have this bareback rider that hooks up with me, but if you're interested, I think we could make a hell of a run."

Grey stood up, stretching out his body. Young or not, three events had left him sore. Putting his bag over his shoulder, he awaited McLain's decision. In a blink, McLain was completely back. "Let's do it. I'm up in Bakersfield day after tomorrow, so I guess we need to get on the road." He grabbed his bag and the saddle.

"No kiddin'? Me too. Sounds like we need to make some tracks. I don't like being late. Let's take my rig. Sponsor pays for the fuel, supplies the truck. Pretty good deal. We can park yours at the house," Grey said, and the two walked out, leaving the contestant haven for the last time.

"I can't believe this, boy. When it rolls it rolls. I'll tell my sister to head back up with the boys. She can take care of things for a spell. Plus I know she's pissed about taking fifth in the finals."

The two superstars walked out and proceeded to do the usual signing of autographs. Grey was pestered more than Jess; nevertheless, fame had rediscovered McLain. Talking with people and shaking hands, McLain looked through the small crowd, noticed a familiar face twenty feet in the background, looking straight at him. Smiling, he politely excused himself from the group and left his bag and saddle with Jason.

In the midst of signing pictures, McLain made his way to a woman, waiting alone by the stands. Although Jess and Amy stood right in front of each other, they might as well have been miles apart. Unable to meet each other's eyes, each struggled for words they couldn't find. Jess saw Natalie, cell phone in hand, standing by not ten feet away. It was an opportunity to break the silence.

"Does she have to be with you?" he asked.

Amy nodded her head and threw her arms around his neck anyway, hugging him hard. Then she slid her hands down around his waist and said, "Forget her. You'll never believe this. Guess what?"

"What?"

"Someone you know has a number-one single. Someone you know is booked with Willie Nelson until December!" She looked into his eyes, hoping he would approve.

"Really now? Well, I expected no less."

Amy grew serious. "Yeah, and that same someone also loves you. A lot. Misses you at night. And all day."

Jess said nothing but drew her closer, kissing her for the first time without inhibition. Releasing her slowly, he had news of his own. "Listen, I want you to know I'm going to try and make the finals. The day was too good to pass this chance up. Thanks for . . . believing in me. Guess I needed you as much as you needed me. Fact is, I'm going to be traveling with Jason Grey. The guy drives me nuts, but it looks like we both have a long road ahead."

"Oh. I was hoping you could spend some time with me before I left," Amy said, regretting the answer. "But they say we have to get on the road soon."

"I wish I could too. But I can't. California is our first stop. Junior there wants to get on the road right away."

The uncomfortable tension had returned and the hard truth enveloped them both. Each understood that the price of dreams coming true is often the breaking of hearts. What they'd both overcome to reach success would now tear them apart.

Amy felt the futility of their accomplishment and hot tears welled up in her eyes as she sought a way to make Jess understand. But she couldn't. Embracing again, their final moment was cut short as Natalie interrupted, always impatient. "Amy, they're waiting. We really need to go."

The girl clicked her cell phone closed and excused herself, leaving Amy and Jess together. Tears flowing, Amy clung to him. "Why does it have to be this way? We're supposed to be together. I'm supposed to be happy right now," Amy sobbed.

Jess forced himself to be strong. "Amy, we'll be together . . . I promise. Look at me. I love you, and I'm pretty sure you love me, so it'll happen. I'm proud of you. It's your time to go now and get the job done."

"I need you, though," she said, hugging him again.

Holding her tight, he answered, "I need

you, too. No question we'll make it."

"Hey, old man, hate to be an ass, but we got to hit the road, chase some white lines to buckin' horses," Jason Grey called from a distance. His was the final pull that would rip them apart.

"Okay, on my way, tiger!" McLain answered. "Look, we'll make it work, okay?" he said, taking Amy's hand and kissing her on the cheek. "Now go! Go and be a star."

As if being led, she pulled away, letting go of his hand at last, and mouthed the words that she loved him. He stood and watched her go. After a few steps, she turned for one last word, one last look.

"Christmas in Purgatory?" she asked. Jess smiled and winked, hands on his hips, creating the picture she had seen so many times in her dreams.

"Nope. Meet you in Vegas: National Finals, December. See you there."

"Deal." She turned to walk away and, as she had done before, leaving Jess behind so she could pursue her dream. Only he knew now, just as she did, that one day she would return.

Making his way back to Jason, Jess held his emotions in check. Grey handed him his bag. It didn't take much to know that if a girl walking away was crying, the guy was probably in pain too. Throwing his bag over his shoulder, Jess grabbed his saddle and the two made their way to the parking area.

"She sure was pretty. Hope it's not over," Grey said.

McLain answered the best he could. "No, not over, but I won't be seeing her for a while. I guess that's how it goes."

"Doesn't make it any easier, amigo. Such is the life of the American rodeo cowboy. I'm sure you two will end up together. I could tell. She seemed heads up for you. I know that doesn't make it any easier right now, though. But you'll heal, cowboy. You'll heal." Grey spoke his feelings honestly.

"Yep, it'll just take a little time — and tears. But we'll make it," Jess answered, smiling at his own pun.

"Hey, I heard that song on the radio coming up here. Some new gal with one hell of a voice," Grey said, thinking he was changing the conversation as he adjusted his hat.

"Yep," answered Jess, "that she does. That's for damn sure."

Acknowledgements

To the riders, the rodeo hands and the stock contractors, some good friends that inspired the characters in my entire series, *The Seven Roads to Cheyenne*.

Although I had to change some names, each horse, or bull was real and a few of them almost killed me. To the bucking warriors of the rodeo world.

Junior Michael Ray

Thanks are due to many for the inspiration, music and details found in the novel *Sanctuary Ranch*.

To Mike Blakely of Marble Falls, Texas for the beautiful song "Slow Fallin Rain" and his Amelia, the subject of that song, who became our Amy in this book. You knew her even before we did.

To Donnie Price of Texas, for walking me through the steps of a recording session — I relied on your wonderful ability to help put the magical process into words.

To Jon Chandler of Colorado, for striking

out on his own and creating some of the most memorable and original songs ever written about the west — such as "Through the Gap," sung by Jess. I'm sure he never did it as well as you.

To Donnie Blanz of Texas *and Ed and Judith Bruce* of Tennessee for the wonderful song "You Just Can't See Him from the Road," reminding us that the cowboy is always there, even if we can't see him. He's always in our hearts.

To Stan Rood of Kansas whose talent and vision created the song "Ride into the Sunset," which describes our hero Jess, and so many cowboys like him, as no other music could.

To Willie Nelson for long having inspired hundreds of musicians to combine country, western, and folk, and just sing. You've defined a generation.

To the Cheyenne Frontier Days General Committee for keeping one of America's greatest traditions alive — and for keeping it safe, humane and accessible.

And to Bill Barwick of Denver, whose refrain to the song "Carolyn in the Sunset," recorded on his "Sons of the Tumbleweed" album, became Amy's mantra, her promise of return. *"When it's time to put your saddle up and finally come on home . . . ,"* words that came back to her as she sought solace in her memories.

Once in a while, a writer gets a chance to take some risks and explore a new world. But you don't usually go there alone. With luck, you get a map, like those that lead to buried treasure, and maybe a friend to turn to when the map is hard to read or the trail grows tiring and long. One of those friends has been Bill Barwick, a man whose music has been like a light in the dark, illuminating the way for all who hear it. His voice makes the very space around it deepen, and his view of the West confirms that it's not where you are, but who you are — not what you do, but how you serve. Not the trail you ride, but how you ride it.

With great appreciation, the refrain of this song recalls Amy's own journey as well as the recognition and admission that there's often something else that calls us. Something, or perhaps someone, we crave to return to.

That knowledge is paramount — and once we know it, we can go anywhere. Only by looking back at the distance that they've come can our characters Jess McLain and Amelia Talbot know for certain that it's time to head on home — a word that finally has meaning for both.

Corinne Brown
August 2005

About the Authors

Junior Michael Ray is the fifth-generation rodeo cowboy in his Colorado-based family. Since 1996, he's been a professional cowboy in saddle bronc, bareback and bull riding. A veteran of the US Armed Forces, an agented actor, and an emerging song-writer/singer with a newly released CD to his fame, he takes the life he's lived and makes art out of it. *Sanctuary Ranch* is the third installment out of a rodeo series in progress entitled "Seven Roads to Cheyenne." This is his first collaboration.

Corinne Joy Brown is a Colorado native who writes about the West. An award-winning member of the Denver Woman's Press Club, a charter member of Women Writing the West and a professional member of Western Writers of America, she writes for Western media, including the publication of the National Cowboy and Western Heritage Museum, *Persimmon*

Hill. Corinne is the author of a highly successful historical novel, *MacGregor's Lantern*, which was published by Five Star Publishing.

The employees of Thorndike Press hope you have enjoyed this Large Print book. All our Thorndike and Wheeler Large Print titles are designed for easy reading, and all our books are made to last. Other Thorndike Press Large Print books are available at your library, through selected bookstores, or directly from us.

For information about titles, please call:

(800) 223-1244

or visit our Web site at:

www.thomson.com/thorndike
www.thomson.com/wheeler

To share your comments, please write:

Publisher
Thorndike Press
295 Kennedy Memorial Drive
Waterville, ME   04901